I0611451

Wakefield Press

ROAD TRIPPING with PEARL NASH

Poppy Nwosu is an author of young adult fiction. She has published three romantic contemporary novels: *Making Friends with Alice Dyson* (2019), *Taking Down Evelyn Tait* (2020), and now *Road Tripping with Pearl Nash* (2021). She is the editor of the 2021 Wakefield Press YA anthology *Hometown Haunts: #LoveOzYA Horror Tales*.

Her work has been shortlisted for the Adelaide Festival Unpublished Manuscript Award and the Readings Young Adult Book Prize, and has been awarded the SA Writers Fellowship residency at Varuna Writers House, as well as an Arts SA grant. She has appeared at Adelaide Writers' Week and Salisbury Writers' Festival, among other places.

Growing up surrounded by cane fields and rainforest, Poppy studied music at university before living overseas in Ireland. She is now based in Adelaide, Australia.

You can visit her at www.poppynwosu.com.

Praise for Poppy Nwosu
Making Friends with Alice Dyson

'Alice and Teddy's journey of self-discovery is charming and sweet –
a heart-warming story of friendship and first love.'
– Melissa Keil

'A fresh, funny novel about first love, friendship and change in the
final year of high school. Alice knows exactly who she is and where
she wants to go – but sometimes love is what happens when you're
busy making other plans. I loved it.'
– Vikki Wakefield

'*Making Friends with Alice Dyson* is a sweet contemporary romance
about growing up, growing apart, and getting to know someone before
it's too late. A tender and true debut about the power of friendship
and the trust it takes to really let someone see the real you. What an
outstandingly lovely tale with solid heart; intimate and enchanting.'
– Danielle Binks

'*Making Friends with Alice Dyson* is a tender, assured novel about the
complexities of first love, friendship and staying true to yourself.
It will have you falling in love from the first line to the very last.'
– Allayne Webster

'This gentle and tender contemporary romance from Poppy Nwosu
finds friendship, compassion and understanding under the weight of
other people's expectations ... Nwosu bypasses toxic and high-stakes
romantic tropes for a refreshingly nuanced and realistic dynamic,
while still giving readers the slow-burn romance they crave: a
gloriously heady mix of tentative self-consciousness, bittersweet
longing and simmering tension.'
– Judges' comments, Readings Young Adult Book Prize

'This is the sweetest story of cautious offers of friendship, little acts of kindness, and vulnerable people opening up to those who love them. It has so much heart! Here for this kind of quality #LoveOzYA contemporary!'
– C.G. Drews (Paperfury)

'A delightfully fresh, funny and insightful novel full of endearing characters and settings that are palpably SA local with the mingled beach-and-industry vibe of the Port Adelaide trainline.
– Katharine England, *Advertiser*

'A story that's quietly thoughtful, joyful and sweetly romantic – in the same wheelhouse as Jaclyn Moriarty's Ashbury/Brookfield books, minus the epistolary style.'
– Angie Schiavone, *Age*

'I really enjoyed this journey we go on with Alice.' – Rhianna Patrick, ABC Radio National OzYay Book Club

'Alice's voice is charmingly open, honest, and kind, and her loyalty to her friends combined with her deep insecurity render her character fascinatingly layered ... An entertaining teen romance.' – *Kirkus Review* (US)

'The rollercoaster ride of Year 12 has never been captured so well as in this excruciating journey of a nerd who finds herself unable to maintain her usual invisibility and is forced to confront the truth about herself and her relationships, and adjust her secret dream for after the end of the year. It's a heck of a ride and I believe many young adult readers will be only too happy to hop on board and experience the peaks and troughs of Alice Dyson's final year of school.'
– Julie Wright, secondary English teacher and member of the SAETA Council

Taking Down Evelyn Tait

'Lottie has the worst of intentions, jumps to conclusions, and behaves badly –in short, she's exactly the sort of character I absolutely adore! I reckon Lottie will go down as one of the great characters of OzYA lit – and deservedly so.' – Gabrielle Williams

'A delicate, layered story about revenge, relationships, and learning to be kind. I adored this one.' – Jodi McAlister

'I loved the slow widening of Lottie's perspective (and world) and the descriptions of seaside/industrial town, and the tomato plants, and the set piece at the Medieval fair. Sharp, sweet, sonder.'
– Simmone Howell

'Lottie is mischief personified and she is a glorious blaze of magnetic energy on every page.'
– C.G. Drews (Paperfury)

'Lottie is a wonderfully memorable character with a very distinctive voice and a whole lot of attitude ... Poppy Nwosu captures the uncertainties and jealousies of high school perfectly, with her story mining similar territory to her Readings YA Prize shortlisted debut, *Making Friends with Alice Dyson*, to excellent effect. This is an utterly delightful read that you will devour like a cheeky bar of chocolate.' – Angela Crocombe, *Readings Monthly*

'Warm, funny and wise, *Taking Down Evelyn Tait* examines disjointed family dynamics, complicated friendships, awkward teen romance and honouring your true self. ... A joyous and accessible read for fans of *To All the Boys I Loved Before* and *10 Things I Hate About You*.'
– Annie Waters, *Books & Publishing*

ROAD TRIPPING

with

Pearl Nash

Poppy Nwosu

Wakefield
Press

Wakefield Press
16 Rose Street
Mile End
South Australia 5031
www.wakefieldpress.com.au

First published 2021

Cover designed by Liz Nicholson, Wakefield Press
Edited by Jo Case, Wakefield Press
Typeset by Michael Deves, Wakefield Press

ISBN 978 1 74305 843 5

A catalogue record for this
book is available from the
NATIONAL LIBRARY OF AUSTRALIA
National Library of Australia

CORIOLE
McLAREN VALE

Wakefield Press thanks
Coriole Vineyards for
continued support

For Gus

Prologue

DAISY
One Year Ago

The concrete driveway is overgrown. And it's dark. Also, the music spilling from the clattering windows is bad. Like, really bad: nothing but repetitive electronic beats. I'm trying to think of more excuses but that's all I can come up with as Daisy drags me toward the front door.

She's definitely not listening though.

I try out some more protests, think of anything I can to save me from the stupidness ahead. Daisy simply rolls her eyes as bass throbs in muffled beats through the thin walls of the building.

House party.

My own brand of personal hell.

Practically every person from school is inside that house. I'll spend the entire evening hovering around the edges, feeling awkward and hating everything.

Yet I still can't bring myself to tell her the biggest reason I want to be anywhere but here. Instead, I ask if she knows that my nana will kill me if I'm not where I said I'd be (at Daisy's house studying for our end-of-year exams). Also, I mention to her that no one in there likes me. They all still think of me as that weird country kid, even after four years of living in the city. I remind Daisy I just got my braces and my teeth still hurt. (And that I look stupid.)

She's not listening. I keep talking anyway.

'Daisy, seriously. I want to go home.'

She snorts, flicking long hair across her shoulder. 'You're already here! Besides, how bad can it be?'

I try to clamp down on the irritation rising in my chest but seriously, I've been through this a million times with her. I speak through gritted teeth. 'I can think of better ways to spend my Saturday. Like a million ways.'

'Stop it, Pearl,' snaps Daisy. 'You agreed to come! I didn't force you.'

She kind of did, but I shut my mouth hard on what I was about to say anyway, push it down deep because I value our friendship and I don't like it when she's mad. Even though she's making me mad. So I don't say the thing that's burning inside my head, sizzling on the tip of my tongue.

I don't want to be a third wheel.

Instead I blurt, 'You don't even know if he likes you!'

She stops her incessant pulling of my arm. Goes deadly still as dim light from the house spills over her face. Her voice turns low. And a little bit wobbly, which immediately makes me regret my words.

'I'll never know if I don't go in there.' She takes a big shaky breath, and it occurs to me for the first time that maybe she's scared. I don't get a chance to ask her though, because a group of boys pushes past us on the doorstep, laughing and shoving as they tumble into the house. I watch them go with a wrinkled nose.

Lachlan, the object of Daisy's affections, isn't with them, but his best friend is. Like the rest of them, he shoves past us as if we don't exist. I scowl, rubbing my side where his elbow connected with my ribcage.

'I heard he couldn't even name one single plant in biology,' I mutter. He doesn't hear but Daisy shakes her head at me.

'You truly embarrass me, Pearl Nash.'

'What?'

'Honestly, you can take the girl out of the country ...' She doesn't even bother finishing the sentence. But believe me, I've heard it before.

I scowl even harder. 'Knowing the name of a plant has nothing to do with being from the country!'

My nana is just into gardening is all. And she teaches me things sometimes.

I sniff. 'Besides, he's one of the worst offenders in there! Walking around school like he owns the whole place. Looking down on everyone.'

'Sounds like you're the one looking down on everyone. You know, you're being pretty judgemental for a country girl.'

I grit my teeth again. But say nothing. Lately, the line between teasing and being mean is getting blurred, I think.

It's hard work, but I let the comment go. Let the irritation that's boiling in my chest go too.

'Fine,' I announce, waving my hand at the throbbing, light-drenched house ahead. I take a big breath. 'Let's do this.'

Daisy grins wide, eyes sparkling in the dark. She launches at me, grasping my shoulders into a tight hug. Which makes me feel better. I whisper into her hair, 'Just promise you won't leave me alone in there, okay?'

She pulls away and nods solemnly. 'I promise.'

I raise my eyebrows meaningfully at her. 'Because last time I had to spend the whole night next to that idiot who doesn't even know how to name a single plant!'

'He's alright, though.'

I'm feeling annoyed again. 'He's not alright! See how he pretended he didn't even see me just then? Came barrelling into me with his elbows? And besides, he totally insulted my braces.'

Daisy inspects me quizzically through the dark and then finally shrugs. 'They do look a bit weird though.'

My mouth gapes open in disbelief, until she laughs.

'I'm just teasing! You look great. And I won't leave you alone in there like last time.'

I'm still frowning. And I'm already cranky, which is hardly the right mood for a party. Also, I'm highly aware that my current state of mind means if Lachlan's best friend says even one *slightly* insulting thing to me tonight, there's no way I'm going to be able to hold back. I take deep breaths.

Lately, I feel like I've been shoved onto the back foot with Daisy. Like something is happening that I don't quite have a handle on yet. 'You seriously won't? You'll stay with me?'

Daisy grins and wraps an arm tight around my shoulders as she shoves open the front door. Music spills across the patio in a heavy wave, dim lights flickering inside. She tilts her head toward mine, whispers, 'I promise I'll stay with you, Pearl Nash.'

1

MYRTLE WATTLE

'You can't leave me here, Nash!'

I certainly can. But I admit I'm wavering. It's the puppy-dog eyes. And the rain, probably. I don't know how I'm meant to stay defensive against all that wet skin and those shivers.

I suspect he's playing me, though. He's good at that kind of stuff. It's summer, for starters. It's not even cold.

'It's a petrol station,' he breathes, eyes widening like this should mean something to me, other than, *yeah*. I am parked outside a petrol station. I had in fact noticed that already.

His palms press flat against the half-rolled-up front window of my Bedford van, wet fingers curled through the gap. As if he'll slide his whole body through the second I unwind it any further.

I glare. 'Call someone else.'

We don't like each other. Never have. It's our whole thing.

'*Who* else?' He gestures with one shivering hand behind him, looking traumatised.

Flat scrubby landscape and one rundown petrol station with a concrete toilet block. The sky is black with pulsing clouds, heavy and low against the flat stretching highway and shingled earth. Twisted, stunted trees in all directions. Middle-of-nowhere shit.

I sigh.

'It's a petrol station, Nash.' He says it again. Irritation creeps into his voice.

'So what?' I snap.

'So what? *So what?*' Obi takes a really deep breath. 'So, every single outback horror movie ever made features a murder scene at a deserted petrol station. I am a young black male, Nash. What do you think happens to the young black male character in horror movies?'

I don't answer.

'Do you want me to tell you?'

'No.'

'They *die*, Nash. They always die. It's literally a death sentence if you leave me here!'

'I feel like you're exaggerating—'

'I'm *not* exaggerating. Look at me, does this seem like the face of an exaggerator?' He shoves his nose real close to the narrow gap at the top of my window. Brown eyes, buzz-cut. He's got bad skin across his cheeks and water dripping from his lashes.

And he's got puppy-dog eyes.

'Do you want me to die, Nash?'

I bristle. 'You won't die. A bus will come through soon.'

'I'll die, Nash.'

He keeps staring through the gap, rain-slicked fingers tapping on the glass, his whole body vibrating as he makes soft, sad sounds, like that's going to change my mind.

The puppy-dog eyes turn into kitten eyes.

Turn into baby-seal eyes.

I can't resist baby seals.

Finally, I let out a defeated grunt.

'Alright,' I snap.

Obi's mouth curls into a wide, sudden grin. Dimples appear in his cheeks. Both sides.

I scowl. Mr Charming turned on like the flick of a light switch. Dimples like that are magic. They even make everyone forget the acne scarring on his cheeks.

Obi sure knows how to work it, and that only annoys me more.

A moment of silence passes as I attempt to control my temper. He shifts from foot to foot, sneakers crunching on the wet gravel outside like nails on a chalkboard. Finally he snaps, 'Are you going to let me in or what?'

So much for trying to charm me.

I raise my brows at him from the driver's seat, elbow on my knee and hand across my mouth.

'It's not locked,' I inform him curtly.

He tries the handle of the sliding door at the side of the Bedford. 'Huh. So ... it was *always* unlocked? You didn't lock me out?'

Things were definitely not meant to go like this.

Daisy was meant to be here, sitting in the passenger seat of my rundown Bedford, engine roaring, feet on the dash, her hair flying in the wind.

Instead I'm stuck with this idiot. In the middle of nowhere.

It becomes clear I'm not planning to answer him, so Obi just shrugs, the lightbulb grin back on. Like the sun shining through rain clouds. Magic dimples and all.

I roll my eyes. That shit doesn't work on me.

Obi shoves two heavy bags into the back, and I don't love how they shower wet grit across the thin mattress laid out in the body of the van. Rainwater leaks from the canvas and soaks into the foam.

I scowl at him. 'Can you clean that first or something? This is my car, *Obiara.*' I stuff up the pronunciation of his full name, I know I do. Not on purpose though. 'It isn't some piece of junk!'

Not strictly true. The van is an utter piece of junk, inherited from my grandpa, a man obsessed with old junk.

He glares back at me. 'Oh-byo-rah,' he corrects, sounding it out.

I curse Daisy again beneath my breath as I curl around in the driver's seat, on my knees now as I grab a towel from the van floor and shove it beneath his stupid bags. We almost knock heads as I get up and remove him from my vicinity with a hand to his sopping wet shoulder.

A jagged flash of lightning flickers across the sky, the heavy clouds almost purple now. In the distance, a sheet of water approaches across the desert, a visible wall of rain.

'Um ... Nash, can I like, get in now?'

'I already said you could, didn't I?'

Obi flashes another of his dimpled grins, almost blinding me. It appears forced though, like he's trying to play nice for the sake of his ride. The sliding door slams shut behind him – too loud for my liking, because I love this car – and then his wet sneakers squelch and scrape across the gravel as he throws himself into the passenger seat.

Just in time.

The wall of rain envelops us, the world outside turning white and misted, water battering the metal roof as a roll of heavy thunder rumbles overhead. Sheets of it slam hard against the windshield and I chew my lip.

Do I want to drive through this on the highway?

I'll barely be able to see.

I guess I think about it too long, because Obi clears his throat. He's still flashing that smile, but it's worn thin at the edges.

'So ...' he says, and then stops.

I watch him as the pasted edges of his grin slowly falter. I can't help but be curious. 'They seriously just left you here? Daisy and that?'

Obi says nothing as rain sloshes against the front of the Bedford. I swear the whole van is shaking from the howling wind.

I try again. 'They seriously just kicked you out at this shit petrol station and told you to beg me for a lift?'

The grin disappears completely, swallowed whole. 'Yeah.'

I scowl. 'She didn't even text me.'

'No reception.'

I point through the roaring rain toward the ramshackle petrol station. 'There is literally a payphone over there!'

Obi blinks. 'What's that?'

'A payphone?' I stare at him blankly. 'What do you mean?'

He rolls his eyes. 'It was a joke, Nash. No one uses payphones anymore.' He rubs an impatient hand across the misting glass of his window, squinting through the rain. 'Look, can we just go, or what?'

This infuriates me even more. Ordering me around in my own car.

But I start the engine.

It sounds sick actually, like it's choking. But I keep my face blank so Obi can't tell I'm worried. Or if not exactly *blank*, a scowl, which is what he's used to from me anyway. Wouldn't want to change things up too much.

'Yeah, we can go?' I mutter, pulling out slowly onto the road. Considering it's school holidays, there aren't many cars around. I'm glad. I'd be too scared to drive this slow old thing in a traffic jam in this weather.

I roll down my window a little because the car is stifling, summer heat hanging heavy in the air, more humid than I'm used to. Rain spills through the gap. It wets the bare skin of my legs and slides down the pale, cracked leather of the seat.

I roll the window back up.

I'm pretty keen on staying silent and just concentrating on the road through the rain, but Obi has other ideas. 'Ouch,' he says. He fishes around beneath his bum and drags out a battered paperback: creased cover and dog-eared pages. He raises his eyebrows. 'What's this?'

I try to snatch it, but he pulls it from my reach. He's grinning again, skin still damp. But the grin looks a little sharper now, so I guess he's just as unhappy with the situation as I am. Outside, rain hisses down. Relentless, flat land seeps away behind us as I drive slow and careful up the highway.

'Give it back!'

He doesn't.

'Is this seriously what you read in your spare time, Nash?' Obi shows me the cover – two people embracing in a wild Scottish-style landscape, his billowing shirt in a low V and her dress half unbuttoned. Judging from the deep dimples appearing in his cheeks, Obi finds it all quite amusing.

A nice story to spread when we meet up with all his friends.

'Put on your seatbelt,' I snap. My face is hot and flushed. No wonder Daisy and Lachlan kicked him out. 'It's my nana's book, okay? Not mine.'

His grin grows wider. 'Sure it is. It's always the country kids, isn't it?'

I shove back my hair, which keeps falling into my eyes.

'*What's always the country kids?*'

I'm pretty sure I don't want to know. But if he says what I suspect he's going to, I'll kill him.

He shrugs. 'You know, the ones you least expect. For example, you dress like a boy. And your mouth is full to the brim with braces. At school you never talk unless Daisy is around to hold your hand. Except when you want to pick at me, for some reason. But the whole time, you're reading juicy romance books about delicate fair maidens. Unbelievable.'

It isn't exactly what I suspected. It's a new variation. New enough that I gape at him.

My mouth is *full to the brim* with braces?

My cheeks flush hotter, and I run my tongue over my teeth self-consciously. Metal ridges and sharp edges. All this mocking reminds me again why it's better to avoid Obi. And Daisy's boyfriend, Lachlan.

And lately ... Daisy herself.

Not that Daisy mocks me exactly. Or at least, I know she doesn't mean to. She just ... gets caught up in the way Lachlan is. And she doesn't seem to protest when other people do.

I attempt to smooth my cropped hair, feeling a little winded. I can't even find the words to cut Obi down, instead saying weakly, 'Can you please just put the book away?'

He doesn't listen to me.

He never listens to me.

Instead Obi kicks both his sneakers onto the dash – *my* dash – and begins reading *Flaming Secret of the Highlander*, a small crease appearing between his brows.

Daisy's sneakers are allowed on my dash. Not Obi's. I wish I could chuck him out of my van the same way she did.

It's hard to imagine Daisy doing that.

Lachlan though – well, that's easier to imagine.

I grit my braces-covered teeth. I'd imagine Obi must have done something truly horrendous to get left behind if I didn't also secretly suspect Daisy and Lachlan were just looking for an excuse for some alone-time. Since they got together, everything's been about alone-time with them. It's been nearly a whole year now, and I feel like I've lost my best friend.

I glance over at Obi.

And gained … whatever awful thing he is.

A nemesis?

I huff. Loudly. And lean over to shove his feet off my dash with a hard stare.

'I'm starting to realise why they left you behind,' I grumble. A bit lame, but the only insult I can find in the spur of the moment.

Obi resettles himself in his seat, attention still on the paperback. 'Only *starting to*, Nash?' He throws a lazy grin my way.

I scowl. 'Put your seatbelt on.'

This time he does.

I keep driving, seething in silence while Obi reads. The Bedford is like a sauna. Sweat beads on Obi's forehead, yet he makes no move to open his window. Good. I'd only tell him to shut it again. The rain outside is hammering down.

The landscape rolls on: flat stony ground and twisted bushes. Every now and then we pass a collapsed colonial house, broken chunks of stone and caved-in rooves. Just flat land. Endless and wet.

It's familiar yet alien, this landscape. I grew up out here, but it's been so long since I was last here, it only half feels like home. An ache rises in my chest.

Eventually the rain eases and then stops entirely, and I roll down the window, desperate for relief. The air isn't cool like I'd hoped, but it's fresh. I breathe deep. It smells like rain, like the desert and hot bitumen. It smells like my childhood. Like my life until four years ago.

I always loved being out here when I was younger.

Staring at the flat, misted horizon, I think maybe I still do. Maybe I miss the big skies and wide landscape.

Maybe I miss the farm, even.

Definitely, I miss my nana. In a way that's crept up on me. Surprised me.

I've just been so busy lately with other things – with exams and school and holiday plans and Daisy – so I didn't even notice. But that's fine, because it's a problem that'll be resolved incredibly soon.

Slowing the van, I pull off the highway onto a smaller, winding road, a glittering bay visible in the distance now the sky is clearing. Sunlight shimmers between the heavy, dark clouds. Dry yellow hills roll down to the hazy ocean and the road curls beside a salt plain, mangroves clinging to the edges. Obi's been reading for ages, every now and then making an amused grunt in the back of his throat. He's lounging like he owns my car.

Finally, I can't take it anymore. 'Can you stop doing that? You're wrinkling the edges of my book.'

'The edges of *whose* book?'

'My nana's book,' I correct quickly.

'That's not what you said.' He glances up with an evil grin but then his eyes widen. 'Oh, the rain stopped. Cool. You can see the ocean.'

'You only just noticed that now?'

He shrugs. 'Your book is pretty engrossing.' He wiggles his eyebrows at me.

'It's not *my* book. I told you. It's my nana's.'

Obi doesn't answer but the smile falls from his face as he blinks suspiciously out the window. He turns in his seat, trying to see behind us. 'Um, Nash ... where are we going?'

'To check on my nana. Her old house is down the peninsula.'

'Excuse me?'

I stare back at him. I say it slower. 'We are going to my nana's house at the end of the peninsula. To make sure she isn't dead.'

Obi gapes at me. He shakes his head. 'Say that again? Dead?'

I roll my eyes. 'No. *Not* dead.'

'Um ... and why are we doing that?'

'Because my parents are making me go. They're worried or whatever. But she'll be fine. It's not a big deal.'

Obi lifts his hands as if to wave me away. 'No, no, Nash. I don't care why *you're* going to see your nana! Why am *I* going?!'

'Because you pissed Lachlan off and he left you behind at a petrol station. And because you were on your knees in the rain begging me for a lift.'

He hisses, 'I wasn't on my knees!'

'You were definitely, at least metaphorically, on your knees. And you definitely *did* beg me.' It's a little vindictive, I admit, but I'm almost enjoying myself now. Enjoying the fact that I'm dragging him somewhere he doesn't want to go.

Definitely *not* enjoying the fact that it will keep us together in my van for at least another billion hours of driving time. That part is less nice.

'But ... but ...' he stutters. 'What about Finn's coast shack?'

I shrug. 'I never said I was going to Finn's coast shack.'

'Yes, you did! When you first rolled down the window, I asked where you were going and you said, "Finn's coast shack".' He puts on a high, fake voice, which I suppose is meant to be me.

I glare at him. 'I never said I was going *straight* to Finn's coast shack. You want a lift to Lachlan's stupid party, then you come with me to check on my nana first.'

Obi gapes at me. 'But I don't *want* to come with you to check on your nana.'

'Well, that is unfortunate. Because that's where we're going.'

'And how long will this detour take exactly?'

'I dunno. Like an extra day?'

'A whole day! Nash, are you fucking serious?' He slams his sneakers against the dash again, hands over his face. 'Why are you doing this to me? This is ridiculous! I don't want to see your weird old country nana, I want to go to Finn's party.'

I recoil. Weird old country nana? How dare he.

'I'm literally giving you a lift right now and you insult my family?' My voice is rising, temper flaring. 'Do you want me to shove you out of this car? And you don't even know anything about my nana! She's a lot better than stupid Finn.'

'And I *don't want* to know anything about your nana!' Obi's voice is getting louder too, rising to match mine. 'Turn this car around right now!'

'No way!'

'I mean it. I'm going back to the servo to get a bus.'

'I'm not turning around!' I yell at him. We've been driving for ages and my nana is waiting for me. 'This is your own fault, you're the one who begged me for a lift! And besides, insulting my nana?' I laugh derisively. 'You don't even know the name of a single plant!'

'What?' Obi's eyes bulge. 'What's that even supposed to mean?'

I'm about to open my mouth to tell him exactly what it means, when the Bedford makes a chugging, groaning sound, the engine rumbling and choking.

Spluttering.

Steaming.

Stopping.

It cuts out. Just like that, my van dies.

2

DESERT PEA

It's growing dark and we're parked beside the road, flat land and scrubby plants rolling all the way to the packed mangroves and extending salt flats. Complete isolation. I can't even see the highway from here.

I'm peering at the engine, the bonnet propped up by a metal rod. Something in there is fizzing; smoke rising before disappearing into the salty breeze. I can't tell if the clouds above are heavy with rain or if it's just the night closing in. Either way, we're screwed.

Obi's wedged against the side of the van; arms tight over his chest, jaw clenched. 'Do you even know anything about engines, Nash?'

No.

'Stop calling me that, *Obiara*.'

'Nash? It's your name though.'

'It's not my *actual* name.'

He scowls. 'Fine. *Pearl*, then.'

I shudder. It's weird when he says it like that.

He hovers over my shoulder. 'So ... *Pearl* ... do you know anything about engines?'

Still no, though I'm not about to admit that to Obi, and also, now I'm wishing he'd go back to calling me Nash.

'You screamed when the engine died,' Obi informs me smugly. Already I can imagine him telling the story to everyone at the beach shack. Together with the romance novel thing, it will be a wonderful beginning to my stay. He'll probably add something about me being a weird country girl with a weird country nana, and everyone will laugh. I kind of want to hit him.

Instead, because this is an emergency situation and I don't want to die stranded in the bush, I take a deep breath and say calmly, 'Give me your phone, I'm going to call my nana.'

Obi blinks at me. 'I don't have it.'

Immediately the pressure returns to my chest and I'm about to explode again. I try hard to stamp it down, my shaking voice carefully controlled. 'What do you mean, you don't have it?' No one goes anywhere without their phone.

'You broke it. Remember? Last week before exams.'

That throws me. Well, yes I did. A total accident. The glass of his screen cracked under my sneaker. But only because he was tying his shoelace and had left it on the floor.

Actually, thinking of it now makes my stomach sink. Not because of Obi's phone. Because I remember Daisy's expression while she watched us fighting afterwards. Disapproval. Looking at me like I was a kid, shaking her head as if she couldn't understand me.

It's what Obi always does. Causes problems. And it always ends with Daisy looking at me like that.

Except all of that happened last week.

And now it's *this* week.

'Well, don't you have a new one?' I fold my arms over my chest, getting defensive now. This isn't my fault.

Obi's eyebrows pull tight as he steps toward me, his damp T-shirt billowing in the rising wind as he waves his hands at me. His voice is getting louder. 'No, I don't have a new one, Nash! Do I look like a phone shop to you?'

I scowl up at him, my voice rising to match his. 'No, but you're meant to *go* to a phone shop and get a new one!'

'A *new* one? That *was* my new one! I was on a three-year plan!'

'What about your insurance?'

'I don't have insurance!'

'Well, that's stupid! It's not my fault you don't have insurance!'

He rolls his shoulders like he's throwing off my words, clearly pissed as hell but holding up his hands like he's asking for a time-out. Trying to calm the situation. 'Fine. Fine! Whatever. You just call your nana then.'

I flinch. 'What?'

'What?' Obi echoes suspiciously.

I say nothing and he slowly tilts his head to the side. 'On your phone, Nash. Just call your nana.'

I open my mouth and then shut it again, running my tongue over my braces. Turning to the engine, I shove my back toward him, waving him away. Or at least trying to.

He's having none of it.

'Nash.' His voice is low and controlled. 'Where. Is. Your. Phone?'

'Um ...'

'Nash!' he barks.

My voice turns small. 'Well, it sort of died because I forgot to charge it.'

Obi gapes at me. Then a strangled yell escapes his throat as he lurches away, sliding onto the wet gravel with his back against the van door. His jeans are gonna get soaked but he doesn't seem to care.

I refuse to meet his accusatory gaze, blankly facing the engine. But no matter how much I stare at it, I still know nothing about cars. The world around us is sinking into dusk, shadows drawing long across the flat, rolling landscape, clinging to the mangroves. I slam the bonnet shut and open the driver's door to roll the window up against mosquitos.

It seems we're going nowhere fast.

Obi's voice rises from the other side of the van. 'Do you have any idea what this means, Nash?'

I don't answer.

'This is *literally* the start to every horror movie ever. We're both going to die.'

I frown. 'We're not going to die.'

'And you know who's going to die first, right? Definitely not the pretty white girl.'

I roll my eyes and ignore him, especially the bit about me being pretty. He's always tormenting me about my braces and short hair, so I'm well aware he doesn't mean it.

Shoving the van door open, I rummage around in my esky. There's a blessed two minutes of silence before Obi starts up again. 'I really dislike you right now, Nash. I can't believe you brought me out here.'

I slam the door in answer and trek to the front of the van. 'Shut up. Come and help me make food.'

That perks him up. 'Food?'

I shove a couple of bags at him and heave the esky up, motioning with my chin to a clearing in the scrub. I dump my stuff beside an old fire pit, filled with leftover charcoal sticks and damp ash, and dig around to make it fresh. It's been a long time since my family went camping. A long time since I've been out here on the peninsula at all. I guess that's what high school does: sucks away all your time.

When I was a kid I used to go into the salt marshes with Grandpa and Nana, down to the wild beaches on the west coast, where the waves crash against massive dunes. My grandpa wasn't a talker, but Nana would teach me about the native plants. She'd spend hours pointing each one out, showing me the texture and the scent as I ran the leaves between my fingers. In the deep night, the campfire would roar and spark.

Good memories.

Quite different to what I'm experiencing right now.

The logs the campers left behind are too wet for a campfire, but I have my grandpa's old camping stove, so I fiddle around with that instead, setting it up slowly.

Obi doesn't shut up the entire time.

'So this is our life now, huh? Until we get murdered? We're just going to stay out here all night?'

I nod, concentrating on the camp stove. 'Uh huh.'

Obi snorts and stands up. 'I'm going to set up my tent.'

I glance at the stormy sky but say nothing. Let him get blown away in his dumb tent. What do I care?

Obi's behind the van for ages, as far from me as he can get inside the line of stunted trees. I can barely see him – just flashes of canvas floating in the heavy desert air, lots of swearing and muttering. I don't offer to help, though it's clear he needs it.

It takes forever for him to come back. And it's getting dark. I motion to one of my bags. 'There's a lantern in there. And mosquito spray.'

Obi is horrified. 'Mosquitoes?'

'City boy.' I mutter the words as if they're a slur. I live in the city now too, of course, but I was born out here. Grew up out here. That kind of thing gets inside you in small ways.

I chew my lips, thinking about it.

It's probably different now, though. After all, I've been gone so long. I haven't set foot in this place since Grandpa died. So maybe I'm a city girl through and through. Or maybe I'm half and half, one foot in either place.

That makes me feel sad, like I'm missing something. Like maybe I haven't visited often enough to still feel like I'm part of it.

Though I still know a thing or two about mosquitoes.

Obi sprays everything, including me, then stumbles around coughing and choking for a while. Probably more than he truly needs to, if you ask me. It might be meant as my punishment for the Nana detour thing. And the van breakdown thing.

And I guess maybe the phone-smashing thing. Which was an accident.

I sigh. We're stuck together, but not for long. Another day tops.

Then I'll be with Daisy again.

Pressure settles on my chest. That thought doesn't make me quite as happy as it once would have. Everything has changed over the past year since Lachlan and Daisy got together – my best friend leaping light years ahead of me, experiencing everything first; a boyfriend, love, sex, a relationship. Or maybe it started changing even before Lachlan came along, I don't know. I grimace, fishing around inside my bag to pull out some bread. I clasp it into the little hand-held grill from my grandpa's set. I have a billy can too, blackened from when Grandpa used to cook the old-fashioned way, in the flames, during our camping trips. Now the billy can just sits on top of the tiny stove, baked beans bubbling away.

'Looks delicious,' says Obi in a deadpan voice.

I can't tell if he's being sarcastic or not, so I ignore him. It's so dark now, the van has disappeared from view, even though it's only a few metres away. The air is heavy with moisture, thick with salt. A hot breeze stirs the stunted leaves on the bushes.

Ruby saltbush. That's what they are. I think.

My nana would know.

I think of her blue-veined hands, fingers covered in earth as she runs papery skin across curling plants, telling me their secrets. Sharing her passions with me. Kneeling in the dry, crackling grass.

I glance at the dark wall of scrub and shake off the feeling creeping across my body. If my dad isn't worried, I shouldn't be either. My nana is fine.

Of course she is.

She's always fine.

I drag a tin plate from my pack but I only have the one, so we have to share. I motion Obi closer, pouring baked beans over the crisp blackened toast.

'Healthy,' he comments and I pull a sour face at him as I hand across a fork. I fold the baked-bean-soaked toast in half, using it to slurp great bites. I don't care how messy I am. He can just deal with it.

Obi sighs and leans close, our heads bent together above the tin plate, which rests precariously on my knee.

'I can't believe this is how I'm spending my Saturday night,' Obi grumbles through a mouthful.

I nod, agreeing for once. Obi snorts. Loudly.

'You, Nash? As if you do anything on a Saturday night, anyway.' He grins and the dimples show in his cheeks again. It definitely doesn't look charming at all right now, though. 'I bet you stay home and read your trashy novels all weekend.'

'I don't,' I protest immediately.

I don't know why I say it. I do like reading on the weekend. It's my favourite thing to do.

Yet I feel embarrassed suddenly. Like I want to hide it. Which pisses me off. At Obi specifically, for making me feel embarrassed.

Yes, I tag along to parties on the weekends with Daisy some-times, but it's not exactly my idea of a fun night. Lachlan and his friends aren't my favourite people. Most of them don't give me the time of day anyway. I'm a year younger than Lachlan, awkward with my braces. Not pretty like Daisy. He doesn't like me.

Clearly Obi doesn't like me either. He's made that clear in the past year.

I turn my back on him, pulling the tin plate with me though he protests loudly.

'Nash! Nash, I'm sorry.'

Sure, *now* he's sorry. Now there's food involved. 'For what?'

'For ... um, insulting trashy romance books?'

I whip around to glare at him.

'I mean, not trashy ones. Just normal ones. That you love.'

I can't help myself, though I hate that I say it. 'They're not mine. They're my nana's. I told you.' I turn my back on him again.

'I said I was sorry. Really.'

He sounds sorry. Or at least as if he's making an effort to sound sorry. I don't answer either way, so Obi is forced to shuffle awkwardly around the campfire in a crouch, until he's in front of me again in the dark. His face is shrouded in shadow. In the distance a ripple of thunder rolls through the air, and the wind picks up, heavy and warm. I allow him to pull the plate closer to shovel beans into his mouth. He grins at me between each bite. I suppose he thinks he won that round.

I guess maybe he did.

I grimace, though when I fear he's going to eat the whole thing, I quickly pull the plate back. Obi plops onto the gravel, hands behind him and chin lifted to the dark sky.

He sighs softly. 'I thought you were supposed to be able to see the stars in the countryside.'

I make a *duh* noise, except it doesn't fully work because my mouth is full. I swallow and almost choke. 'Not if it's storming, idiot.' The plate is scraped clean.

'You've got toast in your braces,' Obi drawls and immediately I snatch my hand to cover my mouth.

I'm self-conscious in an extreme way when I eat around other people. When I first got braces, a boy told me I had bits of orange stuck in the metal rivets and I've been emotionally scarred ever since. When Obi sees my horrified expression he laughs loudly, throwing his head back to the sky.

'Relax, I was joking. It's too dark to see anyway. I mean, maybe you do have toast in there, I dunno.'

I lower my hand and glower at him, appetite gone. 'You are a terrible person.'

'Yeah, yeah.'

Big fat droplets of rain fall, slicking against my skin and hair, getting harder and faster every moment. Obi yelps, swatting at his face.

'I think I felt a mosquito.'

I empty the billy can, getting ready to pack up. 'It's raining, doofus, there's no mosquitoes. Go to bed.'

Obi stands up, frowning at me as he wipes water from his face. 'Don't call me a doofus, *Nash*.'

I roll my eyes until I notice he's tangled his sneaker in the strap of my bag, scraping it deep into the dirt. I stand up to point. 'Can you please get off my stuff, *Obiara*.'

He growls, stumbling back. He seems to have run out of comebacks though, which is unusual for him. He looks like he's about ready to leg it back to his tent to avoid the rain, and I'm fairly annoyed he's not even pretending to help me pack away the camp stove and dinner stuff. I'm irritated enough to call him back to hiss, 'You know three people were murdered along this road last year, right?'

Obi hesitates. 'There's no way that's true.'

'It's definitely true.'

Not true, but whatever, he deserves it.

Anyone that obsessed with horror movies deserves it. It's a stupid hobby. Like ruining the world for yourself so you can never enjoy anything ever again. Want to go camping? Can't.

Seen a scary movie about it. Want to go swimming in the ocean? Can't. Want to get on a plane or go overseas? Can't.

Stupid.

Obi's staring off into the dark as I load two bags onto my back and cradle the camp stove against my chest, tin plate balanced precariously on top. When it almost all unbalances, I snap, 'Are you gonna help me get this stuff back to the car, or what?'

He jumps. 'Oh … um. Yeah.'

Well. I hadn't expected him to agree that easily.

I hand the camp stove to him. Then sling one of the bags over his shoulder for good measure, before heaving the esky up myself. We trudge the short distance to the Bedford and start unloading everything into the back. Obi just shoves everything wherever it fits, while I try to stop him and find some order in the chaos. This is my bed, after all.

He's also rummaging around in my bags.

Which I don't enjoy. 'Can you stop that?'

A grin breaks across Obi's face, half illuminated by the soft blue glow of my lantern; shadows dance wildly across our little clearing.

'Nash, what is this?' He smirks at me in an unflattering way.

He's holding a stack of romance novels, at least five, and quite a few of them are very new. Unread even. The title on the top one is clearly visible: *Forbidden Passion of the Duke*. It's a classic enemies-to-lovers story and I've read it multiple times.

I bite my lip. 'I'm bringing them for my nana.'

He snorts. '*Whatever.* Just admit it. You read trashy romance novels!'

Irritation flares in my chest and I can't help but snap, 'They're *not* trash!'

Obi just laughs and I fold my arms across my chest. If he thinks they're so bad, why did he read half of the book in the car? I refrain from saying it though, because I don't want to give him any more ammunition.

I growl, getting defensive. 'You want me to admit it? You mean, the same way you admitted to Lachlan that you're quitting school next year?'

He freezes. 'I'm not quitting school next year.'

'I was in the office, Obi, I heard you request the paperwork.'

It takes a long moment for him to answer, and when he does, his voice is sharp. 'Nothing's been decided. And it's got nothing to do with you, anyway.'

My stomach swells. I don't answer and instead lean into the Bedford to hide my expression, shoving the camp stove into its designated corner.

Maybe he's right and it doesn't have anything to do with me, but he's the one going on about my books, going on about how I spend my weekends. *He's* the one inserting himself in my private business. I shove the stove hard until it clatters against the van's metal frame.

The air is thick with tension. I'm planning to leave it be. But Obi clearly doesn't have the same idea.

When I turn around, he's looming right there, not moving – even though the rain is falling heavier now. I straighten my shoulders and lift my chin to him. Obi's glaring down at me. He's a good bit taller, too. But if he expects me to back down, he's dead wrong.

We face each other in the shimmering lantern light. The

stony earth crunches beneath my sneakers in the dark. His voice turns low and hard. 'Did you tell him, then?'

I throw my hands up, exasperated. 'Tell who what?' I don't even know what we're fighting about right now.

Obi's mouth grows tight. His dimples have disappeared. This is serious stuff. He leans closer, enunciating each word. 'Did you or did you not tell Lachlan about the forms I requested?'

A rough laugh escapes my throat. 'Why the hell would I tell him that?' Or anything.

Obi bristles, something mean glinting in his eyes. 'True. And even if you wanted to, why would he speak to you, anyway?'

I flinch. I mean, the words are true, but it's the way he's said them. So dismissive. As if Lachlan is on a whole different level to me. Somewhere high up and unattainable. It sends electricity rolling across my skin, my fingers curling into fists. The words are out before I think twice. 'Oh and I suppose the wonderful Lachlan dumped you at a petrol station because you have such a healthy, beautiful friendship!'

It's Obi's turn to flinch now. His voice rises. 'That's none of your business! And he didn't just dump me there.'

'He left you to beg me for a lift! Sure sounds to me like he dumped you!' I'm yelling now, voice pitched to meet his. I swipe rain from my cheeks.

The darkness is swallowing us whole, the lantern flickering and catching like dancing fireflies across the discarded metal grill of the stove. Everything feels close and stifling. The salt in the air, the scent of the mangroves. The distant rumble of thunder crawling across the sky.

Obi's eyes are wide and his chest heaves. He looks like he's about to explode. Barely in control, his voice getting louder with each word. 'What about Daisy, then? You gonna finally quit clinging onto her? Looks like she's been trying to dump you for an entire year!'

I open my mouth but no sound comes out, and for a moment I struggle to breathe.

Obi doesn't notice, he's still yelling. 'Oh right, she already *did* dump you! Because I sure as hell didn't see you driving in the same car as us. Maybe it's time to take a hint, right?'

His words drop heavily into the humid air, hanging there as if suspended. Silence falls between us. Wind howls through the scrub and whips my hair. My hand is splayed across my belly because it feels like he just drove something sharp into my body, like I need to hold on tight to avoid being turned inside out.

Obi looks different now. Still looming, chest still heaving and hands still clenched, but the fury slowly drains from his face. He blinks rapidly.

I can't move. I feel breathless.

With effort, I step back in the wailing wind. Away. 'Tomorrow I'm dumping you at the nearest servo and you can walk the rest of the way for all I care.'

Obi rolls his shoulders, any traces of uncertainty wiped away. He laughs harshly. 'Sounds good to me. Anything is better than being out here with you.'

I turn on my heel and slam the back door shut. The hinges squeal. 'Good luck in your stupid tent.' I glance up at the sky, fat rain droplets landing on my skin. 'And make sure you check inside your sleeping bag,' I add. 'Don't get bitten by any snakes.'

Obi recoils. 'Snakes?'

Let him stew on that one. I stomp away to the passenger side and wrench the door open, climbing inside. Light spills from the lantern across the dark earth and I catch a glimpse of Obi standing frozen in the dark, just the blur of his white T-shirt, before he scuttles off toward his tent, arms held over his head to ward off the rain.

I don't think he even has a torch. I sit seething in the car and stare at the lantern glowing at my feet. Serves him right. I hope he dreams of snakes. And mosquitoes.

I hope he gets blown away in a cyclone.

As I crawl awkwardly into the back of the Bedford, I concentrate on that fizzing sour anger in my belly. Hone in on it. Stir it up and make myself even more furious.

Because hating Obi is a lot easier than worrying that, when it comes to what he said about Daisy, maybe he's right.

The tiniest seed of doubt creeps into my mind. Daisy might have asked me to come out here with her, *begged* me in fact, but she still ditched me at the last minute to drive with Lachlan. She always picks the better offer, and these days, that's never me. And I want to believe she asked me to come in the first place because I'm her friend, but more and more lately I'm beginning to worry that I'm her security blanket. That she keeps me around *just in case.*

No. No way. Obi's wrong.

I believe in Daisy.

Which is why I'm out here to salvage whatever's left of our friendship. My last chance. *Daisy's* last chance.

I know that's what she wants too. Deep down inside.

3

WARATAH FLOWER

I wake to the thrashing hiss of hard rain against the metal van. Thunder ripples in roaring waves and shakes the world outside. Sleep still clings to my mind, to my fingertips, and I curl smaller in my tangled bed, surrounded by luggage and rolled tents. The metal camp stove gleams in the dark on top of my esky.

Dreams shift in the darkness, drawing me back in. I'm about to drift off when the scraping sounds again, a tapping like fingernails on metal.

I sit up. Fast. Totally awake now.

For a moment I don't remember where I am. Somewhere in the howling wind and dark, the whole van shaking. Alone in the night beside some highway somewhere, isolated. The scraping sounds again and I jump with fright, adrenaline spiking to my fingertips, my head and chest buzzing with it now, my ears humming. I try my best to calm my thudding heart. I locked the van. No one can get in. I'm safe.

Which is when the wailing starts.

It's fairly familiar.

I scrunch myself down toward the end of the van and shove my ear against the metal doors. More scraping. Some pitiful whimpering too. He's calling my name, voice lost in the rush of rain and wind. The storm pounds at the van. The windows light up, crackling lightning burning the whole world white outside.

A yelp snaps out from beyond the doors, and pounding starts, fists against metal.

'Alright, alright,' I yell back, undoing the stiff lock and attempting to shove one side of the door open to the wild weather beyond. It's heavy, like someone's leaning against the other side.

'Move,' I shout into the gap. A plastic box is shoved into my back, all this stupid stuff Mum made me bring to store in Nana's old house because she doesn't want to see it anymore. Remnants of my family's old country life she's finally ready to get rid of. I guess we've truly sunk into the city now. I push back hard against the plastic but it won't budge, and I manage to do nothing except bruise my spine.

The desert turns electric white, shadows running across the packed earth. Finally, the door swings outward. An earth-shattering crack of thunder slams through the sky. Rain pools and spills into rivers on the road. A figure surges forward, barrelling into me in the most annoying of ways. Wet skin and dripping clothes, soaked through.

'Get off me,' I shout. He sort of does, but so much crap hems us in that he's still shoved into my side. I drag myself around onto my knees, trying to pull the door closed. Obi's sopping wet, rainwater soaking into my jersey, his jeans cold against my thigh. 'Help me with the door!'

Obi does. Or at least he tries.

I swear he only manages to make it worse, dripping all over me, but between the two of us, we drag the door closed and

I shove at the metal lock, blocking out the shuddering world outside. Obi's hands swipe at his dripping face, water streaming down his skin and catching in his lashes. Another flash of lightning illuminates the inside of the van like it's on fire.

'Holy shit,' he gasps. 'I nearly drowned. And you totally weren't going to let me in!' His tone is too accusatory for my liking.

'I didn't hear you,' I grumble. His stupid sneakers are dragging grit all over my bed and I hate it enough to ask, 'What happened to the tent?'

Obviously, I already know what happened to his tent. It clearly collapsed on him, like I knew it would, but still, it gives me pleasure when he sheepishly admits it.

Pleasure that evaporates when another deafening crack of thunder and flash of burning light shows that Obi's got his bloody sneakers on my pillow.

'Get your feet off that!'

'Why's your pillow down there,' he complains, proceeding to mash his sneaker against it a bit more.

'Stop! Stop.' I lean forward and grab his foot, which is squelching wet, dragging the shoe off. I grasp the other one too, which is impossible to get off. Thunder roars overhead and sheets of rain smash against the roof.

Obi barks out another yelp. Then looks embarrassed. 'This is insane.'

I scowl back at him. 'Your stupid shoe won't come off.'

Obi's squished behind me, his body caught between Mum's stacks of plastic containers, his knee shoved into my side. He grimaces. 'Did you undo the laces?'

I turn to glare at him, my face illuminated by a conveniently placed bolt of lightning flaring through the glass window.

Obviously, I already undid his laces. I don't even bother to answer.

Obi just scowls back, like the whole thing is entirely my fault, showing teeth that glitter in the dark. I kind of hate him right now, the remnants of our earlier fight stirring again inside my chest.

Finally I manage to extricate his dumb foot from his even stupider sneaker, and I twist around, getting a knee in my ribcage for my trouble, as I try to chuck his wet shoes into the front seat of the van. One at a time they sail over Obi's head, his face one moment caught in absolute darkness, the next lit up like it's daylight. He's absolutely soaked through, his T-shirt clinging to his skin.

'Okay, okay,' I say, attempting to slide past him in the narrow space. 'Where's your stuff?'

He looks at me blankly, close in the dark. It's his elbow that's stuck in my side now. I grasp his arm and dislodge it. 'Your clothes. You're soaked.'

'My stuff is in the tent, Nash. Obviously.'

I blink. 'Why? Why didn't you bring it?'

He sits up, our faces close. He's irritated. 'Well, I didn't actually think of that when the tent fell on my head and I was drowning.'

'Well, you're a doofus,' I snap. 'What are you going to wear now?'

He grimaces at his wet jeans. 'You got any spare clothes, Nash?'

I sort of take him seriously, because he *is* completely soaked and it's still dark outside. But Obi's a lot bigger than me and he'd just ruin my stuff.

I shake my head. 'Nope. You'd stretch them. Go on, get in the front seat.'

'The front seat?' He shifts like he's actually going to listen to me for once. 'Why?'

'Well, you're not sleeping here beside me! You're all wet.'

He snorts as he attempts to squeeze past. 'So lend me a T-shirt then.'

'Just get in the front.'

'Come on, Nash.' It's dark but I can still make out the puppy-dog-eyes thing he's attempting to do. I turn away fast.

'No way, stop that,' I say. 'Go away.'

Abandoning the puppy-dog expression, he shifts, dragging his knee under him. Except he manages to knock one of Mum's plastic sealed boxes with his head, which makes him yelp sharply, and then the whole thing teeters like it's going to fall. I yell and reach for it at the exact moment Obi does.

His elbow connects hard with my nose.

'Urgh.' Tears spring as a sharp, stabbing pain erupts across my face.

Hands over my throbbing skin, I push back, as far from Obi's flailing limbs as possible, my back hitting the camp stove and making me hiss all over again. 'Ow ow ow ow.'

'Sorry! Nash. Sorry! Are you alright?'

'Stop calling me that,' I whine. 'You broke my nose.'

'Shit, sorry, I'm sorry.'

I have my hands over my face, lying back on a pile of rubbish my mother forced me to bring, head tipped up. Obi's hands grasp my wrists, trying to see my face.

'It's bleeding.' I swear that it's bleeding. I can feel it.

'Show me. Pearl, I need to see.'

'Don't touch me!'

'Let me see.'

I allow Obi to pull my hands away, his face close in the dark. I'm half-propped against a tower of folded sheets and plastic bags and he's hovering over me. The rain hammers harder against the roof, almost drowning out the sound of his heavy breathing.

Everything feels close and thick and my head is absolutely pounding, black spots dancing in front of my vision. Or maybe that's just the lightning at the windows.

'Stay still.' Obi's breath is against my cheek, his fingers touching my chin. He turns my head this way and that, angling it back. 'I can't ... see anything.'

'It's bleeding.'

'It's totally not, Nash. It's fine. Oh thank fuck, I thought I'd killed you.' I can hear the grin in his words, which irritates me. He sits back. 'What is all this stuff, anyway?'

'It's not bleeding?'

'No, you're alright.'

I scowl. 'It hurts.'

'I'm really sorry, Nash.' His voice sounds like he means it.

Even though I haven't forgiven him for what he said, I relent. The circumstances are pretty strange, after all.

'It's all this rubbish my mum packed.' I sigh, gingerly pressing my fingertips against my sore nose. 'She's sending me to visit my nana.' I pause and then admit, 'Nana hasn't been picking up the phone lately and apparently I'm the cure.'

I shift on the pile of sheets as another ripple of thunder sounds, lifting a hand to Obi's elbow to manoeuvre him out of the way as I push back the plastic storage box digging into my shoulder blade. It doesn't work that well and we end up knocking heads, my skull against his chin. 'Ow!'

When I glare up at him, his dark eyes glitter. He's bent over me now, shadows dancing across the inside of the van, water streaming against the windows. It's loud and heavy, an endless wash of white noise, broken only by the now-distant rumbling of the thunder. The storm is moving away. Wind howls long and low, moaning beneath the Bedford.

My nose still throbs, but not as much. Maybe Obi's right, maybe it's fine.

I struggle to sit, but it's difficult. The space is small and cramped, and Obi's looming very close, his face right there in the darkness, T-shirt dripping water. His lashes too. I reach up and tug the neckline of his T-shirt, just to find out how sopping it is, to decide whether I really do have to let him stretch one of mine.

Obi follows my fingers, watching as I touch him. It's disconcerting enough that I immediately wind my arm back as if scalded, because his expression is weird. I can't tell what he's thinking. I grow still.

This new darkness seeps between us, heavy shadows and rain sounds. And then it happens. The strangest thing. I see it and blink.

Obi's gaze flicks to my mouth. And back up again. And he sucks in his breath.

So quick, I think I imagined it. Am certain I did, because

now he's clearing his throat and breaking eye contact, the air between us suddenly thick and hot and uncomfortable. My skin is humming and buzzing. Obi's leaning back, away, and it must be the darkness, the distant rumbling thunder, or the rain, I don't know what it is.

Not much thought is involved.

I just do it.

Reach for the hem of his T-shirt again, at his throat, curl my fingers gently around it. Obi's dark eyes widen. And I stop moving, stop breathing, stare back at him with my heart thudding against my chest.

I've never done this.

Ever.

This is new. A strange thrill inside my chest, unfurling like a secret. That maybe I can be however I want to be. And right in this moment, there is something I want to do. Something stupid and foolish, but I want it. Now, while the air feels charged and heavy, while the rain lashes against the windows, roaring in my ears.

Slowly, I tug on his T-shirt, stretching it toward me. Obi follows, until he's so close his breath is on mine. And then my fingers dance from his hem to his throat, along his jaw, behind his head. His buzzcut is sharp against my fingertips and I can't believe what I'm doing, what I'm instigating. Can't believe he's so willing, looking at me in a way that makes me shiver.

Our noses touch and we hover there, caught in place with his breath hitching, and I think this must be a dream. Because Obi's chest is rising and falling fast, his fingers moving into my hair. My mouth presses against his, a deep open kiss, lashes against my cheeks and his breath mingling with mine. He pulls me closer until I'm almost sitting on him, his clothes soaking into mine.

And it should be too much, except it's not.

It's not enough.

4

LILLY PILLY

I wake with my face against warm skin.

Sunlight filters through glass and dust dances across the inside of the Bedford. My face is pressed against Obiara Okocha's throat and his shirt is completely gone, chest rising and falling steadily, his chin resting on top of my head. He's on his side, one arm flung over my body. Curled around me.

The inside of the van is stifling, its metal shell cooking us within. Obi's hand is caught beneath my hip and my life couldn't possibly get any worse.

Except apparently it can, because someone is knocking loudly against the window and trying to peer inside.

I yelp and sit up so quick, I accidentally slap Obi in the face. He grunts, still half-asleep, and raises himself on his elbows. 'What the hell, Nash?'

I cower against him, momentarily forgetting the fact that he isn't wearing a shirt and this whole thing is entirely new for me. 'There's someone out there.'

He frowns sleepily, flexing his hand like it's gone numb. Which it probably has. Because until one second ago, I was sleeping on it.

My cheeks burn and I turn away in embarrassment, unable to bear facing him right now. I madly flatten my short hair, which has gone full bedhead, and try desperately to ignore his bare chest. Try even harder not to think of kissing him in the dark and how his hands were …

I shake my head to clear it.

Besides, Obi's clearly not thinking about any of that because he nudges me with his shoulder and asks, like everything is super normal between us, 'So who's out there?'

I gape up at him, our faces close. 'How would I know that?'

'Oh.'

Now he looks more like how he should.

Worried.

Obi opens his mouth to say something else but I just know it's going to be another stupid horror movie scenario so I cut him off, calling loudly, 'Who's out there?'

'I'm just checking up on you,' the voice says. Deep and male. A real bogan accent. 'That was a bad storm we had last night and I saw you parked here so thought I better check. Everything alright in there?'

Crunching footsteps move about outside and the same voice grumbles beneath his breath, 'Bloody tourists.'

'Er … one moment,' I call out.

Obi's black eyes are wide and he silently mouths *axe-murderer*. I shove him away, hand on his chest, pretending I don't feel anything when my fingers touch his bare skin. I hiss, 'Put some clothes on.'

This finally gets through to him, because then he's crawling around the tiny stifling space, searching for his T-shirt and very purposely not meeting my gaze.

Honestly, I don't know if that makes it better or worse.

Worse probably. Because now we're both utterly awkward, except we're also pressed further together with every movement he makes. 'Sorry,' Obi mumbles. 'Sorry.'

And then when he tries to reach around me to collect his damp T-shirt, he finds himself pressed into me again, this time face-to-face. 'Sorry.'

I smack him away and hiss, 'Stop saying that!'

'Sorry.'

He has so much trouble getting the T-shirt back on that I have to actually help him, which is fairly horrifying. But there I am, dragging it over his head and feeding his arms through in the limited space within the Bedford, cracking my own head on the roof. I crumple, clutching my skull. 'Oww.'

Obi actually snorts with laughter. 'You'll have bruises all over if you keep this up. Your nose, your head.' And then his hands are in my hair again, a gesture way too soft and intimate for the harsh morning light. For the fact that we hate each other.

I stiffen, my mind curling with images of the dark van and rain sounds on the roof. Of Obi's breath warm against my neck and his mouth on mine, kissing me in a way that makes my skin warm, even now.

I shove him away, breathing heavily.

I need to get out of this damn Bedford.

Swearing under my breath, I unlatch the back doors and tumble out. And it's like the storm never even happened, the sky bright blue and stretching, a thick wind rustling the scrubby, stunted trees. The sun is beating down. A dry baking heat wafts off the sizzling van. Even though it's still early.

I blink. It *is* still early, right?

I shove my feet into my thongs, standing upright and trying to flatten my crazy hair. An old bloke with a ute is parked beside the baking bitumen road. He raises his eyebrows when he sees me, like I'm not at all what he expected. Too young maybe? I dunno.

'Tourists?' he asks in a low drawl.

'From the city,' I answer, nodding. Straight to the point. No beating around the bush with this guy. 'Over for the week.'

I'm too embarrassed to admit I'm originally from here. Breaking down in the middle of nowhere is such a tourist thing to do.

Obi launches himself from the van behind me, all limbs. He blinks at the guy with the ute, who does a double take and stands straighter. He wasn't expecting me, and he definitely wasn't expecting Obi. The old man crinkles his brow beneath his wide canvas hat. His red skin is like old leather.

'Where are you from, son?' he asks, voice rasping, hand held between his face and the sun.

Obi sighs and I shove at him with my hip. Finally he says curtly, 'We're both from the city. Like she says.'

The old man blinks and chews his lip, staring a little longer. 'Right. All okay here, then? With the storm and all?' He's looking at me now.

'Um ... not really,' I answer, shoving Obi again because he's rolling his eyes. 'If you could give us a lift to the nearest servo we'd be really grateful.'

The old guy agrees, which makes me extremely happy, and I crawl back into the van to grab an old canvas backpack, which I quickly fill with everything I could possibly need. A jumper? Unlikely in this heat, but sure, why not? My dead phone and charger. Fresh clothes. Water.

A book called *The Knight's Betrayal.*

'Food?' says Obi hopefully over my shoulder and I jump, sliding the book quickly into my pack before he sees.

I'm starving too. I add the sliced bread and apples he directs me to. I'm still not used to this whole new thing of us working together toward a common goal and having conversations that aren't fights. Definitely not used to us making out in the back of my Bedford, either. I turn away to hide my flushed face, adding my toothbrush to the pack because I live in fear of getting food in my braces.

Obi runs off to his bedraggled tent and as the old guy watches silently from his ute, he drags the whole thing over to the back of the van. So much for not fighting.

'You can't put it in there like that!'

'Why not?' Obi's indignant.

'Because of my mattress.' Obviously. 'You're making it dirty.'

Together we get the whole tent turned inside out instead, which takes some massive manoeuvring and by the time we're done, we hate each other again. I've almost forgotten the whole kissing thing.

Almost.

The old bloke gives Obi another beady eye and then lets us into his ute. Obi and I fight over who has to sit squashed in the middle of the front bench seat, next to our driver. I lose because I'm smaller, or at least that's why Obi says I lose. I'm not happy about it but I still climb in.

It also means that I spend the entire ride shoved so close to Obi that I'm practically sitting in his lap, which is awkward for both of us, but still better than having my entire side pressed against our old-man saviour.

The bench seat is tiny and the ride is rough, the ute turning off the sealed bitumen road and down a dirt track. I've never seen Obi's eyes go so wide.

He stares at me in a not-at-all discreet way and mouths *axe murderer* again. The road winds through thicker bush and around agricultural fields that roll toward the ocean. The desert stays at our back, wheatfields ahead.

Our driver talks the entire time, some awful story about how his wife left him for some other dude fifteen years ago. I think he's trying to tell me something. About not trusting anyone? Or maybe he's trying to tell Obi, except he mainly seems to be telling me.

I'm stiff with horror at the whole thing and starting to worry that Obi might be right about our saviour being an axe murderer, because we're back in the desert now and there's literally nothing here except the long flat highway.

Finally, after what feels like hours, a rundown servo slides into view. Beside me, Obi is almost buzzing with excitement.

Both of us thank our driver profusely, in part for the lift but mostly because we're so grateful he didn't murder us.

He leaves us standing outside the ramshackle truck stop; huge road trains hauling shipping containers parked in the gravel lot and the sun beating heavily on my back.

I grab Obi's arm and drag him to a big rusted trough with taps, beside the loos, shingled flat desert stretching behind. I'm pretty excited to brush my teeth right now. Having braces makes you paranoid about your face on a whole new level. So I scrub and brush and pick until I'm certain my mouth is perfect and there's nothing anyone can laugh at me about, then I splash water on my cheeks. While I'm in the bathroom Obi heads inside the servo to find a powerpoint for my charger, and then rejoins me at the trough beside the stretching wasteland of desert, retrieving his own toothbrush.

He brushes in silence until I can't stand it anymore.

'So let's just never mention it again, right?' I announce.

Obi blinks at me, toothpaste smeared across his mouth. 'Mention what?'

I don't want to say it aloud but force myself to grit my teeth and get it over with. 'I'm referring to what happened last night.'

Obi doesn't miss a beat. 'And what was that exactly?' He grins evilly, his dimples rising, toothpaste still smeared across his mouth. I kind of hate him right now.

'I'm serious, Obi, you can't tell everyone about this, alright?'

The grin disappears. 'You think I'm gonna tell everyone?'

'Of course! You're a boy, aren't you? It's easy for *you*.'

He flinches, then his expression turns hard beneath the toothpaste. 'And what's that supposed to mean?'

'It's different for me. I'm a girl. You know what they'll say about me.'

'No, I don't. Enlighten me.'

Of course he knows. He just enjoys putting me on the spot. Well, I'm not biting.

'I'm warning you,' I say instead. 'I mean it.' I lift my chin and attempt to look fierce. 'We'll both just forget it. It never even happened.'

He watches me, expressionless. The sun is making me sweat, my fresh T-shirt damp against my back and my jean shorts actually warm to the touch. I shift uncomfortably under his gaze. I snap, 'Well?'

Obi wipes toothpaste from his mouth with the back of his

hand, staring down at me. 'Do you think you can get into the habit of hating someone, Nash? For like, no reason at all?'

But I can't think about his weird question right now. I'm already imagining us arriving at Finn's coast shack, everyone there laughing at me because it's common knowledge at school that I'm a late bloomer. That I haven't had a boyfriend. That I'm a virgin. Boys even try to talk to me about it like it's any of their business. There's no way something like this wouldn't be a focus. Me and Obi making out in a van. I almost sway with the horror of it all, my lashes fluttering shut.

Lachlan and all his friends will think it's hilarious. Finn and Sophia and all them.

'Nash,' Obi presses, like my answer is important, like any of this matters.

'What do you even mean? What are you talking about?' I squint at him suspiciously and Obi squints back, and then finally just shrugs, leaning over to spit toothpaste into the trough. It's gross and I step back.

'Nothing,' he says. 'Whatever. Forget I said anything.'

'Fine.'

'Fine.'

'And forget about last night too,' I add for good measure.

He straightens after gulping water from the tap, towering over me with his brows drawn tight. Then suddenly he bends, leaning close like he's going to ... I don't even know.

But my heart thuds faster against my ribcage and my fingers curl into sweaty fists at my sides. My whole body stiffens when he draws near but all he does is hover with his mouth near my ear, the heat of his body between us as his voice turns hard. 'Fine.'

Turning back to the trough, Obi flips the tap on full, still frowning, and dunks his entire head under it, splashing me with warm water as I stand there stiffly, my breath heavy.

I don't want to be thinking of his mouth or the heat of his body. Or his hands on me in the deep night.

I step back, cheeks burning.

Uncool, Pearl. Uncool.

'I'm going to call my parents,' I announce, already walking away, heaving my bag over my shoulder. 'I'm pretty sure you said you'd rather be dumped at a petrol station than travel any further with me, so I guess this is your chance.'

Obi doesn't say anything, just lets me go.

5

RUBY SALTBUSH

I find my phone where I left it, behind the counter, with a young guy who's busy making chips in a deep fryer. He hands it over as a truckie comes to place an order. I back away to find a quiet table by the window, disappointed at the one bar of battery. It won't last very long.

The air conditioner is whirring, its hum mixing with the crackling oil of the chipper and the drone of the television against the back wall. Obi is still braving the summer sunshine in the car park. Sweat beads my forehead and clings to the hair at the nape of my neck. I dial home and Sam picks up.

'Pearl!'

'Ratbag,' I greet him. He's the kind of little brother who'll either save all his pink jellybeans to give you just because he knows you like them best, or he'll sneak into your bedroom when you're asleep and fart on your head. There's no middle ground with Sam. He's either giving you nightmares or smiling like an actual angel. It gives me whiplash, but also I admit I love it. I don't know what that says about me. I know what Mum says about me, though. She says it's all my fault. Because I encourage him.

'My phone won't last long. Sam, can you get Dad?'

'He's at the pub.'

A long pause stretches between us, where what I want him to do is so obvious, I don't think I actually need to ask it. Except clearly Sam isn't following. 'Well, can you get Mum, then?' I sigh.

'Why?'

'Sam! Just do it! And tell her to hurry, my phone's about to die.'

He hangs up on me.

The ratbag.

Breathing through my teeth and gritting my jaw so hard I think it's going to break, I ring back. This time it's Mum who picks up. The first thing she says is, 'You were meant to call us last night. Your father and I were worried sick.'

'Sam said Dad's out at the pub.'

Silence.

'We were worried sick, young lady.'

I pull a sour face, listening to Sam tear around in the background screaming. The television is blaring too. 'It's not my fault, Mum, the Bedford broke down and my phone wasn't charged—'

'It broke down? Are you alright?'

Now she sounds worried. I'm glad, which feels a little vindictive. But our household is hectic. It's nice to get a bit of attention. Except she ruins it by saying, 'I told your father that van was no good, didn't I? I told him! We should have sold it immediately, why do you need a car anyway? You haven't even finished school! When I was your age—'

'Mum. Mum!' It's very hard to get a word in. 'Listen, what I want to know is if you can call a mechanic for me, if there's one nearby?'

'Oh, here he is. It's your father.' She's not even listening. 'I told you we should have sold that old van.'

I can hear my dad complaining in the background that the Bedford was his father's, that it's precious, it's vintage. Obi's entered the servo now and is hovering over me. He's all cleaned up and changed. White T-shirt and washed face. I completely ignore the fact that he looks very nice and focus only on his bad acne-marked skin.

He gestures to the seat opposite me, as if asking if it's taken. I shrug like I couldn't care less. Mostly that's true. I mean, one make-out session in the back of a van doesn't wipe away a year of nasty interactions. It doesn't fundamentally change who Obi is. In fact, I'm pretty sure everything is exactly the same. Just a million times more awkward.

I wish he'd go away.

Get on a bus and leave like he said he would.

Instead Obi collapses into the seat as a fly buzzes noisily past, batting into the window and then falling to the linoleum floor. I wipe sweat from my forehead. It's just so bloody hot.

'Mum,' I whine. 'Please listen.'

Except it's my dad on the line now and Sam is screaming even louder in the background. 'Pearl, have you seen your nana yet?'

'Hello to you too, Dad.'

'Have you? Sam! Be quiet, Dad's on the phone!'

Obi raises his eyebrows at me and I shake my head like there's nothing to worry about. In truth my battery is getting exceedingly low and talking to my family is like trying to herd cats. I heard someone say that once. Such an accurate description. 'No, I haven't seen Nana yet, Dad.'

'Why?' He sounds quite annoyed for a man who spent the last hour relaxing at the pub. And it's only one pm!

'Because I broke down.'

A long pause. 'And you and Daisy are alright?'

I wince.

'Um ... yes?'

'Yes? Yes? Why are you asking me?'

I clear my throat. 'No, um, yes! Definitely we're totally fine. Totally.'

'Should I call her parents?'

I go into full panic mode. 'Um no. Definitely not. She ... uh ... she says she doesn't want to worry them.'

Obi's watching me closely.

'And actually, she's right here and she's just saying ... oh, you already called your parents, Daisy? Okay. Did you hear that, Dad?' I cringe. This is not a lie I want to get caught in, because as much as their parenting style is *let Pearl figure it out for herself because it encourages independence* they still wouldn't allow me to drive off into the desert with some random boy to go to a party at some other random boy's coast shack. Getting them to let me drive off into the desert to visit my nana with my best friend still took some serious convincing.

Which is why I'm cringing, as in physically curling in on myself.

That's when I notice Obi smirking at me.

I glare at him as I attempt to break through my dad's endless mumbling. 'Dad. Dad! Can we just concentrate on the broken-down part?'

'Sure, sweetie. Sam! Stop that. Go to your mother! Ruth, control your son!'

I hear Mum in the background, 'Oh, so he's *my* son now?'

I whine, 'So what should I do?'

A moment of silence passes on the other end, music blaring from the television and my little brother still screaming. Finally my dad says, 'Well obviously you need to call a mechanic, Pearl. And then you need to go see your nana. And I'm going to give you my brother's number, so you can call him if you have any trouble or need a ride.'

Interesting.

My dad and uncle do not get on. They stopped speaking four years ago, when we moved to the city. We never visit.

Dad rattles off a number while I wave my hands madly until Obi has grabbed a napkin and gone to beg a pen from behind the chipper guy's ear. I hold it and frown. Yuck. An ear pen. Obi grins one of his dimpled sunshine smiles that totally makes you forget about his bad skin.

I blink.

'And Pearl, make sure you tell your uncle to go and see your nana more often. I think she misses him. Lousy good-for-nothing old man that he is.'

'Dad!'

'I'm worried about her, Pearl. She hasn't been herself lately, and now when I call her house I can't get through. She's not answering her mobile either. She needs some company, alright? You know the only reason we allowed you to go on this trip with Daisy was—'

Beep.

Beep.

Beep.

So that's that. My battery is dead.

I fling my phone onto the plastic table and Obi and I both stare at it like it'll do something. I drop my head into my hands. I honestly don't know what's come over me the past few days.

First, the rash decision, so unlike me, to drive halfway across the state to attend a party I don't even want to go to. I hate parties. They're awkward and always leave me feeling stupid, hovering in a corner by myself because Daisy always flits off to talk to other people. And she doesn't seem to care if I'm there or not these days. But she asked me to come. She *begged* me. And she did that thing where her lower lip quivered and she looked at me like she needed me and ... I did what I always do.

I did what she wanted.

I flick my attention to Obi's face because he's made a weird sound. He's got his elbows on the table and his hands over his mouth, watching me suspiciously. He makes the same sound again, deep in his throat, still staring, sort of like *huh*.

'What?' I snap.

The *second* absolutely rash decision I've made lately was to kiss Obi in the back of my Bedford. I must be losing my mind.

'Nothing.'

'What do you mean, nothing?' I glare at him. He's clearly got something to say. 'Just tell me already.'

'Well ... I just never took you for a liar, Nash.'

I flinch. 'I'm not a liar!'

He grins like a cat. 'Did you or did you not just tell your dad that I'm Daisy?'

I grimace uncomfortably. But Obi's not done.

'And did you or did you not gain permission to drive that piece of junk across the desert only because your parents think you're visiting your nana?'

'I *am* visiting my nana!'

Obi erupts into laughter, deep and throaty. 'Yeah, but then you're leaving your nana behind to go stay in Finn's beach shack with a bunch of Year Twelves from school! I bet your dad would *love* that.'

'They're not *all* Year Twelves,' I protest weakly. Like it matters. 'You're not.' I don't mention that's only because he got held back a grade last year. I'm pretty sure that's a very sensitive topic for him and right now, at least, I don't want to make him mad. 'Daisy's not, either. Or Stacey.'

Obi just shakes his head and I cross my arms over my chest, attention turning to the dying fly still buzzing weakly against the grimy glass. Outside, the sky blares bright blue, heatwaves rising off the bitumen. An enormous, shimmering truck roars into the gravel carpark, painted like a shark. Teeth and everything.

I sigh. 'Why are you still here, anyway?'

'Well, I don't exactly have a lot of options, do I? There's no buses coming through here.'

Mmmh. So he did try to ditch me.

He must have asked the fryer dude about buses. For some reason that irritates me no end, despite the fact I told him to leave. I snap, 'You could hitchhike.'

Obi recoils, expression horrified. 'Nash, this is the middle of nowhere. I don't even know where we are, and you want me to hitchhike? Do you even know what happens to hitchhikers in the desert?'

I sigh. 'Do they die?'

'They die! Besides, I can't exactly leave you here by yourself. Like I said, this is the desert, Nash!'

From the way he says it, I feel like it's more about *him* not wanting to be left by himself. His horror-movie fear is setting in. I can almost see him quaking in his boots.

Or sneakers. Whatever.

'I grew up out here,' I snap. 'I'd be fine.'

Obi leans an elbow on the table and changes the subject. That's when I know he's definitely angling for an invitation to wherever I'm going next. He picks the wrong topic though. 'So ... Nash. Why are you so keen on this party anyway?'

I glare at him. 'What do you care?'

Obi's quiet. There's only the sound of the deep fryer and the hum of the air conditioners, the bell at the door ringing as another truckie shuffles in. My skin prickles with sweat, despite the air conditioner working overtime above my head.

'I *don't* care,' he clarifies eventually. There's something different about his voice now. More tentative. 'I just didn't think you liked parties. Or Finn.'

I stare at him across the table, biting my lip. Obi's face is expressionless. Is he genuinely curious, or is this more about collecting ammunition to use against me? He and his friends spend a lot of time laughing at other people.

And he already has enough to laugh at me about after last night.

Clearing my throat awkwardly, I wave a hand between us, pushing back the sudden tension, the heaviness. 'We need to charge my phone again. I have to call a mechanic. And my uncle.'

Obi sways back, leaning into the hard plastic of his chair, an emotion I don't quite catch flickering across his face. It's gone in a moment and he grins at me, his face splitting open, all teeth and dimples. 'Good idea. I don't want to be late for the party.'

It sounds like a joke, except the words have a hard edge to them. Like maybe he's annoyed at me.

I don't know what he has to complain about. (Other than the Nana detour thing, obviously.) After all, I'm rescuing him from certain death in the desert. For the second time.

I cringe as he slides out from the table, towering over me. I follow, sighing. My head barely reaches his chin. Obi starts walking toward the counter. 'What are you wearing anyway?'

I gape up at him. 'Excuse me?'

He makes a face. 'It's a *costume* party, Nash. On the final night.'

I blink, leaving him to walk ahead.

Daisy never told me that.

Actually, a huge part of me feels uncertain about this whole thing. Daisy said she wanted me to come, said she *needed* me to come, helped me organise the big scam of my parents to get us there. And then ditched me last-minute when Lachlan invited her to drive with him instead.

Daisy and Lachlan have been together for a year, but sometimes I get the sense that things between them are ... weird. Unbalanced. Daisy never talks about it, but I notice. Like, she's always the one running around behind him, trying to keep up. Coming when he calls and leaving whenever he gets sick of having a girlfriend hovering around. Which I guess is why she still needs me. Maybe it makes Daisy feel better to have someone running around after her too. Maybe it makes her feel powerful in a way she never does with Lachlan.

Which is a topic I finally got up the guts to talk about with her, the night before we left for this trip. It didn't go down very well. Daisy barely let me get a word out before she stormed out of my house. Next thing I hear, she's riding to the beach shack in Lachlan's car and not answering my texts.

I sigh, glancing at Obi, who's now chatting easily about mechanics with the deep-fryer guy. I hand over my phone to be charged again. Daisy even allowed Lachlan to ditch Obi beside the road. Or at a petrol station beside the road, to be specific.

Which is a little ... uncool.

And unlike Daisy.

Or how Daisy *used* to be.

I shrug it off as Obi returns and we head back out into the beating sun. I shield my face, dry wind ruffling my hair and flat stony land in every direction. No sign of the ocean anymore.

Obi hands over some gold coins, nudging me toward the payphone, and together we crowd into the cramped space. Which gives me way too many flashbacks of kissing him in the back of the Bedford. He's standing much too close, facing me. In the end I can't stand it and shove him out of the phone box again, snapping something about the heat. He just grins at me, one of those too-charming smiles that shouldn't be allowed, black eyes sparking. I think he knows those smiles annoy me.

I huff, turning my back on him, lifting the phone to my ear. I call the mechanic first, using the number the deep-fryer guy gave Obi. It's pretty straightforward to organise a pick-up, and I have a little money saved for the Bedford's repairs. I'm half certain my parents will chip in if I need them to. I'm sure they don't want to leave me out here in the desert forever.

Probably.

Obi leans against the glass, arms folded over his chest and sunglasses on. It's harder to read his expression now.

I watch him suspiciously and wait as my uncle's mobile rings. I'd like to know what Obi's thinking. Or you know, I'd be interested.

For instance, I'd be interested to know if he's thought of last night at all. I doubt it's running through his head like it's running through mine.

When I think about it, he's always hooking up at parties. He's probably used to weird situations like this. Used to having anybody he wants. He probably never thinks about it twice, except to joke afterwards with his friends.

Ugh. I really wish I hadn't done it. I had a moment of complete insanity. The first time I make such a huge mistake and it has to be with Obi.

With Obi!

This whole trip was a terrible idea. And even worse? Every now and then I catch a seed of resentment growing inside my chest, a little ball of bitterness aimed directly at Daisy. All this time, I've held to the belief that the changes in Daisy, and the way she treats me, are all Lachlan's fault. So I've stuck by her, even when her other friends have peeled away. I've waited for her to change back, return miraculously to who she used to be.

But these last few days ... I feel different. Like maybe she should have treated me better. If she actually valued our friendship, then maybe she should have tried to at least listen to what I had to say, instead of storming out of my house and ignoring me.

I shut that thought down as quickly as I can, because it scares me. I don't want to feel this kind of bitterness toward my best friend. But still, it's there.

Shifting and expanding.

Growing.

'Hello?' A gruff voice sounds on the other end of the line. Outside the phone box, Obi jumps up hopefully, opening the door and cramming himself in beside me so he can listen too. I have no idea why.

'Hi Uncle John, this is Pearl. How are you?' I glare at Obi. I don't like having him pressed against me. He grins back, sunglasses on and dust from a passing road train smeared across his skin.

'Pearl?' My uncle repeats my name like it's unfamiliar. Which is crazy, because I grew up next door to him.

'Um, yeah,' I say, taken aback. 'My name's Pearl Nash?'

Silence.

Surely he hasn't forgotten me! It's only been four years, and even if he and my dad are fighting, it's got nothing to do with me.

I frown. Try again. 'I'm your niece, Pearl Nash? My dad is your brother?'

'Right.'

'Right,' I echo awkwardly, when it becomes clear he isn't going to elaborate. Uncle John was always a man of few words but this is ridiculous.

I try to scrape back some of the warmth I remember from my childhood. 'So ... it's nice to talk to you again, Uncle John. It's been too long, right? How have you all been?'

'Good.' Pause. 'I wasn't expecting your call.'

I cringe. 'No. I know. It's quite unexpected.'

He clears his throat. 'And how have you been, Pearl? Good?'

I nod enthusiastically, though he can't see. 'Yes! Quite good. Thank you.'

'And your dad? He good, too?'

Obi leans close, his head bent to mine. He raises his brows.

'Yup. Real good.' I hear my uncle make a *humph* noise on the other end of the line and decide this awkward conversation needs some direction before my money runs out. 'Er. Listen, Uncle John, myself and a friend have run into some trouble, some car trouble to be exact. And we're in your area and I'm hoping you don't mind if we ... um ... pop by? Our car will be in with a mechanic near you.'

'Near me?'

Uncle John is exactly like my grandpa was. Quiet. Taciturn. Men of action, not words. Or at least slow, plodding action around the farm. It's all flooding back to me now.

'Uh ... yes. Near you. Is that ... okay?'

Silence. Then finally a gruff, 'Right.'

I take that to mean a big resounding yes and react appropriately. 'Oh, thank you so much, Uncle John! We really appreciate it. We'll be around later today.'

'Today?'

I hesitate. 'Um, yes. Today. Is that ... fine?'

I wince at Obi, who's still squished beside me. It brings our faces closer and this time it's him who clears his throat and extricates himself from my vicinity, exiting the phone box to wander away into the sun. I watch him go, kind of surprised. Wondering if he's feeling weird too.

Would that make me feel better?

I don't know.

'Fine,' repeats my uncle before the line goes dead. I'm not sure if I ran out of coins or he just hung up on me, but either way I'm wondering how my family managed to get this messed up. It's not just me who hasn't been back here in the last four years. My dad's been avoiding his brother like the plague. I knew things were bad but maybe not this bad.

When we moved to the city, I was still a kid, preoccupied with the uprooting of my entire life to a new unfamiliar place. I can't even remember the fight that ended their relationship.

Frowning, I trail across the dusty lot to the concrete toilet block, peering at Obi. He's sitting in the shade with his back against the cement wall, legs splayed out facing the desert. He's even dustier now than he was before, a layer of fine dirt clinging to his T-shirt and skin. I resist the urge to dust off his head. If it was Sam I would have. Daisy, even.

I'm probably just as dirty, though. I run a hand through my own hair and Obi watches as I sit carefully on the warm concrete beside him. Not too close. The sun burns my legs, so I curl them toward my chest and rest my head on my knees.

'Well, I can't wait to meet this monosyllabic uncle of yours, Nash. He sounds like a fascinating specimen.'

'Hey!' Obi's totally his normal self. No lingering weirdness after all. I scowl, feeling protective despite my own weird feelings toward my uncle. 'That's my family you're talking about.'

'It's fine, Nash. Wait until you meet my family.' He dons an exaggerated African accent and says loudly, 'Why can't you be more like your brother, Obiara? He is so much more responsible than you.'

I stare at him, but Obi doesn't seem to notice. His sunglasses reflect the desert like a mirror.

'And so loud. Like, when my dad took us to community events when I was a kid, I thought everyone was angry at each other. I thought they were shouting.'

I blink. I've never heard Obi talk about his family before. 'They weren't?'

He leans his head back against the concrete. 'Nah, they were just having a good time. Hey Nash, you got any more coins?'

'No. *You* gave me those coins.'

He nods seriously. 'Which is why I now don't have any. I want to buy an ice-cream or something. It's too hot.'

'You don't have any money?'

'Um. I mean, I do. I did. But I used up all my cash. And I don't have my new card yet, so was just using my phone but ... well, you know.'

He glances at me pointedly, which annoys me. Especially because I'm actually already handing him my card. Which is probably why I add more barbs into my next question than I might have otherwise.

'You didn't even bring money for petrol? Maybe that's why Lachlan kicked you out of his car.'

Obi's face shuts down, mouth growing tight. I can't read him properly beneath the black sunglasses. 'No. That's not why.'

I press. 'Why, then?'

He grins, sudden and wide, slinging himself to his feet, sneakers scraping against the concrete. 'That was because he knew I wanted to travel with you, Nash. Lachlan knows how much I love being interrogated by socially inept nerds.'

I suck in my breath, winded by his meanness. And because now I know Obi's definitely not chewing over the events of last night in his mind like I am. Or if he is, it's in an entirely negative way.

Which kind of hurts.

Not because I wanted him to like me. But if I'm honest, it

would be nice to have kissed someone who didn't think I was a socially inept nerd.

I say nothing, just simmer and grind my teeth as Obi legs it across the parking lot in a cloud of dust and baking sun. A hot wind blows over the shimmering trucks and burning metal.

It takes a while for the anger to die down. There's nothing to do except boil, my back against the warm concrete, watching the road trains rumble by.

I find myself thinking about Obi's smile, despite myself. Because for the first time I noticed how it seemed almost like a shield. Not genuine. I wonder how aware he is of his best feature, how often he uses it to deflect and avoid.

Weird.

I've never spent as much time thinking about Obi as I have today. I rub my face, realising even my lashes are dusty. Yuck.

Right then, something cold touches my arm. I glance up to find Obi blocking out the sun, sunglasses still in place and a wrapped ice-cream in his hand.

I huff and don't take it, so he nudges me again. 'Come on, Nash. I'm trying to say that I'm sorry.'

A peace offering?

Probably because he's worried I'll leave him here with no money and no ride.

I take the ice-cream anyway. It's cold and I'm hot. 'Fine. I'll eat it. But it doesn't mean this socially inept nerd forgives you, alright?'

He grins, dimples appearing, and I soak it in for a moment, analysing whether it's real or not, or if he's just using the smile to charm me and get whatever it is he wants.

His face falls, dimples and teeth disappearing. 'What?'

I shake my head, taking a big bite of my ice-cream. Lime spills icy cold onto my tongue. 'Nothing.'

I take another huge bite before it melts and, sitting beside me on the concrete, Obi does the same. A sort of truce, I guess.

We wait like that until an old truck rolls into the parking lot beneath a cloud of swirling dust, the name of the mechanic I called painted across its side. Obi runs off to grab my phone and charger from the servo and I head over to the mechanic to explain the situation. It's occurring to me that we're going to have to ride in a squished front bench seat all those hours back to my Bedford.

Horrific. Especially in this heat.

Our rescue truck is a total bomb. It looks like it might break down itself.

The mechanic wears a stained blue singlet. His long grey hair is balding on top. I'm talking to him when Obi comes running out of the servo, like we were going to leave him behind. The mechanic blinks at him. Asks, 'Where're you from, then?'

'I'm from the city,' Obi answers. He rolls his eyes for my benefit beneath his sunglasses, and when the mechanic isn't looking, he mouths, *he's going to murder us.*

I watch the mechanic closely as he loads our bags into the back and then we're all squished inside the truck, me in the middle again, pressed tight against Obi. The mechanic begins telling us a mad story about some girl who went missing from this stretch of road in the fifties.

And for once I'm inclined to agree with Obi.

6

SWAMP GUM

The mechanic doesn't actually murder us in the end, which is quite nice.

But he does talk a lot.

Like *a lot,* a lot.

We go all the way back to the Bedford (which takes hours) and strap it up and then travel off into the low hills of the peninsula toward the mechanic shop (which takes hours). And the whole time the old man talks.

Eventually I can't deal with it anymore. I selfishly leave Obi to listen, and retrieve the new paperback from my bag, burying my face into it so I can leave the conversation behind. Obviously the rather one-sided discussion still occurs, but it's occurring over my head now. The mechanic is trying to convince Obi just how totally okay he is with Obi being black by describing in excruciating detail the exact shade of pitch-black skin a friend of his used to have. Still has, presumably, but clearly they don't hang out anymore.

Not because of his skin colour, though – the mechanic is pretty quick to point that out.

I'm perplexed by the whole thing, but I guess maybe it's like how if you have a close family member with cancer, everyone you meet will tell you about their neighbour or childhood friend or distant acquaintance who also had cancer. That's what happened when my grandpa was sick.

Except I'm not sure what this situation and cancer have in common.

Not much, presumably.

I'm not really reading, more staring at the same page over and over again, because instead I'm watching Obi out of the corner of my eye. Clearly, he's annoyed, but he's also being polite, nodding along. Maybe it's easier that way. Which feels sucky. I feel like I should do something, but I don't know what.

I suppose I drift off while I'm thinking about it, because next thing I know, I wake with a jolt of the truck, a loud, 'We're here!' and my face pressed into Obi's throat. Again. I'm pretty sure I'm drooling and I'm also pretty sure I have dust in my mouth.

I sit up quick, wiping my cheeks self-consciously, which is when I realise Obi has an arm slung over my shoulder, the paperback open across his knee to a place a lot further along than I got, and that he must have been asleep too. I know this because his sunglasses hang askew and his face is indented with the pattern of the rubber seams from the window. It's hard to see because his skin is pock-marked across his cheeks, but near his temple it's pretty obvious. It makes my chest ache. I don't know why.

He wakes slowly, kind of goofy and sleepy, like he doesn't know what's going on, then sharpens immediately when he notices his arm draped over my shoulder. He snatches it back, turning away and yawning deliberately. The sunglasses come off because it's growing dark outside. Blue-lit dusk falls soft over fields of rolling wheat, the stretching sky a blue so deep and dark that the remaining clouds seem black.

I love this time of day. It's my favourite. Even the ugliest places in the world are beautiful under this soft blue light.

Although. The place we're in front of might be the single exception.

We slide from the car onto a gravel lot, old rusted tractors crowded together and sheets of stained tin and corrugated iron leaning against a barbed-wire fence. A big cattle dog barks loudly, dragging against its chain and snarling.

'Come on, Lola. Stop it. These are customers,' mutters the mechanic, pushing long grey hair from his face and getting to work immediately on dislodging the Bedford from his truck. Lola doesn't stop barking and Obi's mouth hangs open as he takes in the dilapidated shed and the old tin house beyond. He steps closer to me, putting his hands on my shoulders and actually placing me between himself and the barking dog. I glare up at him.

'Have you seen that movie?' he hisses at me. '*Wolf Creek*? Have you seen it?' His voice is actually really loud. Loud enough that I'm worried the mechanic has overheard.

'Do you have a phone we can borrow, Tim?' I bellow, ignoring Obi and marching toward the house. Tim the Mechanic nods and also informs us that he reckons the Bedford isn't so bad, it might only take him a day or two to fix. I'm pretty pleased about this but I see Obi wilt where he waits within easy escaping distance, near the flyscreen door.

Secretly I wish I knew more about cars, because I have a strong feeling from Tim's explanation that the problem with the Bedford might be something highly fixable, if only I knew what I was doing. I make a quiet vow to learn about engines.

If I survive this trip.

My uncle John arrives to pick us up. Another ute with a front bench seat. This one looks like an old paddock basher. We're waiting on the side of the highway in the pitch dark and Obi's shivering. It isn't cold so I figure he's scared. Which is fine, because so am I.

I have the weirdest urge to pat his arm and tell him no one is going to murder him as my uncle cuts the engine and hops out, the headlights flooding the gravelly verge with bright, hot light. I don't though. Obviously.

Instead I shove my bags at Obi's chest and greet Uncle John with a really awkward hug. He reacts as if no one has ever hugged him before.

Uncle John greets me with a grunt and then squints at Obi. 'Who's this? A boy?'

'Uh yeah, Uncle John. This is a boy. A friend. A friend who is a boy.' I'm stammering, which is highly embarrassing. 'This is Obi.'

Uncle John peers at Obi for a long moment without blinking. Then he says, 'Fine.'

And that's it.

He turns and climbs back into his truck, and I shiver even though the thick night is stifling and my T-shirt is damp with sweat. Seeing my uncle again reminds me of the old days in a surreal way. Almost like seeing my dad dressed how he used to, driving an old paddock basher how he used to, back when he was a farmer and not working in management at the factory in the city. Like seeing my mum in boots and a big straw hat, out walking across an empty, flat landscape as the sun sinks low, carrying my baby brother on her hip.

My parents don't talk much about the old days. About the ancient farmhouse we lived in or the newer property built nearby for my uncle and aunt. What it was like living so close to family, all in each other's pockets. They don't talk about the times I'd head into the fields with my dad and he'd teach me how to drive the ute. Or about the big, noisy dinners on the verandah with Grandpa and Nana when they visited, eating vegetables my nana had grown in the earth behind her house.

My brother Sam is growing up in such a different way to me. I don't know if that's a bad thing or a good thing.

Maybe it's neither.

But I can't help but wonder if my dad misses it. This place. This landscape. Maybe that's why he goes to the pub all the time these days. Maybe he's trying to fill some kind of hole in his heart, the way Mum used to fill up her empty spaces with phone calls to all of her city friends.

It's strange being out here again. It makes me think weird thoughts, brings the memories flooding back. All the things I hardly ever think of anymore.

Obi nudges me with his elbow, soft. Raises his eyebrows. He still looks scared. The air smells sweet, like cut grass and the ocean. I follow him to the passenger side of the truck.

We travel in silence, squished into my uncle's truck. This time I sit more comfortably in the middle, closer to Uncle John. He's family.

'How are you?' I try.

'Good.'

'And Aunty Sue?'

'Good.'

'And the kids?'

'Good.'

'Oh ...' I run out of things to say. He was always like this. 'That's ... good.'

Obi nudges me in the ribs and makes a face at me. I batt him away. And then I try again. 'So ... we're here to visit Nana, Uncle John.'

'Right.'

'How is she?'

'Haven't really seen her.'

'Oh.'

We lapse into uncomfortable silence again. It's an odd experience, trying to talk to Uncle John. It reminds me of when I was younger and we all lived on the farm together. Back then he was almost just a blur in the background, a big quiet man who stayed on the edges of things. Lost in a sea of stronger, louder personalities.

Beside me, Obi's trying not to laugh, his whole body shaking. But I don't find it all that funny. Maybe Uncle John is just shy.

I elbow Obi in the ribs to shut him up. He still snorts. Loudly. And I glare at him as we draw off the dark highway onto a long and winding dirt track, just two tyre lines running between tall dry grass beside a wheatfield.

I perk up.

The farm.

Suddenly my skin is prickling and my ears buzzing. My heart thuds softly against my chest.

This place used to be my home.

Rolling hills all the way down toward the cliffs and the ocean, shadowy in the darkness. Fields stretching into the black. Vast skies. It's beautiful and I didn't realise how much I missed it until now. I feel it suddenly like a tangible thing, hissing and popping inside my chest, fizzling to my fingertips.

Home.

Or at least, it used to be home. Now I don't know what it is.

We approach the house beneath the inky blue shadow of night. The ute's headlights illuminate the wavering grasses and a sprawling homestead ahead. Ancient date palms loom out front. A big dirt driveway and a wrap-around verandah held up by carved wooden poles. The roof is tall, nearly as tall as the house itself, chimneys poking out the top.

The lights are on and a warm glow spills from the verandah across the baked dirt yard, revealing ancient tractors gone brown with rust and the kind of old ploughing equipment no farmer in their right mind would touch nowadays. Relics of the past.

Left to rot and rust.

I stare at them fondly. Great for kids to climb on. For make-believe and games.

And tetanus.

I frown. Everything looks different when you're older.

The homestead itself is crumbling stone, paint peeling and wood rotting away, the tin roof dark green to hide the rust.

I jump from the ute when we stop rolling. Twirling around in the yard, I bask in the memories of this place, breathing deep. It smells fresh out here. The air hangs heavy with the day's heat, despite the darkness, but it smells sweet. It's like my feet are rooted in place. Like I'm growing down and outwards beneath the earth, settling in where I'm meant to be. Becoming part of this harsh landscape again. Just like all those tough old native plants that Nana likes so much.

At home we live near a bunch of factories, my school sprung up right beside the beach. It smells like salt at home, thick and humid, and sometimes like sulphur, an eggy scent that makes Sam puke. It comes up with the bore water our neighbours use to water their neatly cut green grass. This place has a different smell.

I take deep breaths. Sink back into it.

Home.

It takes me a while to realise that Obi is watching me from beside the truck, laden with our bags, his face hidden in shadow. I go back guiltily to help him carry the load. He whispers, almost with a kind of reverence, as if he could tell something inside me was shifting, 'What is this place?'

My uncle has gone ahead into the spilling lights of the house. A dog barks in the distance. I heave a bag onto my shoulder. 'My dad was born out here. In that house. And I was too. I lived here until a few years ago when we moved to the city. And my grandpa was born here too.'

'Like ... actually in the house?' Obi wrinkles his nose, and I suspect maybe he's missing the point, maybe he's not really tuning into what I'm feeling at all.

I roll my eyes, but still can't seem to stop talking. 'Yes, in the actual house. Or at least, Grandpa was. Back then it was really isolated out here. There wasn't much in the way of facilities. They would get post delivered, and go into town for special occasions. But my dad always said that growing up, they mostly just stayed here on the property.'

Obi stops walking. 'Huh.' He peers around into the swelling dark and clinging shadows. The vast emptiness beyond the house. 'It's weird to imagine it. Why'd your family move away anyway? They didn't want to stay out here?'

I lean closer and lower my voice, forcing him to bend to hear. Because it's sensitive. 'My dad and his brother, you know, Uncle John I mean, they used to run the farm together, but they had a huge fight. They haven't spoken even once since then. I think it makes my nana sad.'

'What did they fight about?'

I shrug. 'I dunno. No one will tell me. But they hate each other. Hey look.' I point upwards. This is the real deal now. No cloud coverage tonight.

Proper countryside sky. No moon, but that's what makes the stars burn so bright.

Obi sucks in his breath, turning in circles, face upturned to the Milky Way, which shimmers like a thick streamer across the sky. He makes a low sound deep in his throat.

I stare at him and grin, because I like seeing how impressed he is. I feel like it's the first time anything of mine has impressed him.

It feels like this sky is mine. This place too.

Until the moment is broken with squeals from the house. My two little cousins come barrelling out, both of them body-slamming into me, making me spin again. I drop my bags to the ground so I can pick up the closest one. Lily or Rose? They're a year apart and so similar I can't tell the difference between them, particularly because I never see them. I'm surprised they even recognise me. Last time I saw them was … when my Aunt Sue came into the city? So like, a year ago maybe?

'Lily?' I ask.

'Rose!' She's indignant. 'Look at my tooth.'

'Mmmh. Disgusting.'

'It's wiggling.'

'It sure is. Rose, this is Obi. Obi, this is Rose and this here is Lily.' I point to the other girl. Slightly older, she stands at my side, arms wrapped tight around my waist, her hair wild.

'Obi. Obi. Obi,' she says.

I'm embarrassed but Obi doesn't seem to mind.

'My full name is Oh – byo – rah.' He sounds it out for her and she grins cheekily before running off into the house, screaming his name at the top of her lungs.

Rose kicks and bucks until I let her down so she can run after her sister, screaming it too.

'Right,' I say awkwardly. 'So those are my cousins.'

Obi's brows scrunch like he's trying to think of something nice to say. 'They're both really … dirty.'

'Yeah, they were, weren't they?' I rub my hands together. I don't know what Rose was eating but I feel sticky. 'Come on, let's do this.'

I take a deep calming breath, suddenly nervous. Maybe it's the prospect of seeing the home of my childhood that's unsettling me. What if it's not really the same anymore? Because how could it be? Everything felt perfect and happy back then, but I know it wasn't really, now I'm older and looking back. Things were fractured even then. My dad and uncle were fighting. My grandpa had cancer. My mum was going crazy on that isolated property and my nana was bossing everyone around, like she does.

I square my shoulders and decide to take the plunge, marching toward the lit-up house. I'm so nervous about seeing my relatives and old home that suddenly having Obi here feels like a comfort. As if he's on my side.

Weird.

Comfort is not a word he usually brings to mind.

We climb the creaking wooden steps and pass through the ripped flyscreen door into a dark hallway with peeling paint and a huge pile of muddy shoes. The place is more rundown than I remember, like maybe money's a bit tight.

I shake off the thought as my aunt pops out of a doorway ahead in the hall, her hair dripping. I hear my cousins humming loudly behind her, water splashing as they squeal from the bath. She smiles warmly, in a frazzled way, then stops and blinks when she sees Obi.

'Oh. Pearl. John didn't say you had a boyfriend ...' The smile returns, still frazzled. Maybe even more so. 'Welcome. Both of you. It's been too long, Pearl.' She gives me a big warm hug, gives Obi one too and then sends us to drop our stuff in the end room, while she slips back into the bathroom to wash the kids. Uncle John is who-knows-where.

'So ... they all seem nice,' whispers Obi. 'Your aunt was less sticky than the other ones.'

My stomach churns. I'm trying to resist the pull in my belly, but I can't ignore it anymore. I step from the shadowy room back into the bright hall, walking lightly across the heaving wooden boards until I reach another door. It feels like walking inside a dream, a half-forgotten memory. Things familiar, except … not.

Obi hesitates and then follows.

'This one was my room,' I whisper, because he's looming behind me and I feel like I have to say something to hide the strange feeling blooming in my chest. Somewhere in the distance, a dog barks. The squeals continue from the bathroom. I push the door open gently.

A flick of the familiar light switch and the whole room floods with an electric glow.

My stomach sinks.

Two single beds sit against the walls on opposite sides, a small pink plastic desk placed between them. Dolls and building blocks and books are strewn across the threadbare carpet. The walls are painted the colour of candy floss.

It's mayhem. In a friendly, chaotic sort of way.

I clear my throat, peering around.

'Uh, nice room,' says Obi. 'Very … pink. It's quite pink.'

I shake my head, surprised at how disappointed I feel. 'It's different.'

And it is. I don't feel any twinge of familiarity in this place. Nothing reminds me of how it used to be. I don't have any sort of connection.

I kind of thought I would.

Grandpa always used to say that you can't go back, only forward. He said it when he was scolding his sons and their wives. In hindsight, he might have been a pretty difficult person to live with. The only person he didn't scold was Nana.

And me, I guess.

I sigh.

Families are complicated.

And memories are complicated too. When you grow up, your memories shift and change. You slowly realise things aren't necessarily what you assumed they were. Does that make your memories false? It makes me sad to think my old happy childhood memories might get overwritten with what I know now.

Obi nudges my shoulder, tugging me back into the here and now. I blink as he says awkwardly, 'So ... I think your Aunt Sue is calling us to go have dinner with your sticky family right now.'

A small, unexpected laugh escapes my throat and Obi looks surprised. And then maybe a bit pleased with himself. Less so during dinner (a nice roast with veggies), when we're sitting at the dining table opposite Rose and Lily who are both (still) screaming his name at the top of their lungs. My aunt seems very stressed and my uncle very serene, like he hasn't noticed there's any commotion whatsoever. It's all quite interesting.

Until my aunt says, 'So Obi, where are you from?'

She doesn't ask it in a mean way, and Obi simply smiles back, very pleasantly. I can't tell if he's annoyed or not, but it makes me feel on-edge.

'I'm from the city, Mrs Nash.' He gives her one of his big whopping smiles, showing off both dimples in a way that makes me roll my eyes at Rose and Lily across the table. They don't know why I'm doing it, of course, but that certainly doesn't stop them copying me. Which I regret very quickly when their eyes turn back in their heads and they both loll backwards on their chairs.

'Girls!'

I cringe. 'Sorry, Aunty Sue.'

'It's fine. Totally fine.' She smiles at Obi. 'But where were you from before the city?'

I've stopped eating and am watching awkwardly, a piece of carrot waving uselessly on my fork, as Obi clears his throat.

'I was born there actually. I've never been overseas.'

Aunty Sue nods while the girls keep rolling their eyes. Rose is on the floor now. We all ignore her. 'But what about your parents? Where are they from?'

Obi's smile doesn't lessen. He's good at this. 'My dad is from Nigeria and my mum is from India. From the south.'

'Oh that's interesting. How does that work?'

'Er ...' Obi turns to me with wide eyes, like she's asking him to literally describe it.

I slap his arm. 'She doesn't mean how babies are made, Obi. She means how your parents met!'

My uncle startles us all by suddenly roaring with laughter, like what I said was the funniest thing he's ever heard. And then he makes a joke about Nigerian princes and email scams.

My palms are sweaty and I decide it's time to change the subject. I wave my hand at my uncle to get his attention, my voice a little shrill. 'Uncle John, when was the last time you saw Nana, anyway?'

He blinks at me. 'Mmmh.'

'I think in September,' answers Aunty Sue on his behalf, her face scrunched as if she's thinking very hard.

I'm shocked. 'September? That's ages ago!' I'm counting the weeks back on my fingers. 'But she told us she was staying with you back in November.'

Aunty Sue blinks at her husband and both of them slowly shake their heads. 'No. She never stayed with us.'

'But she's been on the peninsula,' I push. 'Just down the road, since like ...'

Mmmh. I can't remember. It was ages ago that she left the granny flat in our backyard. Two months? I had exams and then it was the end of the year and I was dealing with all this weird Daisy stuff and then ... I guess Nana just disappeared one morning. And we were all worried at first – crazy worried – until she texted Dad to say she'd driven herself back to her old house on the peninsula for a while.

At first, we called her often, each of us taking turns. Even Mum. Then we got out of the habit. I guess life got in the way.

And lately, she hasn't been answering the phone. At first we figured she might be mad at us for not calling, or just in a mood. I didn't think much about it: surely it's Dad's job to worry about Nana, not mine. Even though our house felt emptier without her around.

But now ...

Am I worried?

I'm not sure.

I lean forward, confused. Rose is still rolling around on the worn carpet. I spread my fingers on the table. 'So wait, what you're telling me is that no one's *seen* Nana for two months?'

Uncle John and his wife glance at each other nervously and then back to me. Finally Aunty Sue admits, 'Well, we didn't actually know she was out here. We thought she was still in the city with your dad. We spoke to her on her mobile once or twice. But that was ... a while ago.'

Well that's ... even worse.

I sit back, feeling weird. Obi reaches out and pokes my elbow. Like an *are you okay?* sort of poke. Which is weird in and of itself. And I'm not. I think.

Maybe I'm worried.

'Well we thought she was out here with you guys,' I admit slowly. I regret it though because immediately it ignites a squabble between my aunt and uncle, both of them just as confused as me. Both of them blaming each other. But in a sort of good-natured way. While we all eat our veggies.

Obi turns all stiff and weird, which is fair enough. No one wants to get caught in the middle of a family trauma while eating peas and carrot.

'You know losing your grandpa hit her very hard,' says Aunty Sue finally, which makes me raise my eyebrows.

'That was almost three years ago!'

She frowns like I'm being insensitive. Which maybe I am.

'Yes, but there's no time limit on grief, Pearl. I think your nana may be going through a tough time. It might be nearly three years since your grandpa died but it was fifty years of her life living with him before that. It's not an easy thing to adjust to, losing someone.'

I nod like I understand it, but to be honest, fifty years is an inconceivable amount of time. Obi nods too.

While Lily joins Rose on the floor to have a roll around and a scream, my aunt and uncle decide that they definitely, absolutely cannot take the day off tomorrow to go searching for my nana. But apparently Obi and I can, since we're young and responsibility-free over the summer holidays. I'd like to mention the fact that I actually took a week off from my boring job as a check-out chick for this trip, but it doesn't seem like the time. And besides, we were on our way there anyway before the Bedford broke down. So I bite my tongue.

The only problem, of course, is the Bedford. Or lack thereof.

Which is how Obi and I end up with the paddock-basher ute at our disposal.

And also how I find out that Obi can't drive.

Which might have been more of a revelation and talking point if it hadn't just come to light that no one has seen my nana for months.

And that's how our evening meal draws to a close.

KANGAROO PAW

I'm awake on a mattress in the lounge room. It's very dark and shadowy, a faint light seeping from the hall. Obi is lying beside me, close but not touching, and he's snoring very lightly. I notice the steady rhythm of his chest rising and falling in the dark. I wish I could sleep.

The ceiling is high and an unlit fireplace gapes like a dark mouth near my feet. The lounge chairs have been pushed aside and piles of blankets are strewn everywhere.

We spent the rest of the evening watching cricket on the television while I helped the girls build pillow forts on the carpet. And when everyone was finally ready for bed, Rose and Lily chucked a massive tantrum and insisted on sleeping with us on the lounge-room floor. Or at least Lily did, and Rose followed suit. Because, why not?

Which is where they both are now. Rose curled like a cat across my legs. It's less uncomfortable than I would have expected. Lily is squeezed long and squished in the crevice between Obi's and my mattresses.

I glance again at sleeping Obi and cringe. Not because of my aunt and uncle and everything they said at dinner. But because of myself. Just as I managed to get the mess with my nana out of my head, just as I was finally falling into an exhausted sleep, tangled up in my cousins on the floor, this terrible thought suddenly occurred to me. And it shocked me awake good and proper.

And this is it ...

Daisy always had loads of friends. I was just one of them. But she always made time for me, and she always left room for me to sit with her at lunch. She had other friends, but the two of us were *best* friends.

I knew Obi back then and he was in a bunch of my classes, but we never spoke. Though truthfully, I was never big for socialising widely at school. I had everything I needed. I had Daisy and she took me under her wing. She invited me into her group of friends, and though I never hung out with them outside school if Daisy wasn't around, we were all friendly enough for there to always be lots of people to talk to. Maybe I still felt awkward and a bit like an outsider, but they'd all been close since primary school, so what else could I expect? I was new. And it was enough.

Even if I'd been inclined to find new friends of my own away from Daisy, it wouldn't have been with Obi. He was popular, charming, he hung out with Lachlan and Sebastian and those boys. Our circles never intersected.

Until Daisy started dating Lachlan and stopped making time for me. I didn't want to lose her, so I made time instead. To hold onto our friendship, I tagged along to parties, to beach days, to town trips.

I didn't love the whole experience, but I was determined to keep putting myself through it to stay close with Daisy.

And she said she wanted me there. *Needed* me. So I'd hover awkwardly at the fringe of groups, and it was there that I first encountered Obi.

And I remember the very first thing I blurted out to him.

I lie on the mattress and squeeze my eyes shut, trying desperately to wipe the conversation from my mind. It's so utterly awful.

I asked him where he was from. I really, *really* hope he's forgotten that.

Sighing loudly, I attempt to calm myself and sleep, but then realise my legs are going numb. I don't have the heart to kick Rose off, though. It's not like I get to see my sticky cousins very often.

The whole thing with Obi makes me squeamish. I watch him sleep, through the dark. He's different at night. He can't use his dimples or his mega-watt smile to his advantage. He looks more normal. Just a boy with bad skin and a buzz-cut who snores.

I snort. What's so great about Obi, anyway? I have no idea why he's so popular at school. Shifting until I'm staring at the ceiling, I think of his ridiculous attempts to pitch a tent, how useless he was back at the campsite. All those dumb horror movie fears.

'What are you thinking about?' Obi's soft voice breaks into my thoughts and I startle, my attention flicking back to his face.

'Nothing,' I murmur.

He's watching me with a soft curve to his mouth. He shakes his head. 'You were smiling.'

'No, I wasn't.' I shrug. Which is awkward when you're lying down with a small child flopped across your legs. I manage to drag my body onto my side, facing Obi. Rose moans softly but doesn't wake.

Obi is sleepy. Lashes heavy.

He looks nice.

I want to kick myself for having that thought.

I turn away and breathe deep. Eventually force myself to face him again. He's clearly amused. Hopefully not because he can read my mind.

'I'm sorry about dinner,' I whisper carefully. 'About all the Nigerian prince stuff. And the other stuff.'

'Oh, I mean … that's okay.'

I don't really believe him though. 'I guess you get asked that pretty often. About where you're from.' I very purposely don't bring up the fact that I did it too. I hope he's blocked that from his memory.

Obi yawns. 'Mmmh. Not so much in the city. People don't care so much in the city.' He pauses and then adds, 'I get why people ask, it's just … annoying. Because everyone keeps asking it. Like all the time. And I'm just from here. That's it.'

My cheeks are hot but I say nothing.

He yawns again, wider this time with his hand over his face. 'People expect you to be an expert, which is stupid. I don't really know much about it. I mean, my dad used to tell me stuff about Nigeria sometimes, and I guess Mum talks about her parents or whatever, but I've always lived here – always, since I was born – just like you.'

'Mmmh,' I say, thinking about it. I can definitely see how it would be annoying.

Obi breaks the silence, his voice a whisper so as not to wake the girls. Lily is snoring heavily between us, her face squished near my belly. 'Are you worried about your nana?'

I glance at him in the darkness, surprised. Slowly, I bite my lip. 'Yeah. Kinda. Everyone's been so wrapped up in their own stuff, I guess none of us … noticed.'

Another thing to feel guilty about.

'I don't know whether to tell my parents about it,' I whisper. 'They'll feel awful. My dad hadn't called her for ages until about a week ago. And when he realised he couldn't get through, he was too stubborn to call my uncle and see if she was here.'

Obi shifts on the mattress. 'Hence you being out here with the Bedford.'

'Yep.'

'Well maybe we can go to her house tomorrow and decide then? If she's there we don't need to worry your folks, yeah?'

I nod. 'Yeah.'

That makes sense. That seems like a plan.

I like having a plan.

I feel a bit better now, my chest looser and my muscles uncoiled. After talking it through with Obi. Which is weird and new. And unexpected. Suddenly I freeze, mid-stretch.

He said *we*.

I glance across in the dark. So I guess he's planning to come with me tomorrow? Down the peninsula. In the opposite direction to Finn's beach shack and end-of-year party.

We're silent for a while. He looks more like how he does when he sleeps. Just normal. Until he smiles, kind of blurry and soft in the dark, and the dimples come back and remind me of who he is. Popular Obi who everyone loves. Mr Charming who only spares me his time to fight with me.

That breaks the moment enough to remind me that he has no money for a bus out of here anyway. And of course there isn't a bus out of this property. So maybe he's hoping to catch a lift with me to my nana's town, where he'll then beg me for a loan to get him a bus to the coast shack.

Which is fine. Let him do all that.

I don't want him here anyway.

Obviously.

But still, I feel strange, a little askew. I clear my throat, shifting again until I'm on my back. Then I keep turning until I'm facing away from him.

'Okay,' I manage to say. 'Let's go to my nana's tomorrow.'

Obi laughs deep in his throat. 'Okay?' He shifts on the mattress, moving closer, like he's propped himself up on his elbow. He whispers, 'We just had a deep heart-to-heart and that's all you have to say? Just, okay?'

'Yeah,' I whisper back, annoyed. 'Okay.'

I don't know what else he expects me to say. I've got more important things on my mind than Obi. Or his mega-watt smile and what happened in the Bedford. I shiver, attempting to focus. I've got to find my nana, after all. And figure things out with Daisy.

Besides, he'll be gone as soon as we reach Nana's town.

'Alright, Nash. You clearly need a time-out.' He chuckles. 'You're not even picking a fight with me.'

'No,' I breathe. I don't really want to pick a fight with him. Which I must admit, is a little unusual. I must be tired.

'Go to sleep then,' he murmurs. He sounds like he's already taking his own advice, his voice turning slow and thick. 'I'm wrecked anyway. Today was full on.'

He shifts again behind me, the mattress dipping in and dragging me backwards. My whole body feels heavy and strange.

Things turn silent. Just the sound of breathing, slow and

rhythmic. From my cousins. From Obi. But I can't help the curiosity rising in my chest. I've wanted to know the truth since yesterday.

'Obi?'

'Mmmh?'

'What did you do to get left behind at the petrol station?'

Silence. 'Why do you think it was me who did something?'

There's something in his voice that makes me roll over, so I can see his expression. We're lying facing each other now. Close. His eyes glitter in the dark.

'I just ... made an educated guess,' I finally admit. 'Was I wrong? Did they do something to you?'

Obi stares back at me, face blank. Eventually he shrugs, letting out his breath in a rush. 'You know how they are, Lachlan and Daisy. They just wanted some space. My presence was unwanted. And I can take a hint.' He raises his brows. 'Unlike some people I know.'

I ignore that barb about Daisy and me, though it stings. I'm not sure I quite believe him, but whatever. I'm keeping enough of Obi's secrets already.

Which compels me to ask, 'Are you really gonna quit school next year?'

He grows very still, barely breathing. 'Nothing's been decided.'

'But why did you request the forms then?'

I'm fairly certain he's about to snap that it's none of my business. I'm waiting for it, watching him bristle and his brows furrow. Except then it escapes him, soft and small, like he doesn't mean to say it. 'I got offered an apprenticeship. I mean ... my mum sorted it out for me. If I want it.'

'Doing what?'

He won't meet my eyes. 'Electrician.'

'Oh cool.' Except now I'm frowning too. I don't get what's going on with him. He's acting weird. I try a different angle, though I'm not sure exactly why I'm being so pushy. 'But you haven't told anyone at school. I mean, like Lachlan and them. Your friends.'

He still won't look at me. 'No.'

'I don't get it. You have an apprenticeship. It's a good thing, right?'

Obi shifts on the mattress, folding his arms across his chest. Curling in on himself. He lifts his eyes, and a strange smile curls his mouth. Different to his mega-watt one. This one is sharp and mean, except it doesn't feel directed at me for once.

'You think that's how everyone else is going to see it? Like it's a good thing?'

I blink. Say nothing because I still can't grasp whatever it is he's trying to say. Soft light from the hallway flickers across Obi's face.

'Besides, have you *met* my brother? He's a total genius.' He stares back at me, his mouth smiling, but not his eyes, which are hard and flat. His voice turns into a whisper, almost lost in the quiet, dark room. 'You *know* what everyone's going to say, Pearl.'

I chew my lips and don't answer. I'm not sure if he's right or not. I mean, kids have left school to go to TAFE or start an apprenticeship before this. It's not like it's unheard of. Though maybe they don't have an older brother who won every academic district award there is, whose framed photo sits in the trophy cabinet in the reception area.

But still, they're his friends: Lachlan and the others. I don't think friends would be like that. Or at least Daisy wouldn't. Whatever else has gone wrong between us, she'd never hurt me on purpose.

I think.

Daisy just seems ... oblivious to the whole thing. To how I've been feeling.

It kind of shocks me a little. I thought she was pretending not to notice how unhappy I've been. That it was obvious stuff between us was going sour. Had been, for a long time. But I kept telling myself there was plenty of time left to fix it, hoping Daisy would return to normal. Except she hasn't. And when I finally tried to talk to her about Lachlan and how I've been feeling, she shut me down immediately. She didn't want to hear me.

'That's why this whole party thing is a big deal,' Obi is saying softly, bringing me back to him. Reminding me I'm not the only one with problems. 'Because it'll be the last time I hang around them all like this. Next year, if I go, everything will be different.' His gaze flicks back to mine, almost accusatory. 'You know it will.'

I pause. 'Maybe they'll be happy for you,' I say carefully. 'Lachlan's graduating anyway.'

A small, hard laugh escapes him. 'Yeah. Maybe.' He rolls over, away from me. All I can see is the curve of his shoulders in the dark.

My cousin, still squashed between us, stirs softly in her sleep. Everything is feeling weird. It sounds like Obi's struggling. And maybe his friendship with Lachlan isn't all that far off mine with Daisy. A little broken.

I stare at his back in the thick darkness. When you're in a

habit of digging at someone every chance you get, it feels weird to be serious with them. I'm considering saying something comforting until I remember that we aren't friends and that Obi is right.

Next year everything *will* be different.

Obi probably won't go back to school and I'll never see him again. Lachlan will be graduating, so things will go back to how they were. No more tagging along behind Daisy. No more being the eternal third wheel, with only Obi around to fight with.

Yet it suddenly occurs to me for the first time that even if things with Daisy go back to how they were, even if she starts treating me like a real friend again, the truth is I don't know if I'll *feel* the same.

Suddenly, I am cold. And I force myself to focus on anything except that ball of bitterness tucked inside my chest, growing again. Expanding. My feelings around Daisy and what I want from her, shifting irreversibly. I ignore it and squeeze my eyes shut, wondering if this is how Obi feels, too. Wretched. And now that I've thought of Obi's failing friendship again, I can't get it out of my head.

I whisper, 'Obi?'

He barely stirs.

I try again. 'Are you okay?' The words drop into the silence of the still room, and disappear. I feel stupid the moment they leave my mouth.

I don't think it's right that I'm suddenly finding myself on Obi's side. I am fundamentally opposed to being on his side, considering how annoying he's been all year. Except the words are already out.

The muscles in Obi's back have gone stiff. Slowly he turns,

until he's lying on his side facing me again. His head rests on the edge of my pillow and I can't read his expression. I watch him, looking for … something. I dunno.

Obi stares back.

Finally he says, 'Go to sleep, Nash'.

I blink, both of us lying in the darkness, face to face. Until his eyes close, lashes heavy.

I'm about to follow his lead, despite the fact my blood is humming in my ears. But then Obi breathes something so low, I'm certain I imagined the words.

'I liked it better in the Bedford.'

I freeze. Chest tight as I search his face.

Yet Obi doesn't stir, no matter how long I watch him, waiting, my heart thudding in the dark.

Eventually I roll over. Away.

I don't know how to deal with being on Obi's side.

I don't know why he just said that.

And I don't know how to deal with the fact that I kissed him in my Bedford last night and clearly, despite what we decided at the servo, he hasn't forgotten about it at all.

8

LOW HORIZON
Three Years Ago

Sun warmed my shoulders as we all sat in a circle on the dry, parched grass. Daisy was beside me, and Stacey Green was talking about Georgie's last football game. I thought she was pretending to be interested, if I was honest.

'Who cares about football?' said Daisy, voicing my thought aloud.

'Lots of people!' said Georgie, outraged. 'It's the best game in the world.'

Daisy snorted. 'I feel like you're a little biased, Georgie.' She rolled her eyes at me and giggled. 'Right, Pearl? Like, maybe being from an *entire* family of footy-obsessed maniacs has made Georgie biased?'

The wind was hot and brushed my hair over my eyes, carrying the scent of the sea. I could almost taste the salt on my tongue. If I lifted my chin from my hands, I could just make out the waves breaking over the dunes, at the far end of the oval. I grinned back at Daisy. 'Right. Maybe.'

I didn't really know what to say. My dad loved footy, but I didn't. My little brother didn't, either. He liked playing sport on his video games, but not in real life. Drove my nana crazy.

Mostly because Sam played his games in her granny flat, usually right when her favourite show was about to start.

It was quite annoying actually, because though I'd never admit it to Nana, I quite liked that show too. It was much more fun than watching my little brother suck at playing virtual footy, anyway.

'What do you think, Pearl?'

I blinked. Everyone was staring at me expectantly, waiting for an answer.

'About what?' I said slowly, embarrassed to be caught spacing out.

Stacey giggled. 'About Georgie's beautiful game, of course! Reckon Georgie has what it takes to do it for a career?' She wiggled her brows enthusiastically as she spoke, and for a moment I thought she was making fun of me, but then I realised she was actually looking at Georgie. And she was only teasing. She shoved Georgie's arm playfully.

Georgie scowled. 'Very nice. Let's all take bets, shall we? If I flunk out next season or not? What a great group of friends I have, eh?'

I laughed along with everyone else. Even Tory looked up from her homework with a smile.

'I don't know much about footy,' I said finally, gathering up my courage. My heart was pounding. I felt exposed.

It was weird how easy I found it, to be myself in front of only one other person. Or my family. Or Daisy. But as soon as it was more people than that – as soon as it was multiple faces all turned my way, all listening to me, concentrating only on me, with *my* voice the only sound at all – I got awkward. Fast.

Like right at that moment.

I had thought maybe my brother's video game obsession was amusing. It was to me. To Daisy too. And I reckoned it *would* be amusing to all of them, if I was telling the story properly, but instead I realised I was rambling. That I *had* been rambling for quite a long time. And about my dumb little brother of all things. No one cared about my brother! But I couldn't seem to stop, digging my hole deeper and deeper. 'And then my mum chased him into the garden and banned his games from the house. Mum's more into natural new age stuff, you know, like organic brunches and crystal shops. She hates technology. And my nana dislikes Sam's video games too, except she dislikes my mum even more, so she lets Sam play in the granny flat. But still, Nana grew up real rural and so she can't help but tell him every time, *Play real footy outside! Kids these days* ... and all that.'

I trailed off. I had even put on a high-pitched voice to pretend to be my nana and now I felt like an idiot. I wished I hadn't said anything at all. I could tell the others felt the same way. Though they laughed loudly at my embarrassing story, I was sure they were cringing inside just the same as I was. Then it was like my weirdness was just brushed aside. There was more quickfire teasing between Stacey and Georgie. Tory put her homework away. Blake and Mish, who'd been quietly chatting between themselves on the edge of our circle, joined in. All of them were laughing together now.

No one asked me any more questions and I got real quiet. Leftover adrenaline pumped through my body. I calmed down enough to follow along with the conversation again, but I didn't add anything. I always felt a beat behind, like my laugh came a moment too slow. I was sweating and flushed under the hot sun, and still feeling embarrassed.

Then Daisy nudged my shoulder with her own, eyes sparkling.

'So, Pearl, what did you think of yesterday's episode of *Billionaire's Secret Penthouse*?' Her voice was pitched low, so no one else could hear. She grinned, showing teeth.

Her expression made me laugh. Made me feel a whole lot better, too.

It was really such a stupid show, but soon we were both chatting together, giggling and hypothesising about what would happen on tonight's episode. Until it was nearly time for our lunchbreak to end, and Daisy stood up under the swaying pine trees and announced she had to go see Mrs Kang about an art project.

I followed when she beckoned for me to join her and Daisy linked her arm through mine. We giggled our way across the oval, under the blasting sun, dry grass crackling beneath our sneakers.

It occurred to me that I never worried about what I said or how I said it when it was just the two of us.

I grinned at my best friend as the school building loomed ahead.

It didn't matter that I had to work so hard beneath the surface to keep up with the others, to make my weird country self seem normal – not so long as I had this. It was enough.

Daisy was enough.

9

BOTTLEBRUSH

We careen along the farm driveway, Obi with his elbow hanging out the passenger side and me sitting as high as I can to see over the driving wheel of the paddock basher. It's enormous. And has no power steering.

The sun is high in the sky, and it's already late afternoon, even though I'd wanted to set out early. I've been distracted all day by a strange feeling in my gut every time I think of Nana.

Today drove me crazy. We were wrestled into babysitting all morning. Which involved a breakfast of toast while standing in the kitchen, Obi not meeting my eyes but still handing me slices over Lily and Rose's heads as they jumped as high as they could to snatch them away. Not because they wanted toast, but because we had it and they didn't. At least three pieces ended up on the cracked linoleum floor.

We had to wait for my aunt to come in from the paddocks before we were allowed to go, our morning spent inside blanket forts and playing with Barbie dolls in the dirt. But by then it was lunchtime, so the whole family had to sit together to eat on the verandah, flies buzzing around our heads under the sticky heat of summer.

I don't know why I'm the only one freaking out about Nana. Every time I brought her up, and the fact that we probably should be hurrying, my uncle just grunted and said a different variation of 'She's a tough old nut, my mother'. Then he'd wave his hand and we'd go back to eating.

Now sunlight is pouring over the fields, dust trailing behind the ute as we roar along the track toward the highway. Finally on our way.

I'm tired because I didn't get enough sleep. I lay awake thinking about Daisy, and how we used to be. And then I was too wired with the knowledge that Obi was *right there*, sharing the same dark space I was, to go back to sleep. His proximity put all sorts of ideas inside my head. All sorts of images I'd managed to banish during the day under the sunlight, but which came creeping back in full force once darkness rolled over the hills.

My imagination ran wild.

I guess I've been reading too many romance novels. That's what Daisy would say. If she were here.

Which she's not.

If she cared.

Which she probably doesn't.

Instead it's just me and Obi, cruising down the winding overgrown track, hot wind blowing and clouds of dust kicked up in our wake under the beating sun. Obi has his black sunglasses on again, and he leans across to flick on the radio. Music fills the dusty cab.

He said that weird thing last night and I haven't been able to get it out of my mind. He was clearly messing with me. A nice, pointed reminder that it was me who kissed him first and he's not going to let me forget it.

Which I haven't. Hence my severe lack of sleep.

Obi, on the other hand, slept soundly.

And in the meantime, we're barely speaking. I don't even know why. Last night was the first time we've ever had a real conversation that wasn't disguised as a fight. And still we ended up this way.

We spent the day avoiding eye contact and each other: quite a feat while babysitting two wriggling little girls. And now the cab of the paddock basher feels too small.

I glance over at the passenger seat. This is ridiculous. I've got way bigger problems than worrying about Obi.

Like the fate of my missing nana.

The words leave my mouth before I've fully thought them through, a little harsher than I mean them. 'You can leave as soon as we reach my nana's house.'

Obi looks dazed. 'Huh?' Or at least as dazed as someone can look under black shades that hide half their face. He runs a hand over his buzz-cut.

'The bus,' I snap. 'You can catch it to Finn's beach shack.'

'But I don't have money.'

'I'll lend you money!' I lean hard into the steering wheel, using my whole body to turn the paddock basher safely onto the stretching bitumen highway at the end of the track. Manual steering is hard work. My muscles already ache.

Obi looks taken aback. 'You'll lend me money?'

He says this softly enough that I glance over at him. The weirdness is still there between us, but it feels different now. More awkward and less angry. Maybe it's been like this all day, and I simply interpreted the silence wrong?

He's making me feel very confused.

'Yeah,' I say slowly, my irritation deflating like a balloon. 'I mean, if you want.' I change gears and stomp my foot on the accelerator as we pick up speed on the long, flat highway.

Obi doesn't answer. His elbow rests on the open window and his fingers are pressed to his lips. 'Maybe ... I don't know.'

'You don't know?'

Why doesn't he know? I thought he'd be desperate to leave this place behind. To leave me behind. I keep stealing quick glances.

'Anyway,' he adds slowly. 'Wouldn't it be too late for a bus by the time we get there?' I think he looks almost hopeful at that prospect.

A reply drops from my mouth like it comes from someone else. I hear my words from far away.

'Yeah. It'll be too late for today.'

I blink and stare straight ahead at the expanding highway.

Obi grins his huge, dimpled smile. He looks pretty pleased about it. 'Oh no,' he says. The words don't match his expression.

Easing back in the passenger seat, he adds, 'So maybe I can stay the night at your nana's and then tomorrow we can see what's what?'

I nod numbly.

Seems he's not as excited to reach Finn's beach shack as I initially thought. Perhaps Obi's scared. Especially if he's planning on making a decision about school and his apprenticeship, and maybe telling Lachlan about it.

I hadn't really thought of that before. Obi being afraid of his friends. It makes me look at him differently.

Right now though, it's hard to think about it clearly. It's

possible *I'm* the one feeling afraid. Because there definitely is a night bus.

But right in that moment, I didn't want Obi to leave.

We drift through a town built on the edge of the highway and sandwiched in by the sea. Streets hang on clifftops overlooking the roaring ocean, wild and rocky far below.

People have little rundown shacks out here, lining the hills above the churning water. A few of the houses we pass are glitzy: special holiday homes belonging to city dwellers who only come for a week during the hottest time of year. Most are smaller, more rundown. Rusted car bombs in the front yards and sheets of tin hidden by overgrown dry grass, peeling paint and crumbling verandahs.

We leave the town behind and keep driving, listening to the crackling radio while I ignore the fact that Obi looks happy to be driving in the opposite direction to Finn's beach shack. Also ignoring the fact that I told a lie to keep him there.

Obviously, we're both feeling a little afraid. Him of telling his friends the truth, and me of being alone when I finally knock on Nana's door. I can't explain it any other way.

After all the fighting we've done during the past year, I'd never have imagined we'd end up like this. Choosing the safety of each other over the unknown.

But that's a safer thought than the images that kept me awake last night. Or his steady breath warming my neck, his closeness in the dark. I stare out the window. Even now, it makes me blush.

I did things with Obi in the back of the Bedford I've never done with anyone. Not the whole way or anything, but still … more than I would have expected.

Do I regret it?

Yes. If Obi's going to tell his friends about it and make fun of me forever. Definitely yes.

If he's not?

I blink at the bleached landscape racing by. Right now, in the late afternoon heat, roaring through the wheatfields with Obi in the passenger seat while I freak out about Nana, I'm not certain about anything.

My heart beats fast and I grip the steering wheel harder.

Lots of big banners flash by on the side of the road, fluttering in the wind and tied against towering eucalyptus trees. I squint trying to read them.

Save our grain line. No drilling. No more cuts.

Slogans whisk by in the bright sunlight as fast as the wind, but make me wonder about the dark circles under my uncle's eyes and the way he tuned out our conversations, as if lost in his own world. Makes me think about the peeling paint and the crumbling stonework of the old farmhouse.

Maybe things out here are just as hard as in the city.

Maybe everyone has their own struggles.

Finally, we turn off the highway and onto a slip lane leading into a small town. This place is built on rolling hills, heritage stone houses lining a bay with a deep-water port. A heavy-duty jetty stretches into the dark-blue sea. Grain silos loom in clumps along the shore, coloured graffiti etched across the white paint near the overgrown ground. Behind the town a quarry casts deep shadows over the road, the sun still caught behind the sandy ridges and scrubby bushes. The quarry looks empty and deserted from down here, its open spaces revealing a deep well of gravel and a gaping bottom that disappears from view.

It's late in the day, the sunshine waning. Obi lifts his sunglasses as we pass an empty tennis court alongside a rundown fish and chipper. Weeds poke through the cracked cement of the court. Torn plastic sheeting flutters from the wire fence, the only barrier between the town and endless yellow wheatfields. We pass a clump of kids on bikes, riding down the wide empty streets without helmets. All of it reminds me of growing up out here. How different it was.

No shoes, no limits. Endless space to explore and long days spent under the vast sky. Swimming in churning sea water and examining small, curling, slimy things in rock pools with my grandpa. Learning the names of all the spindly native bushes and trees while out walking the coastline with Nana, her voice whipped away by sharp winds. Driving the tractor with my dad down the dirt track, dust rising like a cloud trail behind us.

Mum crying in a dark bedroom because the isolation was slowly killing her.

Dark and light. Sweet and bitter.

My childhood.

'This town hasn't changed at all.' My voice is hushed, hair blown wild by the hot, salty breeze rolling in off the ocean. I catch Obi watching me, but I can't figure out his expression beneath the sunglasses, so I just grimace awkwardly before turning back to the road.

We pull into a wide street of dry, overgrown yards and sloping houses, towering eucalypts turning the verge into a carpet of loose bark. I struggle with the steering wheel but manage to turn us into the crowded driveway of a tiny weatherboard bungalow. 'My grandpa's old place,' I say. 'Him and Nana bought it when the farm passed to Dad and Uncle John. We all lived near each other on the property before that, but then Grandpa and Nana moved here to retire and Uncle John and Aunty Sue went into their old place.'

'That … is confusing. How many houses are we up to now?'

I frown. 'It's easy. So listen, there's the big homestead where we stayed last night, yeah?'

'Yeah.'

'So that's where I grew up. But there's another house on the property too, behind that one. Smaller but more modern. That's where Uncle John and Aunty Sue lived after Grandpa and Nana left it to come here and retire. But when we left the big house, they moved back in. Simple, right?'

Obi shakes his head. 'Right.'

I huff as I cut the engine.

With the radio gone, my ears are ringing in the silence.

The whole town feels dead. Even now in summer, when it should be booming. Maybe it's too far away from the city. Maybe it's struggling. I picture the slogans painted alongside the highway. I dunno.

I slide from the cab, sneakers hitting the crackling bark and dried leaves carpeting the driveway. I have to squeeze between the bonnet of the paddock basher and a huge wattle tree that clearly hasn't been trimmed for years. I'm holding my breath by the time I approach the front door, nerves jangling. I don't even know why. Everything is fine. My nana is fine.

I pull on the flyscreen, which opens easily. The main door is locked, so I knock, though already I have this awful creeping suspicion no one is home. There's no answer, so I press my ear against the peeling wood, listening. Letting my lashes flutter closed.

Nothing.

I glance at Obi and he must see something on my face, some of the fear swelling inside me, threatening to overflow. 'Let's check around the back,' he says confidently, like there's nothing to be afraid of. His sunglasses are gone, so I can see his big brown eyes. No hint of a smile.

I nod. Follow him to the side gate. I'm feeling sick, like I might burst into tears at any moment. I whisper, 'She's not here.'

'Maybe she went to the shop.'

I shake my head. 'She's not here. Something's wrong. And none of our family even noticed.' I think of Uncle John at lunch, telling us over and over what a tough old nut Nana is.

She's still old, though. Maybe he hasn't realised that yet.

Maybe my dad hasn't either.

'Okay, no one's answering.' Obi stops pounding on the back door. He raises his brows. 'Spare key?'

Right. Yes.

Spare key.

I scramble off to the front of the house again, squeezing by the overflowing wheelie bins. A big pot of tangled succulents sits beneath the front-room window and I heave it to the side with effort. The concrete base scrapes over the pathway and leaves marks. I find the key. It's caked with dirt and grit, but it's there.

My hands are shaking so hard, I have to hand the key to Obi. I stand behind him on the small verandah, closing my eyes. I can't breathe. Can't think. I'm imagining terrible things, awful things. Like what if Nana *isn't* out, what if the house *isn't* empty? Maybe we just left her alone and she had a fall and no one came to visit her and—

'Pearl. Pearl! Look at me.'

I gasp. Obi's face is right there, hands on my shoulders. He's grinning, the door still not open. 'There's no car here.'

I blink. 'What?'

'Her car isn't parked here, right? Which means …?'

I breathe heavily, playing along. 'She's driven off somewhere. She's not in the house, she's with her car.'

Obi's grin flashes wider. He's putting on a good show for me, but relief blooms in his expression too. I notice how he draws in a deep, shuddering breath before stepping over the threshold into the dark house.

He pulls me gently inside by my forearm, his fingers warm and calloused.

The back windows of my nana's house are big, overlooking her overgrown garden, the Hills Hoist covered in a curling creeper with great yellow flowers. No one has mowed in ages and the grass floods the pathways in an ocean of green. I put my hands against the flyscreen and breathe deep. It smells wild. Of plants and green and salt.

It smells like my nana.

But it doesn't look like her.

My nana loves her garden, loves pulling things from the earth and carefully planting seeds and saplings. Her favourites are the native plants, because she always says those ones were born for this dry, parched landscape, belong to these hills the same as she does. They don't get thirsty like city flowers. They don't die under the harsh sun. So she planted native trees and bushes and delicate native flowers, and she carefully tended them, trimmed them, shaped them. Neat lines and straight flowerbeds. And vegetables. It's how this place used to be.

I can't see her touch in this overgrown garden. It's dry and crackling and tangled. Gone back to nature.

Gone wild.

Dusk descends on the world outside the window. Usually, I love this time. This place. This house was such a huge part of my childhood. Visits to Grandpa and Nana's home for sleepovers and movie nights. But today I'm just scared.

A click sounds across the dark lounge room as Obi opens the front door and comes back inside. I don't turn around.

He drops the gritty key on the kitchen table. Then he's standing beside me.

'She was here, Pearl,' he murmurs. 'Living here. Up until a few days ago. Then she went off in her car.'

'Is that what the neighbours said?'

He nods, leaning against the wall, facing me now. I have to lift my chin to meet his gaze.

'Yeah. They said she seemed fine. Healthy. But the neighbour on the right said she seemed sad.'

'Sad?' I blink.

Sad about what? She didn't have to be out here, being sad and lonely. She could have stayed with us in our granny flat. Our house is loud. Chaotic. She'd never be sad if she'd stayed living with us.

Obi's voice turns soft. Gentle. 'Didn't you say your grandpa passed away?'

I snort. 'Yeah. But that was ages ago.'

Three years is ages, isn't it?

And it's not like I wasn't sad when it happened, too. I was. But when he died we'd already been in the city for a year, and he and Nana still lived out here on the peninsula, in this house, and we hardly ever saw them anymore. So although I *was* sad, it was in a removed, numb kind of way. Like it was sad if I thought about it, but also it didn't impact my day-to-day life. Nothing changed for me when my grandpa died, which makes me feel guilty. But it's true. I didn't feel like I lost a family member. Really, it was like I gained one, because Nana moved in with us the next day.

I shake my head. 'She seemed fine. Just spent all her time with us, with Sam and me.' I breathe, remembering those early days after she first moved in. 'We'd hang out in the granny flat after school. She had a little garden. Or we'd go walking down the beach. No one ever talked much about Grandpa, so I just ... didn't either.'

I'm uncomfortable suddenly. Like maybe I did something wrong. Like maybe I should have given her a chance to talk about him. Encouraged her to remember. 'I stopped thinking about him, too.'

It kind of shocks me to realise it.

Obi shrugs, like he can't figure it out. He flops down at the table. 'Do you think it's weird the electricity is turned off?'

'My dad pays those bills for her.' An awful thought pops into my head. 'Maybe he forgot. Maybe her power turned off and she knew he forgot to pay it. Maybe that's why she's been ignoring our calls and left. She's upset. Because everyone forgot about her.' I breeze past Obi to show him the shelves against the wall in the kitchen. 'There used to be a big photo here of Nana and Grandpa on their wedding day. And another of them on their honeymoon. But they're both gone.'

'You mean she took them?'

'Maybe?' I don't like the words that come out of my mouth next. 'She packed clothes too, but it's the photos that worry me. Like maybe she wasn't planning on coming back.'

Obi chews on his lip. He's clearly stressed out, his fingers twitching across his chin, rubbing non-existent stubble. Like he wants to say something.

A sharp stab of dread pokes against my ribcage, like a knife sliding beneath my skin. 'What?'

He takes a moment to answer. When he does, his voice is slow and clear. Overly casual. 'The neighbour said he saw her car turning off toward the quarry. A couple of days ago.'

'What?!'

Obi lifts his hands quickly. 'It doesn't mean anything, Nash. I shouldn't have even mentioned it.'

'Yes, you should have!' I'm already grabbing the car keys from the kitchen counter, storming toward the front door in a whirlwind of absolute panic, my ears humming and my mouth gone dry. 'Why didn't the neighbour call the police?'

Obi grasps my elbow as I pass him, lightning quick. He drags me backwards. 'Hey, hey. Stop. Think for a second.'

He's still sitting, holding me still with his hand wrapped around my arm. My gaze flicks to the door.

It's getting darker every moment and I can't stand this sitting around. This doing nothing. I take deep gulping breaths. Tears spring up and my heart thuds so loud I'm certain it'll make the whole house shake, from the foundations to the roof.

'Pearl, there's a lookout up there, right? That's what her neighbour told me. He didn't seem to think anything of it. Said people go there all the time. So it doesn't mean anything.' Obi stands up, unfolding his body. There's a lot of him. He seems to take up the whole room.

'And you said yourself, she took her clothes. She was going to stay somewhere, right?' He beams one of his charming smiles down at me. Reassuring. Calming. I know he's acting but I don't care. I find myself nodding along with his words anyway.

But I'm still afraid. 'Obi, I need to check for myself.'

'Right, and you will. It's easy. We'll go up there and see if her car is around. Okay? But you need to calm down before you drive.' He grins at me, close. 'I can't drive, Nash, so it's all on you. And I don't want to end up roadkill.'

I know what he's doing. Making jokes. Using his dimples. Trying to suck the panic from my lungs.

I let him.

Swiping the tears from my cheeks, eventually I agree.

He lets go of my arm, steps away. It leaves a great hollow space where he was. In the kitchen, Obi fills a glass with water from the tap, makes me drink the whole thing. Makes me sit for a few minutes at the table. Not long. My feet are dancing and my fingertips are tapping the scarred wooden tabletop. I need to move.

But I'm calmer now.

So I drive.

10

PINK ROCK LILY

We stand side by side at the top of the quarry. Wind buffets my hair, turning it wild. Ripping at my clothes. The sky above is deep, dark blue, almost black and the gaping mouth of the quarry far below is black too. I can just make out the shimmer of water reflected at the bottom. An unearthed lake.

The lookout is deserted. No cars. No Nana. Just the whole sky overhead and the sloping wheatfields, the silos looming over the town. The houses are the only break in a huge expansive landscape, never-ending rolling hills and a wild, rough sea the colour of tar.

I feel better up here.

Maybe Nana came here, but she's gone now. She's probably somewhere better, somewhere safer.

Standing in the sharp wind, the air heavy with brine and earth from the exposed quarry, I can't believe I thought those things. What felt possible back in Nana's dark, empty house feels impossible out here where it's wild and open. White breakers cut through the black ocean surface like oil. Dry grass wavers wildly by my sneakers and Obi's T-shirt whips back and forth. Everything is alive with movement. It wipes the fear from my heart.

My nana's not the type to do anything unsafe.

She's somewhere. I'll find her.

Obi tries to hold his T-shirt down as it billows. It's almost impossible. But he tries, and I like the expression on his face.

He's just as relieved as I am.

'She's not here,' he says, dropping his hands. The wind whips his voice into the growing dark.

'Yeah.' I laugh suddenly. Relief, I guess. Feeling stupid, but in a good way. In the best of ways. Because things aren't as bad as they were a half hour ago. 'You know, Obi, I reckon I remember Nana talking about those photos. The ones from the wedding and her honeymoon. I reckon they were taken around here. They got married in town, but their honeymoon was down the coast. In a conservation park. I reckon I know where it was.' I'm grinning now, brimming over with hope and ideas.

'What?' says Obi. 'What did you say?'

He frowns, leaning closer, but I don't bother saying it again. Instead, my body buzzing with relief, my heart humming with it, I curl my fingers around the collar of his T-shirt, stretching it as I bounce on my toes, reaching to press my mouth against his jaw.

A *thank you* kiss.

I grin up at him, hair wild as I step away. His eyes are wide, filled with surprise. 'I'm going to call my dad,' I shout. 'Ask him what I should do. I have an idea.'

Obi nods slowly, distractedly. His gaze burns into my back as I jog toward the ute, climbing into the driver seat and fishing my phone from the dash. There's reception up here, on top of the world. My dad picks up after only one ring.

Obi stands where I left him at the edge of the deep drop,

watching me. His T-shirt whips in the wind and his eyes glitter in the dark. Slowly he lifts a hand to touch the place where I kissed him.

Back at my nana's house, I stand at the stainless metal sink in the dark, washing dishes from a small meal of heated-up leftover roast that my aunt packed for us. Obi's sitting behind me at the table and the room is lit only by my camping lantern. Light bounces off the walls and ceiling, the corners pooling with darkness. It gives the place a strange atmosphere. Soft and close. Quiet. Like both of us are more hushed than we would be if the lights were blazing and the television was on.

I turn around from the sink, catching Obi's gaze on me as I wipe my hands on a tea towel. He's been doing that a lot since we got back from the quarry. Watching. Turning away when he realises I've noticed. It fills the air with something thick and unspoken. I probably wouldn't have done it, if I'd known how weird it would make him. I didn't think it through. It was a spur-of-the-moment thing, an outpouring of emotion.

The kiss I gave him.

It flipped something, and I'm kind of desperate to flip it back. Mainly because we're alone in this house in the dark and everything is strange and off-kilter. Which is the same feeling I had blooming in my chest that night in the Bedford, lost in the desert in the dark during a rainstorm. Like anything could happen.

And look what I did that time.

I'm determined to avoid doing anything that stupid again,

because it wouldn't exactly be real. Heightened emotion and all that. Us alone here in the dark. It does things to your mind. Like inside the Bedford.

But Obi is making it hard for me, staring like that. Asking me questions out of the blue like, 'Nash, tell me why you used to hate me.'

I stop moving and grow still, the tea towel gripped in my hands. I notice very clearly the way he said *used to*, like it's a thing from the past. Like he's absolutely one hundred per cent confident I no longer feel that way.

If you'd asked me a week ago, I would have still said we hated each other.

Now I'm wondering *why* we do. Did?

It kind of reminds me of my dad and uncle. Hating each other for years and years, except they never speak, and me and Obi talk way too much. *Fight* way too much.

Maybe that's what Obi was getting at near the water troughs back at the servo. *Can* hating someone become a habit?

I peer at him through the flickering shadows and it's as if the walls draw closer, like he takes up more and more space. It makes my heart beat fast because it occurs to me he's right.

I don't hate Obiara Okocha anymore.

So what changed?

Was it the Bedford?

No.

The servo?

The mechanic? Today when he stood beside me in front of my nana's house?

Something.

Things have shifted.

I suddenly get a sense of him being on my side. The idea is so new and raw that I can't examine it too closely. I tuck it away for later.

Leaning against the sink, I stammer, 'I used to hate you because the first time I met you, you insulted my braces.'

Obi's dark eyes widen. 'Yeah. Your *braces*. Not you. I didn't insult *you*.'

I frown. 'The braces are attached to my face, Obi. They *are* me.'

'Nah. They're just *temporarily* you. Besides, I was only teasing, and I didn't know back then.'

I'm already re-thinking my earlier idea about Obi being on my side. I scowl at him. 'Know what?'

'Well ... how you felt. Now I do.'

I cross my arms over my chest. 'And how exactly do I feel?'

'Like you always cover your mouth when you eat. And check your teeth out in a mirror afterwards.' He shrugs, leaning back in his chair. 'Back then I didn't know you were so self-conscious about it.'

I bark out a disbelieving laugh. 'Obi. *Everyone* who has braces is self-conscious about them. There are literal metal things stuck in my mouth. I'm aware it looks weird.'

He shakes his head, focusing on his folded hands with the ghost of a smile pulling at his lips. 'It doesn't look weird.'

I lean my head to the side, skin prickling but saying nothing. Obi doesn't speak either, still not meeting my gaze. The silence draws out.

I say softly, 'You?'

He glances up.

'What made you hate me?' I ask. 'Back then.' It gives me a small thrill to say the words *back then*.

Obi lifts his chin, leaning back in his chair as he grins at me, all teeth and dimples. 'I never said I hated you, Nash.'

I snort and suddenly he's changing the subject, giving me whiplash when he asks, 'So why are you so desperate to go to this party anyway?'

'Why do you care?' There's no bite to my words though.

'It's just not like you, is all.'

'You think you know what I'm like?'

He lifts his hands, backtracking. 'That's not what I said. I mean you don't *normally* want to go to these things.'

I frown. 'I've been going to parties all year.'

He smiles in a way that reaches all the way into his eyes, crinkling small. He raises his brows at me questioningly but says nothing. The words are on the tip of his tongue.

Yeah, but you don't enjoy them.

He doesn't say it.

I don't either.

Doesn't make it any less true.

I sigh. 'It's Daisy. We had a ... a sort of fight. Kind of.' I pull myself onto the kitchen counter, bare feet dangling above the kitchen floor, kicking softly in the dark. The lantern light flickers like it'll go out, shadows dancing everywhere. I'm slow because it's hard to say. 'I tried to tell her some stuff. About how I feel. But she wouldn't listen.'

Obi is still. 'How do you feel?'

'Like she doesn't even like me anymore. She just wants me around to fill the gaps when Lachlan gets sick of her, and then she wants me to go away again when she doesn't need me.' Now I've started, it just pours out. Except everything I'm saying to Obi is new, stuff I couldn't even voice back when I tried to talk it over with Daisy, things I didn't even realise I was feeling until now. Until this trip. And now I can't stop talking. 'She makes no effort to spend any time with me at all. Not real time, doing the things we both enjoy. She just hangs with Lachlan and that's it. Or asks me to go with her to places Lachlan will be, so she doesn't have to go alone when he's in a mood.' I push hair from my face. 'Her other friends have been saying it too, you know. Not just me. They've sort of cut her off. I don't think Daisy's even noticed yet. But she will.'

Obi watches me carefully in the dark. Waiting. His silence draws the words out of me. And I continue talking, telling him the dark things that have been plaguing my mind.

'See, I figured out something she hasn't. Lachlan has graduated now, right? So when we go back to school next year, he won't be there. And all her other friends have given up on her. They're pissed at her.'

And now that Daisy's other friends have stopped hanging around her, it's hit home how disconnected from that group I really am. I always knew I was there because of Daisy, and not necessarily because I belonged with them, but it feels unsettling to have to face it properly. It feels like losing something I never quite had. And that hurts more than I expected.

'Are you pissed at her, too?'

Obi's question snaps me back. Something about his voice makes me peer closer at him, scrunching my brows. I guess he knows a thing or two about disintegrating friendships. Lachlan dumped him on the side of the highway, after all. I wonder if Obi's angry, too. Or maybe he's started outgrowing his friendship with Lachlan in the same way Daisy's outgrown me. Either way, his question strikes me hard.

'Yeah,' I breathe, letting the confession escape in a rush of air. I'm surprised by how much I mean it. 'I'm pissed at her. And next year when she realises she's got no friends left and she's all alone at school, I figure she'll come back to me. But I'm just … I feel so angry with her that I …'

I stop. Shrug.

This trip is my last-ditch effort to smooth things over. I tried to tell Daisy how I felt, but she wouldn't listen. So I figured I'd follow her out here, confront her at the beach shack, and force her to listen.

Because I still can't bear to let it go.

'It's her last chance,' I say finally into the silence. 'I need to know that Daisy wants to be my friend now, when she doesn't need me, when Lachlan's still around. I need to know that next year, it's not just me because there's no one better. I'm giving her one last chance. And then … I'm stopping. Being her friend. I'm gonna stop.'

It sounds awful to hear those words said aloud, in my voice. Raw and harsh. It almost makes me flinch.

Yet it feels true too. All the good stuff has been leaking away for months.

'I don't even know if I like her anymore,' I say aloud.

This time I do flinch.

But maybe there's a point where you have to let go.

You have to try, hard. But then you let go.

It makes me feel wretched, though.

I lift my gaze. Obi's still watching me and there's something sparking in his eyes, like maybe he understands exactly what I'm saying. Again, it makes me think of finding him at the servo, so I ask, 'What happened in the car with Lachlan and Daisy? Why did you get left behind?'

He opens his mouth like he's going to say something and then closes it again. Squints at his hands. 'Nothing really. I mean ... it's complicated.'

It's like a solid wall slides between us, and I'm almost winded. I told him all that. Everything. Shared everything about my nana too, and he says that it's ... complicated?

I shift on the kitchen bench, slide to the floor. He must sense it, the change in temperature. That he's done something wrong. Because suddenly he's smiling at me, trying to make light of it.

'Lachlan was just mucking around, being an idiot, that's all,' he says, turning it into a joke, turning our whole conversation into a joke.

I don't laugh. Because it's mean of him, after everything I just shared. Yet Obi just grins wider, all dimples and teeth, trying to charm me the way he charms everyone else.

He's doing it on purpose. The mega-watt smile. The confident drawl in his voice. The way his body lounges so casually, arm slung over the back of the chair and chin raised. He knows how to switch it on.

I'm not fooled. I glare at smiling, charming Obi and slap the tea towel onto the benchtop, about to walk away. He lurches to his feet. His chair scrapes back and his smile scrapes away with it. His face is blank now.

Serious.

The pale glow of the lantern dances across the ceiling as the table wobbles, shadows creeping across Obi's skin. His chest rises and falls faster than before. Something brewing in his eyes.

His voice is low. Wavering in the same way the dry grasses did on top of the lookout, buffeted by the wind. 'Sorry.'

The air rushes from my lungs and I lean back against the sink, my body growing still. I don't say anything. And he doesn't either, his own secrets locked up tight after I poured mine out all over the floor. I lift my chin. 'I'm going to bed.'

He stares, unmoving. Expression deep and complicated. And then slowly he breathes, 'Where should I sleep, Nash?'

There's something about his voice, the way he asks the question. Almost an invitation in his eyes. But he's nervous too. Shy, even.

I shouldn't have kissed him on the lookout. It's blurred the lines. Because kissing someone and liking them are two different things. And I don't know where I stand.

It occurs to me that I could, though. Cross the room in a few small steps, reach for him in the shadows and press my mouth to his.

Kiss him.

He wants me to.

It hits me with a clarity that surprises me. And my gaze flicks to his mouth and back up again, in a way that gives me away. He doesn't laugh though. Doesn't tease or smile. Just stands there. Expression strained. His chest hitching in the dark.

Kissing someone and liking them are two very different things.

And I haven't figured out those differences yet. Not for me. Not for Obi. And while I'm caught here in the middle, uncertain, everything feels dangerous. Like wading in molasses, thick and heavy.

I told him my secrets but he didn't tell me his.

Drawing in a deep shuddering breath, I turn around until I'm facing the sink again. I run the cold water over my hands and say, 'Couch. You can sleep on the couch.'

11

GOLDEN WATTLE

I make sandwiches for breakfast and exhaustion creeps through my limbs. For the third night in a row, I haven't slept well. All because of Obi. I sigh and shake it off. Or at least I try to. Morning light spills gold through the glass windows, heat already broiling the small house.

Sleepiness is making my head fuzzy and hot, making words tumble softly from my lips. Besides, I know I have to ask. 'Do you want me to drop you at the bus stop?'

I lift my gaze to Obi's. He's sitting at the kitchen table, munching away on a sandwich. Just watching me. Silence fills the room and he doesn't answer.

I clear my throat, awkward. 'I mean, that'd be good, right? If you head off now you can go straight to Finn's place. I'm driving pretty far in the opposite direction.'

He puts his sandwich down slowly. 'You gonna drive all the way to the end of the peninsula by yourself?'

He's still staring and I realise I'm holding my breath waiting for his answer.

Obi's gone all still and I can't read his expression. Maybe he's angry with me and he's going to choose to leave. Maybe he feels like he went out on a limb last night, and I just rejected him straight out. Yet I feel like he asked me to make a leap that was way too big, way too far. Especially when I don't even know what I'm leaping for.

I have no idea if he even likes me.

I mean, I know he wants to *kiss* me. But that's a whole different thing. And I don't know how I feel about kissing someone who might not actually like me.

Last night, before we went to bed, I felt a little less like he was on my side.

I'm still holding my breath though, waiting.

Eventually he turns his attention back to his breakfast, stuffing his mouth with bread and Vegemite. He shrugs. 'Nah. It feels wrong to leave you by yourself. My dad would kill me if he knew. I'll come with you.'

I let out my breath and nod, turning to the breadboard, my back facing Obi. 'Cool,' I say, keeping my voice steady.

I admit to myself that I did want him to come with me. And I got what I wanted. It makes my heart race and my cheeks flush warm.

I just don't know if that's a good thing or a bad thing.

Things feel different with Obi now, as we drive down the long coast road, past more half-empty holiday towns, through the middle of farming communities brandishing new desperate slogans. We slide past open stretches of wavering yellow wheat paddocks.

Obi's got his sunglasses on and both of us are fresh. Clean

clothes and showers because the water was still working at my nana's place.

At least *something* was working at my nana's place.

I keep stealing glances at Obi across the bench seat but he's turned away, watching the world stream by through black sunglasses. He's been weird all morning – during breakfast, while we got ready to leave – like he could hardly meet my eyes.

Maybe he regrets saying he'd come with me. Maybe he thinks he made a big mistake.

I force myself to dismiss all of it, because it's not important. There is only one actual important thing in this whole situation and, in the light of day, I'm less certain that my hunch about Nana was correct. I could be going on a wild road trip for nothing. Nana might not be there at all.

Besides, if Nana really *was* so sad about Grandpa, and about all of us forgetting her, would going to where she had her honeymoon make her feel better? Or would it make her feel worse?

I chew over it in my mind. Chew my lips too.

I talked to my dad again in the early morning, and he's reported her missing, so the police are involved now. Apparently, he called my uncle too. The first conversation they've had in four years and it was over a missing mother. I'm almost sorry for them.

But mainly I'm just sorry for myself.

If I don't find her down the end of this damn peninsula, then I'm worried I'll run out of hope. And I don't want to run out of hope.

So I hold on to it, pushing the rest back. Hold on tight, and don't let go.

She'll be there. She'll be waiting for me to figure it out.

There's nowhere else she could go.

Even my dad agrees when I stop to call him again. And that makes me feel a lot better. It even starts me being nicer to Obi. Because who cares if he wishes he was elsewhere? He still came with me, and that's cool. It's better than being by myself. And who cares if he likes kissing me but finds me annoying as a person? People do that all the time. I find him annoying, too.

Mostly.

Besides, I've put all that weird stuff behind me. From now on, we're just two sort-of friends stuck in a car together. Driving around.

So to cheer him up I ask random questions and keep pushing him to talk to me, breaking through the awkwardness. He's still acting weird, but mostly he answers my questions, albeit with short one-word replies.

Favourite book?

Dune.

Favourite movie?

Dune.

Favourite band?

Don't like music.

I call him a monster, turn the radio up loud, and we stop speaking, until finally we stop for lunch at what feels like the end of the world. A tiny fish and chipper sits in an old fibro container alongside a wild stretch of isolated beach. Scrubby bushes and sand dunes give way to miles and miles of flat shingled earth.

Desert.

I breathe deep. It's beautiful out here. Desolate. But stunning too. The way the sunlight drips through the wafting clouds, creating great swathes of brightness that run over the endless landscape. The way the ocean breaks against the headland in a wash of white water and crashing waves. A dry heat blows in from the desert, scented like wildflowers. I've never been this far before. My family always stopped at the farm and at Nana's house. We never ventured any further.

Yet here I am. At the end of the world.

With Obi.

We sit on a chipped wooden picnic table, careful of the jutting rusted nails and jagged splinters, and we stuff our faces with greasy chips and battered fish. By the time we're done, Obi is grinning at me again, like maybe the strange magic of this isolated place is breaking down the walls we put up last night. It's good to have him smiling at me again: the genuine smile that crinkles his eyes small.

Though who knows, maybe it's just the hot food making him so happy.

The woman from the fish and chipper brings us sizzling potato cakes for free, her dark hair flying in every direction. I burn my fingers on the hot oil as I crunch through salty batter. I can't help myself: I grin at Obi and don't even care if there's batter in my braces. I think he probably doesn't care either.

'You're lost.'

I snort. 'I'm not lost. There's literally one highway and this is the way it goes. How can I get lost?'

'Well, where is it then, Nash? Where's the turn-off?'

'It's still coming up.' I glare over at him. He's the one with the map! 'It's right up ahead.'

It's not.

I *am* lost, but I suspect it's Obi's fault. Eventually we do find a turn-off, but I have a bad feeling as we follow the winding dirt track. It's heading up, up, up a set of rolling hills and I'm pretty sure we're meant to be heading down, down, down toward the ocean again.

Except we're not.

Also there's this whirring noise, like a wall of sound washing down the hillside, getting louder and louder until my ears are buzzing. Like the whole world is humming. Obi's staring at me with wide eyes, a very similar expression to when Tim the Mechanic's big cattle dog was barking at him.

The hillside is steep and I'm getting worried. If the road turns too tight, I don't know if I can handle it like this, without power steering and on such an angle. Driving the paddock basher is like wrestling a giant beast. I glance at Obi. My expression probably mirrors his, jaw tight. He grabs the dash with straining knuckles.

And that's when we reach the top.

What we find has me gaping, slowing the ute automatically with my foot on the brake, pressing down without even thinking. We're crawling along now as I lean forward in the driver's seat to peer up through the dusty windshield. Obi's got his entire head stuck out the window, mouth open. 'Holy shit,' he breathes.

The dirt track is little more than two tyre marks curling along a wide plateau on a cliff's edge, jagged rock jutting out into the ocean in layers, a vast coastline zig-zagging ahead. The ground is all stone and grit, and dry wavering clumps of desert grass. Sunshine pours between soft clouds and behemoth dark shadows move slowly across the wild blue ocean.

And right above us, towering like skyscrapers and dotting the entire coastline into the hazy distance, are wind turbines.

The roar of the massive propellers echoes that of the ocean against the rocks, and competes with the howl of the wind. The wash of white noise is so consuming, it almost sinks into the background. Becomes part of the landscape.

I push my foot on the brake. Cut the engine. And then slowly, still gaping at the sky, we slide from the old truck.

I've never seen anything like it.

The landscape here is so big, the sky so wide and open, it could almost hide the mammoth white whirring structures, but we're right against the bottom of one of them. The rest whir away into the distance along the jagged clifftops, facing the wild breaking ocean.

I have never felt so small in my entire life.

I love it.

Gravel crunches at my side and suddenly Obi is right there, shoulder touching mine. His T-shirt whips around his body with a vengeance, just like my hair, which I'm attempting to hold back from my face. He lifts his sunglasses and we just stand there soaking it in. It's like crashing into an alien landscape.

I step back. Once. Twice. Until the back of my leg connects with the towbar at the front of the paddock basher. I keep gaping at the horizon, not even wanting to blink as I slowly drag myself onto the cooling bonnet of the ute. I sit with my legs splayed out in front, sneakers dangling off the rusted edge as the sun wanes and shadows leap and bound from the mammoth structures.

Obi crawls up beside me, saying nothing. Just watching as the sea burns orange like fire, reflecting the sky. His hand rests on the hood beside mine, close but not touching. I glance at him through the whipping wind. His face is swathed in yellow dancing light, strange shadows criss-crossing his skin from the windmill above, a pattern too intricate for me to understand. He doesn't look at me. Just stares at the world. So I do too. And it's huge. Everything. The landscape. The cliffs. The ocean and sky. The windfarm. Bigger than my imagination.

Obi leans close, motioning me inwards because of the whirring noise and roaring wind, the crashing waves. 'Have you ever seen anything like it?' A rush of warm breath against my hair.

I shake my head and he falls silent. But I can tell that something's bubbling up inside him. When he finally says it, he's acting casual, like it means nothing, but I can tell it's a big deal. That he's only pretending not to care.

'You know,' he says finally. 'I keep thinking about next year. How weird it's going to be when everyone goes back to school. If I don't, I mean.'

'Lachlan's leaving next year, too,' I point out. I have to lean close to be heard above the deafening white noise of the singing landscape around us. The warmth from the sun seeps from Obi's skin. His billowing T-shirt keeps fluttering against my arm.

Obi huffs, almost a grunt deep in his throat. 'Yeah, but Lachlan is *graduating*. I'd be quitting. It's different.'

I'm surprised. He thinks he'd be quitting? Like ... failing?

I beckon Obi closer and he leans toward me in a way that suddenly reminds me too clearly of how he was inside the Bedford, how I tugged his T-shirt and he followed like he'd been waiting for me to ask. I shiver. Force my mind back to Obi now, here beside me on the bonnet of the ute.

'You have an apprenticeship,' I say. 'That's not quitting. You're *choosing* to leave to go learn a trade.'

He shrugs and this time he leans away without speaking, attention back on the ocean and the cliffs. He pops his black sunglasses on in a way that makes me wonder if he's trying to hide. Too casual. Too nonchalant.

I don't like it.

'Tell me what your brother's like,' I say.

Obi leans back, lifting a hand beside his head, miming that he couldn't hear my question. His mouth curls into a smile like it's funny, being here where it's so loud. Like this is it. Conversation over.

The dimples deepen in his scarred cheeks, but I'm ready to bet there isn't any joy in his eyes. I'm certain they're not crinkling behind his reflective glasses. I have him figured out now.

I can tell when he's acting.

I imagine Obi as a kid. Figuring out that people find his dimples cute. Figuring out how to use them to get what he wants. And now he's older, he uses his sunshine smile a lot. He knows it makes him handsome, charming. Sexy. And maybe he also knows that when he isn't smiling he's just ordinary, a boy with acne scarring and pockmarked skin.

I grab his face firmly, feeling as wild as the landscape around us, as I squeeze the fake smile off him and lift his sunglasses with my other hand. He's surprised enough that he's slow to react. By the time he's reached to pull my hand away, I'm already facing him on the bonnet. I say it again. Loudly.

'What does your brother think about your apprenticeship?'

Obi's brows draw close and I think he's going to deflect again, but he doesn't. Burning orange sunlight reflects off the ocean toward his face. He doesn't turn away. 'He thinks it's good.'

I nod, hair wild and whipping into my eyes. Now he's begun, it's like Obi can't stop.

'And my parents think it's good, and probably if I decide to go for it and tell everyone at school, they'll all think it's good, too.' It all leaves him in a rush.

'So what's the problem?'

'The problem is everyone knows I'm doing shit in school! My brother is some kind of mad genius and I'm shit. I'm bad at everything except shop classes and he's started uni with a full scholarship and is going to be a rocket scientist.'

'A rocket scientist?'

Obi rolls his eyes. 'Or whatever. I mean, I don't even understand whatever the hell he's studying.'

'But your brother doesn't care?'

'About what?

'About you taking the apprenticeship. He doesn't care?'

Obi squints at me quizzically. We're close together, heads bent inwards, but never touching. The wind pushes my hair into a frenzy.

'No, he doesn't care,' Obi answers slowly. 'David is happy for me.'

'And your parents are happy for you.'

He makes a face like he already said that and won't be repeating it for me because I'm slow. I pull a face back at him while I shout over the wind, 'It seems to me like *you're* the one who cares.'

'What?'

I try again, louder. 'You're *ashamed* of yourself. Even though no one else is.'

He glares at me, clearly pissed, as if I've just stuck my finger into an open wound and wiggled it around. It's a little bit fierce. 'Yeah,' he confirms through gritted teeth. 'Happy now? I'm ashamed.'

I scoot closer across the bonnet, my sneakers scraping metal. I beckon him inwards, until his whole body is curled toward mine, blocking the wind. I can talk in my normal voice. No shouting. 'If you're so ashamed of it, why did you tell *me* you were thinking of quitting school?'

'I didn't tell you. I tried to hide it.'

I snort. 'You didn't try very hard, Obi. You practically waved those forms in my face!'

'No, I didn't.'

'You really did. You knew I was in the office when you were requesting them. You saw me. I remember.'

He pauses but doesn't move away. Stays still, his breath heavy, so I stay still too. The wind is howling but it's like we've found our own little pocket of calm.

Eventually Obi says, 'Maybe I did, then.' He lifts his gaze to my face. 'Maybe I wanted to see how you'd react. Like a test group, or whatever.'

Progress. 'And how did I react?'

Obi chuckles. This time when he smiles, it reaches his eyes. 'You shouted at me that you didn't care about my problems.'

I frown. 'No, I mean, after that.'

'You told me your little brother wants to be an electrician too.'

'And?'

'And what?'

I stare at him. 'And I asked if you liked it. What you'd studied for it so far in shop. And you said?'

He leans away and a sudden wall of wind hits me. Obi doesn't notice. He leans back on the bonnet and tilts his head to the side. He snatches the sunnies out of my hand and slips them back on. 'And I said that I did.'

I nod with satisfaction. 'Cool,' I say. 'And anyway, you not doing well at school is a completely separate thing to you wanting to take an apprenticeship. They're unrelated. Don't you think?'

It feels simple to me. He likes it, he should do it. The rest of it is just noise. I slide over the bonnet and off the hood, sneakers crunching in the gravel. Dried grass sways against my ankles and husks get caught on my socks. I try to pick them out.

I peer back at Obi. He's still sitting there with his sunnies on, leaning back on the hood. I think he's watching me but it's hard to tell. I raise my brows. 'You coming or what?'

'Yeah, I'm coming.' He slides off the bonnet too, almost slamming into me. He ruffles my head as he passes. I duck away, scowling.

He walks backwards to the car, grinning. 'Your hair looks great.'

I attempt to flatten all the flying strands as I head to the driver's side and hop in. Slamming the door, I glare at him. 'You know, my situation is a little more stressful than yours, right now.'

'I know.'

'We have to find my nana.'

'I know.'

'She could be dead.'

'She's definitely not dead, Nash.'

'Well, don't touch my hair.'

'Okay.'

I start the engine and then, still muttering, pull a less-than-smooth U-ie back toward the entrance road. I'm sad to be leaving the windfarm behind. Maybe when we find my nana we can come back.

I hope we find my nana.

12

BANKSIA

We make it to the conservation park at the very end of the peninsula just before dark. Dusk shrouds the dirt track and Obi is poring over the map by the light of my phone, which has long since run out of reception bars.

The landscape is different here: scrubby bushes and tough grasses, small hills so you can never see more than a few metres ahead. Everything is harsh and dry and tangled. Proper bush. Sand creeps at the edges of the road, dunes rising behind curling stubby trees and piles of saltbush growing wild and tangled in the dark like barriers.

I'm driving at a snail's pace. It's creepy out here, the headlights shimmering over sand and plants, everything sharp and dangerous. Desolate. I don't love it like I loved the windfarm at the top of the cliffs. But maybe it'd be scary there at night too.

It's not helping that Obi cannot shut up about horror movies right now. He's already told me the plot to three in a row. No matter how many times I tell him to be quiet. Now I'm certain a serial killer or a murderer or a supernatural force is going to come leaping through the tangled saltbush to strangle me.

I'm breathing heavy and my hands are sweating, the window

rolled up though it's stifling inside the cab. I notice Obi has his rolled up too, so maybe his fears aren't far off mine. In the end I distract him from the endless horror chatter by asking him to describe the plot of *Dune*.

It doesn't make me feel much better though. Something about fear being the mind-killer.

A twinkling light erupts in the distance, just visible between the hulking dark dunes, and Obi immediately goes silent. We both glance at each other and my snail's pace descends into practically not moving at all.

'It could be my nana,' I say hopefully.

'Mmhmm. It could be. Or it could be a complete psycho murderer who lives out here and hasn't seen another human being in four years and desperately craves the taste of human flesh.'

That's quite specific but I can't exactly disagree. 'Mmmhmm. It could be.' My heart is beating hard against my chest. 'I need to know.'

I flick off the engine and it dies. Utter silence. Like, ear-throbbing, head-humming, dead silence. Obi's expression is panicked, the dim glow from my phone underlighting him like a shadowed ghost. 'Whoever it is would have heard the engine! They could be crawling through the bush to come and get us!'

That freaks me out. 'Crawling?'

'Yeah, I think we should go.'

'Where?'

Obi's sliding across the bench seat toward me, seatbelt discarded. 'Back to the highway, Nash. We'll sleep in the car on the main road, and then come back fresh in the morning.' He's leaning close so he can plead with me. He's trying to do that damn puppy-dog eyes thing again!

I refuse to let him, facing the grimy windshield and the half-lit bush beyond. 'But what if Nana is out there?'

'Well then she'll still be out there in the morning, Nash.'

'But that means if it's a serial killer they'll still be here in the morning too!'

'No way.' Obi shakes his head like he knows a thing or two about serial killers. And maybe he does. Apparently he doesn't like music but he does like podcasts. Especially true crime ones. I've spent the last two hours hearing all about them. *All about them.*

No wonder he's so freaking afraid of everything.

Obi is still talking. 'Serial killers don't hang out in isolated patches of bush in the daylight, Nash. There's no one around for them to kill. That's when they go home. To rest. They're like night owls.' He's muttering now and not making a whole bunch of sense.

I shake my head. 'I have to check.'

'I don't really think you do.'

I open the car door even though I can't see the distant twinkling light anymore. It's disappeared behind a hulking sand dune. Obi launches himself sideways on the bench seat to grasp my elbow. 'Stay in the car, Nash.'

I turn to him, my mouth set. 'My nana could be out there!'

He doesn't let go, his face turning serious now. Like actual real-life afraid. He's not playing around. 'Look. Pearl. I am *not* letting you go out there until we can see. We don't have to go back to the highway but we *do* have to stay in this car. With the windows locked. And that's it. No arguing.'

I glare at him and he glares back, his grip not slackening. He looks fierce, like there's absolutely utterly no chance in hell that I am getting my way right now.

I peer out again at the very creepy sand dunes and all the creepy crawly shadows and the dark spaces that could hide probably a million serial killers and axe murderers and bunyips or whatever. Slowly my scowl slips away.

Yeah, I'm very worried about my nana right now. But if I had time to stop and enjoy the view at a windfarm then I have time to stay in the car with the doors locked until dawn. I pull the door shut again. Lock it.

'Okay,' I say.

Obi sighs with relief. 'Okay.'

I flick the headlights off. We sit in silence. I'm breathing heavily, like the rush of adrenaline is leaving my system. I'm glad I'm still in the car. I scared myself with the idea of going out there. I'm just about to suck up my pride and actually thank Obi for stopping me when I catch sight of his face in the dark. The mobile glow sends dancing shadows across his features, his skin turning sick and pale blue. I don't like it.

I also don't like the way he's scrunching his brows together and squinting out the windshield. He hisses, 'Did you see that?'

I freeze.

Slowly I peer through the grimy glass, holding my breath.

I let it go all at once. He's teasing me. I see nothing. Only darkness. The shape of dunes and trees. Obi suddenly scoots over to my side, pressed against me as he leans across to the headlights. His arm is under my chin as he flicks them on again, tangling me up as I try to lean out of his way but also press forward so I can still see what's going on outside.

White light illuminates the overgrown track and the sand dunes. The saltbush and the dry grass.

And the figure standing in the middle of the track.

I scream. Loud. And so does Obi, both of us grabbing wildly at each other. My chest grows so tight I can't breathe and my whole body buzzes like electricity is crawling across my skin.

It's a woman. Just standing there with her hands on her hips. Wearing an old tracksuit. With a tiny fluffy white dog running circles around her legs.

It isn't actually that scary.

It's kind of a bit stupid.

Also, her hair is curly and pink. I can't believe it's still pink after all this time. It's been ages since I helped her dye it.

I slap Obi's arms off me, because they seem to be everywhere, as I watch the old woman walk carefully across the sandy track to my window.

'Obi. Obi! Stop it. That's my nana. It's fine. She's my nana.'

Nana has a torch, which dances circles across the dunes at her feet. She lifts her hand to knock on my window but I'm already winding it down. 'Um ... hi Nana.'

She purses her lips. 'I thought that looked like John's ute.' She pauses and raises her eyebrows. 'Who's this?'

'Oh. Um ... this is Obi. Obi, Nana. Nana, Obi.'

'You're sitting in his lap,' Nana informs me disapprovingly.

She's actually correct. I make a horrified noise deep in my throat as we rocket away from each other, Obi coughing loudly. He presses himself tight against the far side of the cab.

'Er ... what are you doing out here, Nana?' I ask it because I'm rather interested and also because I want to change the subject. 'Is everything alright?'

'Of course it is.'

I narrow my eyes at her through the gap in the window. Then I turn off the headlights, plunging us into darkness except for Nana's flashlight and the soft glow of my phone in Obi's hand.

She does seem alright. In fact, she seems quite fine.

A small bubble of anger ripples through my chest. My voice turns low and dangerous. 'Obi, wait in the car.'

I don't wait for his answer, opening my door and slamming it shut behind me using all my weight. The crash echoes through the quiet, only the soft moan of the wind in the distance. My nana is much shorter than me and much wider. But I'm much crankier.

'I need to talk to you,' I hiss, and then I turn on my heel, kicking up sand as I stalk off toward the ocean, presumably in the direction of Nana's car and camp. Or whatever it is she has out here. Her dog, Potato, is running excitedly beneath my feet, yipping happily like something utterly exciting is happening. I don't bother to check if Nana's following me. She better be.

Soon the track gives way to proper beach sand as Nana's car looms from the darkness. I stop walking and spin around to face her. She's a lot closer than I expect. I flinch and Potato starts barking like crazy. In that one unexpected moment I lose all semblance of self-control, and instead of screaming at her in fury, which was definitely what I intended, a great big sob claws its way from my throat.

'Do you even know what I thought?' My voices rises shrill and loud in the silence, thick with tears. It's dead quiet out here and I know Obi will be able to hear, but I can't seem to hold it back. I attempt to swipe my cheeks clean. 'When I got to your house and you were gone, do you know what I thought?'

Nana is clearly shocked that I'm scream-sobbing at her. Her flashlight dances wildly across the dunes. The ocean glitters beneath dim moonlight at the edge of the shore. Slowly she shakes her head and I just sob harder, great heaving gasps and hiccups.

'The neighbour said you were sad! And Dad forgot to pay your bills. And the neighbour saw you drive to the quarry!'

Nana's turning pink. 'Oh. Oh no. It wasn't like that, at all.'

'Then why did you even go up there? What have you been doing all this time?'

'Oh, Pearl. Stop crying.' She reaches up and drags me to her level, enfolding me within the circle of her arms. She's soft and nice and smells like my nana.

'I missed you,' I sob. 'And Daisy's been acting stupid and I don't know if we're even friends anymore.' I cry into Nana's shoulder until her faded trackie top is wet. She makes comforting sounds while she pats my hair.

Which is nice, because Nana isn't usually the soft, loving type. But I guess she feels guilty.

Eventually she pushes me back, leaving me sniffling and wiping forlornly at my cheeks. Nana's hands are on my face. I reach for her crinkly pale-pink hair, which has clearly been re-touched since last I saw her. 'Who helped you dye it?'

She smiles, her thin lips curling and her expression calm, though I know from experience that Nana has bite, too. 'I dyed it myself. Do you like it?' A swell of pride crosses her face, maybe because she always insisted she needed my help even though I complained and tried to get out of it. Turns out she didn't need me after all.

'No, I don't like it,' I answer petulantly as Potato circles our legs. 'I would have done a better job.'

Nana throws back her head and roars with laughter. Patting my cheek, not as softly as I would have liked, she smiles and says, 'You better go get that boy out of the car and come down to the beach. I'll feed you both.'

I nod pitifully. 'We came a really long way to find you.'

'Did you, now?' She squints at me suspiciously. 'And how long did it take to realise I was missing?'

I gulp. Choose to avoid the question and just tell her the good news instead. 'Dad noticed first. He was really *really* worried. That's why he sent me to look for you. He was so worried he even called Uncle John!'

That softens her expression. 'Did he, now? Well that is something.'

'Also he called the police.' I let that bit of news out in a big rush.

'What?'

Watching her reaction makes me glad it wasn't *me* who called the police. Dad is in for it now.

'He called the bloody police?' She sucks air through her teeth. 'That ridiculous boy, wait until I get my hands on him. Call him. Right now, Pearl. Right now!'

I bat her away because she's searching my jean-short pockets like I'm hiding a satellite dish in there. 'Nana,' I complain. 'I can't, there's no reception out here. You know that, it's why no one's been able to call you.'

She blinks. 'No reception? No. My phone's still on. I've been charging it in the car like you showed me.' She sniffs. 'It's true I was ignoring your dad's calls back at the house. I wanted him to stew for a while. But when I got here, he stopped calling!' She looks very offended.

I roll my eyes. 'Your phone being on and it having reception are two completely different things, Nana. Everyone's still been trying to call you. They've been freaking out.'

'Oh,' she says. She's become quite pink. Almost as pink as her hair.

I raise my brows. 'So. Do you want to ... you know, go? Go home? Or go back to Uncle John's or whatever?'

'Go?' She gapes at me like I'm being completely silly. 'I can't drive in the dark.'

I bite my lip. That is true. I did once drive with Nana at night and it was very scary. I made her pull over and swap with me. 'Well, I can drive you.' Even as I say it I feel nervous. Everything around here is sand tracks and steep rises. Easy to get lost. Or bogged. Or drive off a cliff into the ocean. Quite scary.

Nana clearly reads it on my face. 'What about your boy? The one in the car?'

'He can't drive.'

She snorts. 'Useless.'

I snap my head toward the ute, hoping Obi didn't overhear that comment. I only just wrestled him back from truly believing he *was* useless.

'Nana!' I hush her.

'Well, it's true!' She sighs. 'Fine, we eat. We sleep. And at first light we go call your stupid father.'

I nod. And then Nana stops dead still, as if she's heard something, erratically pointing her flashlight toward a stunted, rustling nearby bush.

I freeze, terrified. Waiting for a serial killer to jump out and murder me.

Except the bush just shifts softly in the wind and does nothing else. Finally, Nana nods and announces with satisfaction, 'That's a myrtle wattle. Look at it. Look at it, Pearl!'

She makes a low sound of approval, as if the bush being a myrtle wattle is a very good thing, and then she storms off toward the ocean, leaving me with whiplash and a pounding heart. Potato is a tiny white ghost at her heels.

They melt into the night and I blink after them, nerves frayed. Eventually I pick my way back toward the ute in the dark. It's sort of impossible and after a few seconds I stop and shout, 'Obi! Obi. Obi! Obi!'

'Jeez, what?!' he bellows back.

'Bring the camping lantern, will you?'

And then I have to stand around and do nothing for ages while I wait for him.

He's pretty worried when he finally shows up, big eyes shimmering in the dark. 'Are you alright? Where is she?' He shifts from foot to foot. Maybe he's a little scared of my nana now. He probably heard her call him useless. I feel quite bad about that.

I take his arm and navigate the track, using him to shine the lantern where I want to walk. 'She invited us for dinner.'

'So we're staying?'

'Just until the morning.'

He glances down at me. 'Were you crying?'

At first I think I'm going to lie, tell him *of course not*. Except then I reckon he probably heard me sobbing anyway. I glance up at him. Besides. It's only Obi. And, somehow, he means something to me now. I don't know what. But something. And I don't want to lie.

'Yeah,' I answer. 'But only a little.'

He's solemn. 'Do you feel better now?'

I think about that for a moment. 'Yeah. I do.'

Obi's face cracks open into a grin. A real one. His eyes crinkling small. 'Oh, good. Cos I'm starving.'

I blink at him, and the idea that he's back on my side again uncurls within my mind. It makes me smile up at him. For a moment at least, until I remember that my dad has set the police on Nana, that Daisy is ignoring me and things between Obi and I are still ... complicated.

'Yeah,' I agree. 'I'm starving too.'

13

SPINIFEX GRASS

Obi's sitting cross-legged in the sand, a fire of driftwood crackling away behind him. My nana is crouched and poking at it with a stick.

She's cooking fish, I think. Not like ocean-caught fish. More like fish someone *else* caught in the ocean, took to a store, then sold to my nana so she could bring it back to the ocean and cook it. Round and round in circles. She has a big canvas tent set in the shelter between the sand dunes and Potato is beside the water, yapping at the inky waves.

Obi holds up a creased novel in a shower of sand and shows me the cover, which has a big muscly dude on it. He's wearing a kilt and not much else. *The Highlander's Revenge*. A whole pile of similar books lies beside him. He raises his eyebrows at me as I return from the tent.

'I *told* you they were my nana's,' I say, flopping beside him on the sand. Nana has lent me one of her sweaters and it's nice and soft and smells of her.

'Liar,' says Obi absently, opening the paperback to the middle and thumbing through the pages. 'You love them.'

I rescue the book from him but he just picks up another.

This one has a pirate on it. 'Um Nash, these are pretty steamy.'

I roll my eyes but I can't help but blush too. 'Alright, alright.'

'No, really. This stuff is—'

'They're romantic too, though. That stuff's not the *point* of it. It's the happy-ever-after that's the point.'

'But seriously, listen to this passage—'

'Shush, Obi, stop it!' I can't believe he's actually about to embarrass me by reading out loud. Especially in front of my nana! She already doesn't like the fact that I was (sort of) sitting on his lap, and she's definitely not going to like that he's reading me sexy literature.

I launch myself at Obi to cover his mouth with my hand, but he pulls the book back, out of my reach. His eyes crinkle as he drags my hand from his mouth. 'Admit it. The books are yours and you love them.'

'Give it back!'

'Say it.'

I shove him away. 'Fine. It's true. Those ones are my nana's but the other ones in the car were mine.'

He inclines his head, very serious. 'And you love them.'

He waits.

I clench my jaw and stare back, lifting my chin. 'Yes. I *do* love them. So what? What? Do you have a problem with that?'

Obi drops the paperback on the scattered pile. 'Nah, it's cool.'

I blink. It's a bit anticlimactic. 'So that's it? You're done tormenting me now?'

'Yeah, I think so. I mean, I read that whole book when we were being driven to the Bedford.' He shrugs. '*Dune's* better, though. Have you read *Dune*, Pearl?'

I honestly can't tell if he's messing with me. I watch him

suspiciously until I catch the grin creeping at the edges of his mouth, and then I smack his shoulder and go to help Nana.

She frowns over at Obi where he's still reading by the light of the camp lantern. I'm pretty certain he can hear us but that doesn't stop her. 'Who's this boy you've brought with you? I don't like what was happening in the car earlier.'

I try to hush her, my cheeks burning, but Nana's voice is very loud.

'Is he your boyfriend?'

'No,' I hiss, wrapping an arm around her shoulders to turn her away. 'He's a ... he's a friend?'

That doesn't seem quite right either.

I glance back over my shoulder at Obi. He's very intent on reading that romance novel right now and very purposely not looking our way.

'A friend! Psshh. He doesn't look at you like a friend should, girl. Have you had sex with him?'

'Nana!' I'm horrified, my face flaming.

Please don't let Obi hear, please don't let Obi hear.

I glance back at him over the crackling fire and his carefully blank expression means he totally heard. Dammit. 'Can we just drop it, please?'

My nana opens her mouth to say something worse, probably, so I shush her, trying a different tack, hands on my hips. I attempt to appear fierce. 'What *I* want to know is why you came out here in the first place?'

She pouts. 'Well, how did you know I'd be here?'

'The photographs. And you and Grandpa came here for your honeymoon. I remember you telling me.'

'Well, there you go then.'

Potato comes bounding out of the shallow, inky waves and shakes himself all over my legs, speckles of cold water and sand spraying everywhere. I yelp.

'What a good boy,' says my nana, patting the dog's head. She's sitting in front of the fire, poking at the skewered fish. 'These aren't quite ready yet. What's your boyfriend's name again?'

'He's not my boyfriend, Nana.' I drop to my knees in the sand. 'And his name is Obi.'

She squints at me suspiciously across the crackling flames. 'You kissed him, though, didn't you?'

'Nana,' I whine, dropping my head into my hands. The fish is sizzling and blackened. Woodsmoke pours over the dunes in the warm breeze.

'Thought so.'

I say nothing, my chest tight with embarrassment as I stead-fastly refuse to look across at Obi on the other side of the fire. I can't exactly deny it. I can't even say it was him who kissed me.

It was me.

I did it.

I suck in my breath, my face flushing hot, and we sit in silence for a while, night sounds in the background. The soft whoosh of the waves and wavering of tough bushes. The fire crackles and pops, orange sparks floating into the stretching sky as the fish turns to charcoal.

It doesn't look very appetising but I don't say anything about it, or even complain when Potato comes and crawls onto my lap, dripping salt water and wet sand. I just pet him softly, scratching behind his woolly ears. He's gritty and smells like salt and stinky dog. But he's happy, open-mouthed and licking me.

Gross.

'Nana,' I start slowly. I bite my lips. I don't even know how to ask these questions. I wish my dad were here. He'd do it better.

'Yes, hon?' She pokes at the blackened fish.

I scratch Potato harder, lowering my face over his white woolly body, hiding my expression. 'Did you come here because we didn't call you enough? Because you were lonely?'

She huffs. 'Well, your dad did forget to pay the power bill! He forgot all about me.'

'And he feels so guilty!'

'Humph.'

'Really, he does!'

She's softened a bit, so I repeat it for good measure. 'Just *so* incredibly guilty.'

Nana nods, looking rather pleased now. 'Yes. Quite guilty. Good.'

But it still doesn't explain everything. I clear my throat, feeling awkward. 'But why did you leave the city in the first place, Nana?' I hesitate. 'Because you were feeling sad? About Grandpa?'

This time Nana doesn't answer, the stick in her hand releasing a shower of sparks. They float up, up and away, curling into the night sky. The stars out here are spectacular, like a glimmering, airy ocean. I've never seen anything like them. No light pollution. I whisper, 'It's alright if you were.' I pause. 'Sad, I mean.'

She shrugs, but already I can see the signs. I know her too well. The way her knuckles go white, clasped around the fire stick. Her mouth grows hard, drawn into a thin line. She blinks.

We never talk about Grandpa.

Not anymore.

I continue carefully. 'I think maybe because it's been so long since he passed away ... maybe we forget that you're still ...' I search for the word.

'Grieving?' My nana peers at me, flames sending patterns dancing across her skin.

I nod.

She frowns, lifting a hand to swipe her eye. She does it like there's something caught there, like sand or a bug, but I know the truth. Eventually she rasps, 'Don't you think it's so strange that everyone always says *passed away*?'

I blink at her. 'But he did pass away.'

'No, he didn't, love. It wasn't like that. He *died*. That's the truth. And it was so awful, Pearl. You weren't there and I'm glad of it. He wouldn't have wanted you to see him that way. But he was so sick, and it was awful. There was no peace. He didn't just ... pass away. There was nothing gentle about it. He died.'

I say nothing, frozen in place. I watch her hands. Short stubby fingers, her skin pale and wrinkled, veins popping. She twitches and kneads them, as if she can't stay still.

'I feel like I have to say *passed away* to everyone I meet, because if you say *died* people think it's too blunt, they feel upset. So even when I talk about my own husband, I have to put it in a way that doesn't upset *other* people. It makes me so mad.' She peers at me. 'Three years isn't very long, Pearl. We spent fifty together.'

Guilt blooms hard and hot inside my belly. I didn't ask how she was. Didn't sit with her in the granny flat and listen to stories about Grandpa. I was busy.

I thought three years was long enough.

I felt impatient with her. I didn't want to hear about him anymore.

'Sorry, Nana,' I breathe, tears stinging my cheeks.

'Don't be sorry, love. None of it's your fault. It's just complicated, is all.'

I bite my lip. 'How?'

An invitation.

Because I'm here now. I can listen now.

At first I'm certain she won't explain. But then it's like she changes her mind, flips a switch and once she's started, I don't think she knows how to stop.

'Since he's been gone, I don't quite know who I am. We had routines and things we liked to do. And for the last three years I kept trying to do them, because I thought they were what I enjoyed. But maybe it was just him who liked them? I don't even know what I like. And now I'm supposed to be finding out, but it all feels a bit late to be discovering yourself at this age. And I feel tired of it.'

I shift on the sand, suddenly afraid. My nana is old. Whenever I see old people I think they have everything figured out, that their life is easy. But my nana is crying on a beach at the end of the world.

I say in a small voice, 'You don't like living with us?'

'I love living with you, hon.' She lifts her head and smiles through her tears. 'That's not the problem at all. The problem is ... different. Come here.'

So I do. Crawling through the sand to wrap my arms around her. She's soft and warm and smells of the sea. Her pink hair is wiry and scratchy against my cheek.

'I love living with you, Pearl. I do. It's just this year ... people kept saying that the third would be easier and I was holding out so much hope for it. Just counting the days like I thought I'd turn a corner and just not be sad anymore. But it never happened. I kept finding myself wishing things could be how they were. So I came back to our old house.'

'Did it work? Do you feel better?'

Nana shakes her head. 'Not really. That's why I drove down here. To this place.' She smiles. 'Your grandpa brought me out here for our honeymoon. A secret place. Spent the entire trip teaching me all about the bushes and plants. What you can use them for, how they grow.' She breathes deep. 'Banksia and bottlebrush. And the flowers. Desert peas and waratah flower. We had a good time here. I remember it.'

I don't even know what to say, but listening to her makes my heart hurt.

Turns out Nana doesn't need me to say anything at all though. She's already emerging from her memories. Her eyes cloud over and she mutters, 'But it doesn't feel the same out here without him. Why would I want to come now he's gone? It's lonely here now.'

I sink back onto my knees, flames flickering and heat from the fire burning into my back. 'I'm here now, Nana.'

'Yes, you are, sweetheart.' She swipes harshly at her cheeks. My nana doesn't like anyone to see her cry. Like Uncle John said, she's a tough old woman, for all her soft, round edges. She grew up on a farm in the middle of nowhere. No electricity. No running water. Helped her dad run it until she married my grandpa and helped him run his property instead. She's told us the story so many times.

My grandpa was tough, too. Stern. With everyone except Nana.

He was stern with my dad, but he still left me his Bedford when he died, even though I was too young to drive it. Back then it was a total rust bucket, but my dad loves cars so he slowly fixed it up. Sometimes I think my grandpa really left it as a present for my dad, in a roundabout way. My dad needed a project, and it was something we would do together. Just to pass the time. Nana sat on a deck chair in the garden or pottered with her plants under the sun. None of us spoke. I read novels on the grass and handed my dad tools when he asked and he worked for hours.

Everything had felt heavy back then. Until the Bedford was up and running and Dad spent the summer driving me and Daisy down the beach every day and things started to feel light again. It never occurred to me that maybe I'd left her there.

Nana.

Maybe I'd left her behind in the heaviness.

I peer at her, my chest constricted, but Nana squares her shoulders and sits straight, blinking the last remnants of tears away. Her voice is all business. 'What's your young man's name, again? Ob ... Obby ...'

I roll my eyes. 'Obi.' I forget to tell her he isn't my young man this time.

She shouts, 'Obi! Come here and eat.' Way too loudly, considering he is literally *right there* and has obviously already heard every scrap of our very private conversation. His head pops up and I notice he appears a little less afraid of her.

When he's settled by my side, Nana hands him a tin camping plate with some very blackened fish on it. Nana was always a terrible cook, but this is extreme.

Obi stares at it, stares at me, and then says, 'Thanks.' And then he actually tries to eat it.

My nana nods approvingly, which makes me choke on my

own charcoal fish, coughing and spluttering until Obi thumps me hard on the back. He's sitting close enough on the cool sand that our knees are touching. Probably he's hoping I'll protect him from my nana, but I worry she already has enough ammunition to use against us so I move further away, until we aren't touching anymore.

Nana is watching him with narrowed eyes. Around a mouthful of fish, she says, 'So Obi. Are you in school?'

'Uh … yes.' He glances at me with a *help me* expression, but honestly there's nothing I can do.

'What year?'

'Same as Nash.'

'Mmmh. Nash.'

Obi's eyes widen. 'Pearl! I meant same as *Pearl*.'

Nana's mouth tightens. 'And what are you planning to do after school?'

Obi turns to me wildly, then promptly stuffs the last of his fish into his mouth so he doesn't have to answer. I clear my throat.

'Obi is thinking about starting an apprenticeship in the new year. He might be leaving school.'

Nana doesn't take her focus off him. 'An apprenticeship! What for?'

'Electrician,' mumbles Obi through a big mouthful.

'Mmmh,' Nana says. I don't know if it's a good *Mmmh* or a bad *Mmmh*, until she claps her hands, thin lips drawn back in a wide smile. 'That's very good. Good.'

It's Obi's turn to cough now, and my turn to thump him on the back. Despite all the spluttering, I think he's pleased, if a bit taken aback, by her reaction. Nana totally flips her approach to him now, as apparently she's decided she approves of Obi despite the whole sitting-on-lap-in-car thing. Maybe she's forgotten about it.

Except she hasn't, because when she marches us all off to bed later, she sticks a finger in my face and says fiercely, 'No funny business with that boy in my tent, you hear me?'

Obi has a hand over his mouth, choking again. I'm offended because she said it to me and not him. My nana always presumes everything is my fault. Although, thinking about that night in the Bedford, perhaps she's got a point.

'Look,' Obi says, holding the tent flap open for me to enter after Nana has stalked away. He points at the sky, grinning.

The world above is immense, stars and planets in thick clusters of white-gold light, a tapestry of constellations and unimaginable patterns, all blurring together around a pale crescent moon. The light catches on the surface of the inky ocean, a reflection of the sky, soft waves and shadows dancing.

I breathe deep.

14

MULGA TREE

I wake to the sound of waves and the scent of the ocean, cloying darkness pressing in. Potato's small, warm body is curled against my side, every now and then making little doggie snorts as he dreams his little doggie dreams. Nana is snoring softly in her sleeping bag on one side and Obi is sprawled on my other, dead to the world.

I'm in the middle again, but I don't mind it. Nana is safe and Obi is ...

I shift carefully onto my side to face him, slow and quiet because I don't want to wake anyone. The blankets we share are bunched below his chest, exposing him to the cool night. He's only wearing a thin T-shirt, so I slowly pull them back up to cover him again. He stirs, moaning softly in his sleep.

I'm certain I've woken him, his lashes flickering and his breathing changing, becoming faster and shallower. But his eyes remain closed and after a while his chest rises rhythmically again. Slow and steady.

I lie back down, barely daring to breathe. Facing him. I watch him sleeping, his fluttering lashes and soft mouth, the sharp edges of his jaw and the soft beat of his pulse beneath his throat. What does it mean that he's here beside me at the end of the world?

Nothing. It means nothing. To either of us.

Still. In the dark I reach for his temple, the far edges of his eyebrow, brushing soft fingers against the indents and scarring along his cheekbone, down to the corner of his mouth. My fingers rest there for a long moment.

And then I take my hand back, curling my fingers under my chin. I squeeze my eyes shut, breathing heavily.

Stupid.

I wanted to touch him. It's like being caught inside a spell. My chest is tight and my blood is humming loud in my ears. I take a deep breath and roll away, onto my other side. It's embarrassing.

I'm embarrassing.

What does this mean, wanting to touch him in the middle of the night?

What does it mean?

I keep my body turned away from him and try to sleep, but every time Obi stirs behind me, it's like electric pulses going off beneath my skin.

We rise with the dawn, me with dark circles on my cheeks and a massive bedhead. I know both of these things because Obi informs me straight away. I glare at him and cannot believe I wasted an entire night thinking about him instead of sleeping. Again. This whole thing is absolutely wrecking my head.

I stalk off down the beach with Potato yapping at my heels, spraying sand behind me until I plunge my feet into the ocean. It's wilder today. The waves breaking bigger. The sun is up, beating on my back. Sweat beads on my forehead. The water is cool on my skin. Splashes on my clothes.

'Breakfast!' Nana screams. I flinch. The woman is so loud.

Taking one last look at the soaring sky and crashing ocean, one final deep breath of salty air, I stride back across the beach toward the now-disassembled tent and the campfire. A shower of grit and tiny delicate seashells kicks at my feet.

When I sit beside Nana, she peers down her nose disapprovingly at me. 'Wet,' is all she says, scowling at the sand stuck to my T-shirt where the water splashed through.

I nod, distracted, because Obi is looming over me. He sits close, not touching this time, but close. My nana sniffs, clearly not pleased with my lack of response, though she still hands us both tin plates.

We stare at them.

More fish.

Practically charcoal.

My nana starts eating, sighing blissfully like she's eating the most delicious meal of her life. Obi wrinkles his nose, leaning close to whisper against my ear, 'Is it meant to be this burned?'

I shake my head and whisper back from the corner of my mouth so Nana doesn't hear. 'No. She screwed up.'

His breath is warm against my skin as he replies. 'Oh. I thought maybe it was a special recipe.'

I snort, brushing sand from my skin, hand on my cheek where his breath touched. And then we eat. Well, we try to. It doesn't taste very good.

'How did you both sleep?' Nana asks.

I shrug. 'Bad. I couldn't sleep at all.' I don't feel weird to admit this. Neither of them has to know what I was thinking about all night.

Except then Obi chimes in, 'Yeah, me too. I didn't sleep at all.'

I snort. 'Whatever. You were sleeping like a dead log.'

'A dead log?' He chuckles, a throaty sound. 'I'm pretty sure that's not how you're meant to say that, and no I didn't. I didn't sleep at all.'

I stop eating. 'At all?'

He's staring at me, a slow grin spreading across his face, dimples appearing out of nowhere. Nana nods with approval at the dimples, like she understands everything now and says, 'Aaah.'

I glare at her, before turning back to Obi. 'Not at all?'

My heart is sinking, the already-dry fish turning to ash on my tongue. He didn't sleep at all? Which would mean he was awake when I …

'Not at all,' he agrees. Then he turns to Nana. 'Thanks for breakfast, Mrs Nash.'

'Very polite,' Nana tells me. I push hair from my face and ignore her. Ignore Obi too. My heart is thudding inside my chest in a way that is distinctly uncomfortable. I say nothing for the rest of breakfast. I can't eat all the charcoal fish and Obi takes my plate, finishing my meal as well as his.

'Aaah,' says Nana again, nodding at him. She likes people who don't leave leftovers. 'A very good boy.'

Obi grins, which makes me roll my eyes.

But it works. Nana loves him now, apparently. Which is why

she makes me load the tent and the cooking crap into her car while she and Obi sit by the dying fire and drink tea.

I grumble the whole time, listening as Nana tells him a really long, boring story about how she planted some dumb kangaroo-paw plants in her garden after she first got married. They died apparently.

I think there's a moral in there somewhere but I can't figure out what it is. Neither can Obi clearly, because he keeps flashing 'help me' eyes in my direction.

I ignore him. That ship has sailed. Along with my dignity. I shudder just thinking about what happened last night.

Soon it's all over and Obi and I are trekking in uncomfortable silence back toward the paddock basher over the dunes. We decide we'll wait in the car for Nana to drive by and then follow her out of the conservation park. I don't want to give her a chance to get away.

It's weird, but I reckon I'll miss this isolated stretch of beach: the wildness and the waves. It isn't hard to imagine them here, my nana and grandpa fifty years ago. Making a campfire and watching the stars together on their honeymoon. I bet the place hasn't changed much. It's so beautiful in its empty, desolate way.

I get why Nana and Grandpa liked it so much.

'You know,' says Obi abruptly. 'I kind of thought your nana would be like this wise old woman.'

I bark out a laugh. 'She's definitely not.'

'No. She's a bit scary, actually. But cool too.'

I peer at him. He says it like he means it. 'I'm ... glad you like her.'

Obi shrugs and smiles as we walk on in silence. It's hard work trekking over the shifting dunes and avoiding all the sharp, scrubby bushes. Soon I'm sweating despite my damp T-shirt. My hair is being blown into what I can only imagine is a curly and insane mess, flicking into my face. The sun blasts overhead and the sand burns my feet, getting caught inside my rubber thongs. Finally I murmur, 'Thank you for eating all that disgusting fish.'

Obi grins down at me, eyes glimmering like stars. 'My mum is Tamil, Nash. I know all about eating whatever you get given. Leftovers means you didn't like it. It means you're ungrateful for the hard work of the cook, right?'

'I dunno if she worked that hard,' I counter. But still, I store that information away. Then I catch myself. Why? Why do I need to remember that? For if I meet Obi's mum?

What is wrong with me?

We kissed *once* in the back of the Bedford. That's all!

More than once. We kissed for a very long time.

Which is beside the point.

I've stopped walking and am staring at him. Obi's observing me curiously, his head tilted to the side. 'You alright, Nash?'

He asks this in a nonchalant way, like none of this stuff is affecting him in the slightest. Even though I'm quite positive now that he was awake and knows exactly what I did in the tent. Which makes me very queasy.

I'm so stupid.

Obi likes teasing me. He likes kissing me.

It doesn't mean he likes *me*.

'Yeah,' I mutter. 'Fine.' I turn away and walk fast, drawing ahead to reach the ute. I hop in. And when he slides into the passenger seat I keep my focus straight ahead, turning the key in the ignition.

'No serial killers around to steal the ute, I guess,' says Obi thoughtfully.

At first I don't even want to answer, my head is in such turmoil. Except I don't want to give him the satisfaction of knowing that. Obi is used to people fawning over him. I won't be one of his fan club members. So I shove it all to the back of my head and mutter, 'Or maybe they didn't want it. It's total junk.'

'It's okay.'

'It won't start.'

Truth. The freaking engine is dead. The car is screwed. I sit back in my seat and cross my arms, taking deep, shaking breaths.

'No way! Two cars in three days? No way.' Obi shifts over the bench seat. 'Let me try.'

'You can't even drive.'

'But I can turn a key, Nash.'

Turns out he can't. I lean through the open window and show him how to push the clutch while he turns the ignition on. It seems Obi's mum doesn't let him near their family car unless she's there to drive it.

'She thinks I'm gonna crash it,' explains Obi.

No matter how much he tries, the truck remains dead.

'Probably the battery,' I say as Nana pulls up. She's got an old station wagon with rust stains up the sides. It's a bomb too. It's definitely going to break down next.

I hate old cars.

I sigh. 'The ute broke, Nana.'

She nods solemnly, the engine of the station wagon still

running. 'Of course it did. Your grandpa left that old thing for John when he died. Surprised it lasted as long as it did.'

I notice she said *died* and not *passed away*. Guess she doesn't need to pretend with us, anymore.

I inspect the ute suspiciously. Grandpa left me the Bedford and Uncle John the paddock basher. It makes me wonder if my grandpa is teasing me. If he's a ghost floating around and playing havoc with my life. I shake my head. Silly. If my grandpa was a ghost, I'm pretty sure he'd have better things to do. Like take care of Nana.

'Alright,' says Nana, clapping her hands. She's climbed out of the station wagon to rifle through the ute's engine, head lost under the bonnet. 'It looks like the battery. Not much we can do. Let's get this show on the road.' She motions for Obi to close the bonnet and climbs back into her own car. 'Hop in and I'll drive you. John can come get this old piece of rubbish later.'

We move all our stuff between the two cars and I give the ute a final pat before we depart. It was a good ute.

It helped me find my nana.

15

PENINSULA GUINEA-FLOWER

It's dusk by the time we pull into a car park by the sea, after hours spent driving long stretches of flat road and passing tiny isolated settlements. We're in a small community just off the highway. Typical country town. It's got a jetty, two pubs, a petrol station and a corner shop.

And a huge fair set on the grass beside the esplanade. Flashing lights and a carousel loom ahead. Frightening clown things spin nearby, the ones where you put the balls in their mouths. Whatever they're called.

I stand with my hair blowing in the warm sea breeze and stare, neon blue and green light filtering over the grass and reflecting vividly on Obi's sneakers.

'Why is this here?' I ask Nana.

She's been complaining of exhaustion non-stop. She wouldn't let me take over though and also refused to stop. Until it got dark. She can't drive in the dark. So now we're parked here. In the middle of nowhere. Surrounded by trucks and cars and swelling crowds of people. Obviously, it's not quite so middle-of-nowhere as the conservation park. But when you think of it in relation to the nearest city, it still is.

But I guess when you compare it to the city, everything here is small-scale. The carousel is half-size, dodgers and a train ride are both baby-sized for kids under ten, and three food trucks sit at the edge. A blow-up castle swarms with children.

Still, after coming from that camp at the end of the world, that complete isolation, it all feels like ... a lot.

I suspect Obi agrees. He's blinking at the people and the lights: his face swathed in blue neon, his teeth glowing purple from the slowly turning carousel.

'I need a coffee,' snaps Nana. She's stressed now. Mainly because my dad yelled at her on the phone. And told her the police were searching for her last night. And also that he and my mum and Sam are all currently on their way to wait for us at Uncle John's farm, where I suspect tensions will be running thick and high. I'm honestly not that excited about it.

I wish we didn't have to go back.

Though truly, I now have a much bigger problem.

I take Nana's arm and propel her toward a coffee stand, Obi trailing behind. 'So Nana, I have a little issue. Um. So, like ... maybe Mum and Dad don't, you know ...'

I glance back at Obi, who is now burning orange and pink in flickering patterns as we pass the baby train.

'No. I don't know,' snaps Nana. 'Say what you mean, Pearl!'

I should have waited until she got her coffee. She's tired and cranky and I suspect even Obi's dimples won't help when she hears what I've got to say. I motion back at him to smile anyway. He does, and I have enough grace to feel a little guilty. After admonishing him in my head for using his charming smile as a weapon, I'm now attempting to utilise it myself.

But I need all the firepower I can get.

I grasp him by the elbow, pulling him close beside me so Nana can see how sweet he looks.

'It's just that, Nana, like ... Mum and Dad sort of think that ... um ... that Daisy's with me. Not Obi. They actually sort of don't know Obi. And I kind of ... um ... lied ... because there was this ... party ... in a beach shack ...'

I trail off because Nana's eyes are blazing.

'Um,' I say.

She explodes. 'You mean you've been driving around this entire peninsula for days with some random boy your parents never even met? I thought he was *vetted*, Pearl Nash!'

Obi's dimples disappear and he shrinks beside me. I am very aware of the way he positions my body in front of him as a shield, his hands on my shoulders as he cowers behind.

'Er,' I say.

'I cannot believe this.' Nana turns to the food stall and shouts at the man behind the counter, 'Coffee!' He flinches and then scurries to do what she asked.

Glowering at me the entire time, Nana breathes heavily through her nose, her mouth locked in a thin, tight line. I grasp Obi's arm harder. I can already tell his flight mode is kicking in.

Eventually Nana leads us to a chipped picnic table near the scary moving clown game. Obi watches the open-mouthed painted faces moving back and forth, mesmerised. Or perhaps acting mesmerised so he doesn't have to take part in our conversation.

Nana sits opposite me, her wiry pink hair tumbling in the wind and her skin flashing green and blue. She's like a rainbow. 'Tell me everything, Pearl Nash.'

I gulp.

And I do.

Except the thing about making out with Obi in the back of the Bedford. Obviously. I word that part of the story in such a way that I imply, without implicitly saying so, that Obi slept separately in a tent all night beside the road.

'Mmmh,' says Nana, when I'm finished. 'Mmmh.'

Once again, I can't tell if those are good mmmhs or bad mmmhs.

She taps her fingernails on the table, making me wait. Her face is pink now, to match her hair. The little baby train chugs by, parents standing behind the fence and waving wildly as it very slowly clicks across the tracks.

My mouth is dry and my ears hum with the noise of the fairground. I realise I'm still gripping Obi's arm, so quickly release my fingers. He rubs his skin and rolls his shoulders beside me, glancing nervously at the black shadowed ocean. I wonder if he's trying to map out an escape route. It probably won't work.

My nana is faster than you'd expect.

Though when she does finally clear her throat and speak, Nana doesn't say what I think she will.

'That Daisy! How dare she ditch you!'

I blink.

'I always knew there was something wrong with that girl! She never appreciated you, I told you from the start!'

She didn't.

'I always said you'd be better off without her hanging around, didn't I? And what was the point of spending all your time with that one girl instead of meeting new people? Didn't I always tell you that? Make new friends, Pearl Nash!'

I grimace. She did not always tell me that, and actually it's making me kind of mad. Because I feel like it might have been quite good advice for me to hear at the beginning of the year, but it doesn't count in retrospect. 'Alright, alright,' I say, lifting my hands to stop her. I don't need her to keep listing all the ways my life is screwed up. I already know them.

It's clearly a mistake to interrupt her though, because Nana glares at me with a tight mouth and beady eyes. I sweat silently under her gaze, deflated.

I love my nana, but she scares me.

For instance, last year when she found out I hadn't studied for a science exam, she chased me around the backyard with a broom handle. My mum had to come out and save me. Actually, Mum was quite angry because she doesn't believe in punishing children with violence. Even when Sam is being the absolute worst ratbag he could possibly be, he still never gets a smack. But Nana's parenting style is old-school.

I really miss my mum.

Her and Nana don't get along. I mean, they sort of do, but the problem is that Mum's approach to life involves yoga and avocado smash and treating your children with respect. She believes I'm an old soul in a young body.

Nana, on the other hand, believes that's complete rubbish. And she's very vocal about disapproving the use of precious money on expensive 'hippy' mashed avocado. Doubly so if she has to sit on an overturned milk crate in a trendy warehouse café while eating it.

When she's talking to Mum, most of Nana's sentences begin with, 'Back on the property, you could never have [*insert the thing Mum is doing here*].'

Their relationship is very complicated, softened only by the fact that they both love Dad. And me, I guess. (And Sam.) Though right now I'm not really feeling the love part. Just the fury. All of it, directed right at me.

I clear my throat. 'I think we should leave for Uncle John's house immediately.'

'Do you, now?' snaps Nana.

I plead silently, nodding. My mother is waiting for me at Uncle John's farm. She will protect me from Nana. That is where we need to go.

'I think you forgot something, Pearl.' Nana raises her eyebrows. They're dyed pink too. She jabs her chin in the direction of Obi, who wilts in his seat beside me. He's sweaty and is also breathing very heavily, staring wide-eyed at Nana. It occurs to me that Obi is scared of a lot of things. Dogs. Servos. Serial killers.

My nana.

'Are you planning on bringing *him* back to the farm to meet your parents? And explaining where Daisy is?' Nana sculls the last of her coffee, which must be very hot, and crosses her arms over her ample chest.

'Er,' I say helpfully.

Actually, now that I think about it, won't Uncle John have already told my dad that I was in his house with a boy and not Daisy? My heart beats faster. But then slows. Potentially not. Hopefully. Maybe they're too busy yelling at each other, instead of sharing information about me.

I hope so.

'Um, I don't really want to tell Mum and Dad about the party,' I admit. I don't mention the Obi part of it.

Potato's running around the picnic table in circles, a little white glowing doggy that keeps changing colours. Neon-pink to match Nana's hair and then blue to match Obi's face. A man lurches out of the darkness and we all jump in fright. Until I realise he's old and small and not exactly threatening.

'Is that your dog?' He peers over the top of wire-rim glasses.

Nana frowns. 'Yes. That's my dog. Potato, here boy!' She lifts him from the grass and clasps him against her chest like this man might be trying to steal him.

'It looks exactly like *my* dog,' the man exclaims. He appears quite amazed. I don't know why. Potato looks like every dog. He's small and white and hairy. Lots of dogs are like that.

Nana's frown deepens. 'Well he's not. He's my dog.'

The man just smiles. 'Oh yes, wait until you see.' He walks off into the dark and Obi wrinkles his nose at me, though immediately smooths his features when Nana turns back to us.

She huffs and holds Potato tighter against her body, rocking him like he's a baby. 'Tell me where this beach shack of yours is, Pearl Nash.'

I'm a little frightened, so I do.

As soon as the words have left my mouth, Nana's whole demeanour changes. Her brows smooth out and her mouth curls at the edges. She seems rather pleased.

Which is weird. I exchange a glance with Obi. Clearly it's not just me who notices.

Nana coughs. 'I'm going to ask you a very important question, Pearl Nash. Answer me honestly.'

I shiver. 'Er. Okay.'

'Do you still want to see Daisy?'

I've already told her everything (except the Bedford) so

there's little point in hiding the truth now. I nod slowly. 'Yes.'

It feels important to give Daisy this final chance. I want her to recognise that our friendship is disintegrating, I want her to own up to it and face it. Face me.

At this point, it would be better if it ended with a screaming fight than if our friendship just melted away like a whisper of smoke.

Because no matter how it all finishes, it wasn't nothing to me. Those years.

Daisy was special.

I'm still coming to terms with the fact that she isn't anymore. Still hanging on, even though I know my heart has already turned bitter toward her. The truth is that what we had is poisoned beyond repair.

At least, I think it is.

Like everything else in my life right now, it feels complicated.

I draw a deep, shaking breath. Emotional again. 'I do really want to see her,' I admit.

'Mmmh. Mmmh. Right.' Nana claps her hands. 'Leave it with me. I'll think on it. We'll sleep in the car and then start driving again at dawn, before it gets light.'

I raise my brows. 'Driving in the dark?'

Nana tosses the keys at me. 'You can do it, Pearl.'

I'm touched. Maybe the fact that I came all this way to find her means something.

'I need another coffee,' she says, standing and stretching her back. Right then, the weird old man comes back to show us his dog, which actually doesn't look a whole heap like Potato at all. Nana yells at him to go away, loud enough to make Obi flinch.

And then she walks off to buy another coffee.

Obi and I stay where we are. After a few moments of just sitting side by side and staring blankly into the distance, I finally break the silence.

'She's so loud because she's very old. It's like … because of her hearing.'

'Yeah,' Obi breathes, clearly a bit shell-shocked. 'And because she's really scary.'

I agree. We sit awkwardly for a few more moments and then I extricate myself from the table. Guilt swells in my chest. Which feels weird, but honestly, I do feel kind of bad. Obi's had to put up with a lot because he asked me for that lift. If he'd stayed in the car with Lachlan and Daisy, he'd have been at that coast shack days ago, partying it up with all his friends. I glance over at him.

Instead he's here. With me.

And I bet he's really regretting everything now.

I sigh.

'Come on,' I say. 'I'll buy you a coffee. To apologise for … you know. Nana.'

He wrinkles his nose. 'A coffee?'

'No?'

'An ice-cream!'

I bark a laugh, the sound bubbling in my throat. I choke it back. 'Fine. An ice-cream.' I'm walking backwards across the shimmering grass and his face splits into a grin. Dimples and everything. He follows and I look away.

After I've bought the ice-creams (chocolate for me and mango for Obi), we sit on the long, wavering grass beneath the carousel, listening to the churn of the crowd and basking in the flickering lights. Obi's face turns green and red and then pink, and he keeps glancing at me. His ice-cream is gone in seconds, while I eat mine more slowly, enjoying the cool relief from the warm wind. Even at night, the air is thick and stifling, the ground still holding the day's heat.

I catch him watching me. 'What?'

He shrugs. 'You seem different. Out here. Not like how you are at school.'

'What do you mean?'

'Being in the country suits you.'

'Whatever!' I make a face. 'I'm exactly the same. You just don't actually know me that well, Obi.'

'No?'

'No way. And I don't know you well either. Seeing someone at school every day isn't the same as actually knowing them.' I roll my eyes. 'I'm always like this. Just not usually in front of you. Obviously everyone acts different around the people they're comfortable with.'

'People you're comfortable with,' he repeats slowly. 'So like your nana, you mean.'

'Yeah.' I lick my ice-cream.

'And me.' He looks pleased with himself.

'Yeah.' I stop licking and blink. 'No ... what?'

He laughs, but I sit very still.

Could that be true?

I guess things have changed a lot between us over the past few days. Is that how I feel now? Comfortable?

I glance at him sideways.

He's not smiling anymore, peering at me closely, his head leaning in. I don't know what he's doing. The air grows thick between us. My mind turns blank, breath caught in my throat.

Obi grasps my wrist and swoops in for an absolutely enormous bite of my ice-cream.

I'm horrified. I mean, after I remember to breathe, anyway. 'Hey! That's mine.' Half of it is gone!

Obi swallows happily. I glare at him, hiss, 'I hope you get brain-freeze.' He shows me his dimples.

Nana calls for us and I climb to my knees in the grass, still huffing. I shove the final bits of my ice-cream into my mouth, crushing the wafer against my tongue. It doesn't taste as sweet as it should. I stand, looking down at Obi sprawled in the grass. He's smiling and relaxed.

I'm not.

Because of him.

There's something wrong with me.

I open my mouth to tell him to hurry but something else slips out instead, something sharper and tinged with resentment. 'Just because I've been hanging around you on this trip doesn't mean I'm comfortable with you, Obi.'

He flinches and stares up at me, eyes pooling black. Like it hurts.

It's how it's always been with Obi. Two third wheels shoved together because our best friends are dating, and all we do is slice each other with our words.

Now though, if I'm honest with myself, I wonder if my antagonistic feelings toward him were seeded in part because he just happened to turn up in my life right when Daisy started leaving it. I desperately needed someone to be angry with, an outlet of sorts, and it couldn't be Daisy. And there Obi was, smirking and saying insulting things.

It was rather convenient, really.

Obi sucks in his breath and instead of returning my barbed words, he just nods weakly. Saying nothing, he climbs slowly to his feet in the wavering grass.

I feel ... strange. My ears hum and my chest constricts.

I've spent so much time thinking it's me against Obi that it's almost impossible to reframe it any other way. Impossible to imagine that maybe I feel different about him now.

My mouth goes dry.

Honestly, what had I been expecting? Before, when he leaned in over the grass to steal my ice-cream? What had I thought he was doing?

Something different.

I'd thought he was about to kiss me.

My cheeks burn and I can't meet Obi's gaze. We walk back to the car, leaving the swirling colours and sounds of the fairground behind.

16

BONESEED
Two Years Ago

Burnt sugar smell clung to my clothes. Nana's cooking again. I couldn't figure out why she bothered. My dad should have removed the camping stove from the granny flat ages ago. I told him so, but Nana insisted she needed it. Reckoned Mum wouldn't let her use the proper one inside the main house. Which of course was true, but I was on Mum's side in this latest war between them.

Nana had a penchant for burning things.

Frowning, I flicked the off knob on the camping stove. The rings slowly turned from blue to red to black as the metal cooled. 'You can't just leave this on, Nana!'

Though why stop at burning cookies when there's an entire house to burn?

'Look how well they came out. Delicious!' Nana beamed at me from the couch. Daisy was beside her, practically swallowed by the crochet cushions Nana insisted 'brighten the place up'. My best friend was bravely attempting to eat one of the smoking chocolate-chip biscuits. They looked like charcoal. I shook my head at her, making dramatic warning gestures behind Nana's back. I could hear the cookies cracking between Daisy's teeth, they were that hard.

I winced. Daisy's screwed-up *yuck* face was no joke. I didn't even know you could turn cookie dough into (sort of) actual biscuits on a camping stove. Turned out you (sort of) could. Who knew?

A funny smell clung to the crochet-saturated granny flat. Like burning plastic? I didn't know what else Nana had managed to burn, but I hunted around, trying to investigate. Making sure everything was safe.

'Sit down, Pearl Nash!' my nana snapped. Daisy choked on her cookie, hiding her laugh behind a hand. '*Billionaire's Secret Penthouse* is about to start!'

The television was a bit staticky. It's hard to get good reception here. I heard the factory across the street interferes, though I didn't know if that was true or just an urban legend.

Either way, the factory loomed over us, humming and groaning twenty-four hours a day. The noise was what I hated most when we first moved to the city. From everything. An endless wash. Cars streamed by during the day, the big container trucks at night, and behind it all, the factory my dad worked at. Groaning and humming. He'd be there all hours, there right now as dusk fell, leaving Mum in the main house with Ash. I thought they'd gone for a walk. If we weren't shut away in the granny flat, I'd have said it was to get away from Nana.

I flopped down next to Daisy and the old couch groaned just like the factory does, the rusted springs popping and stretching beneath the crochet. We giggled, our shoulders touching. Discreetly, she handed me her blackened cookie and I tucked it into the pocket of my school skirt, winking.

The show was starting, but Nana wasn't paying attention. She had her head lifted like a dog, imitating Potato, who was lying belly-exposed on the floor. Nana sniffed the air.

Her brows furrowed. 'What's that burning odour?'

I widened my eyes at Daisy. We both knew my nana burned everything she cooked, but the smell didn't usually bother her.

Nana sniffed again. Hard. 'It's your mother, Pearl Nash! She's burning plastic in the house.'

'Your mum's doing what?' said Daisy, as Nana launched herself off the couch, leaving us bobbing on the squeaking springs. I shushed my best friend. There was no point protesting when Nana decided Mum had done something wrong. I did try, though. Out of loyalty to Mum. A little half-heartedly maybe, but only because I knew it wouldn't work.

'Mum's gone out, Nana. The smell is from the camp oven. You left the plastic wrapping from the cookie dough too close. The corner singed.'

As expected, Nana ignored me, muttering something about Mum's cooking as she stormed out into the dusky garden beyond the granny flat. The top of the factory was just visible through the window above the tin fence. All burning lights and whirring chutes, a tangle of towers and silos and huge looming chimneys. I shrugged as Daisy dissolved into a fit of giggles. Her white school shirt was unbuttoned at the throat, dotted with charcoal cookie crumbs.

The school uniform was the thing I hated second-most when we moved here. I was home-schooled throughout primary school. No uniforms. No set hours. Lots of running around wild and helping out on the farm, as long as I got my homework done in time.

In the city everything felt buttoned-up and constrictive. And the uniform was itchy and looked weird.

I got used to it, though. Eventually.

Mainly because of Daisy. She showed me all the good things about living in the city. Back then, embarrassingly awkward thirteen-year-old me walked into a school filled with girls all blooming faster than I was, with social rules and in-jokes I couldn't keep up with, all of them locked into the same friendship circles since kindergarten. Daisy took me under her wing. She saved me.

'Gosh, I love your nana.' She reached for another burnt cookie and then changed her mind, putting it back on the porcelain plate. Good decision.

'Why?' I pretended to be shocked, hands to my cheeks, but my question was serious. I mean, she was my nana, so I loved her, obviously, but she was kind of ... 'She's not exactly loveable.'

Daisy grinned at me as the show got underway, flickering blue light seeping from the TV. It was Nana's favourite. Soapy and over-acted, filled with elegant rich women bemoaning their dramatic lives. Nana had no room in her life for nonsense. She only liked practical things. And practical people. This show, though, must be her exception. I kind of loved it, if I'm honest, even though it was bad.

Secretly, I think Daisy did, too. Why else did she come here after school every day? It definitely wasn't for my nana's cooking.

'Nah, she's the best,' Daisy said around a mouthful of juice. 'Your nana makes me laugh.'

Daisy's parents were kind of strict, which was maybe what she found so appealing about my chaotic, messy family. Maybe about me, too. Daisy practically lived at our house these days. I grinned at her, avoiding the burnt cookies and shoving some crisps in my mouth.

Daisy was the first thing I *loved* about moving to the city. For the first year, when Grandpa was sick but far away, and then the second year, after he died and Nana moved into the granny flat, she was my one bright spot.

I remembered how it felt at first. My freedom was gone. The wide spaces of the farm were gone. I was forced into a uniform, pushed into a shape I didn't fit. A school where I didn't belong.

But through Daisy, I learned that a city had as many hidden secrets as the countryside. She showed me dusky beaches and overgrown laneways, crumbling warehouses and soaring buildings. Introduced me to the joy of libraries and sipping milkshakes at the kiosk near the sea. She'd drawn me out of my misery.

And she said I made her laugh.

My house, my family, we all made her laugh.

Daisy shifted closer on the couch and gave me the side-eye. Her voice turned hushed. 'She get any more romance books, lately?'

Now she was making *me* laugh with her eagerness. 'Yeah, Nana brought home a few. Wanna see?' Not my favourite kind, though. I loved the historical books best, but both Nana and Daisy went for the rich millionaire ones. I wrinkled my nose and reached for the library bag beside the couch. Nana didn't know we read them. I don't think Daisy's parents would have approved.

'Nah, not yet. After the show,' Daisy said happily, settling back into the crochet cushions. 'It's your favourite in the whole world, after all.' Her voice was teasing, but in a pretend way. Without the edge to it that would come later.

In another year, she won't say much to me at all that won't have a razor in it.

I don't know why it happened. The shift between us.

One day Daisy read the same books as me, watched the same shows as me, spent her free time in the granny flat. And then it changed. But I can't trace it to a moment.

It was just a gradual slide.

One day I made her laugh with abandon, her eyes shining and her head flung back. The next day, she laughed but it felt different.

The sound had sharp edges.

17

LAVENDER GREVILLEA

Glass rumbles against my face, cool on my skin. I'm in the passenger side of Nana's station wagon, the plastic seat vibrating beneath me and my neck so cramped, I gasp when I move. I push hair from my face and sit up. I blink back my dreams, all of them filled with Daisy. Blink back tears, too.

Nana is driving now and it's daylight. Filtered blue light and dusky horizon. Early morning. She's got her big black sunglasses on already.

I frown. Then peer out my window. Then out Nana's window. Nothing but flat desert, earth stretching in all directions. Shingled red-rock landscape flashes by the highway. I twist and find Obi passed out across the backseat, his seatbelt tangled and digging into his neck in a way that looks truly painful. Out the back window, the desert recedes into the distance. The ache of my dreams ebbs away.

'Uh, Nana?'

'Yes, hon?' She sips from a styrofoam cup with a thick yellow straw. I take it from her and have a swig. A milkshake. We obviously stopped while I was asleep.

'Where are we?' I rub my bleary face, reach behind into the

back seat and poke Obi until he groans and wakes, rubbing his neck. I'm awkward around him now, because of what I said. And what I thought. I can't quite make myself meet his gaze. I shouldn't have been so mean. He sits and takes the cup I offer.

Nana clears her throat. 'We'll be at your beach shack soon.'

I gape at her as Obi chokes on the milkshake in the back seat.

'What did you say?' My mind is spinning. 'What about Mum and Dad? And Ash? They're all waiting at the farm!'

'Oh, psssh,' drawls Nana. 'Let them stew over at your uncle's. About time this family sorted out their shit. Not speaking to each other for four years! What rubbish!'

I peer into the back seat, wide-eyed. Obi has a similar expression. I'm too busy being shocked at my Nana to feel awkward with him right now. I bite my lips, uncertain I'm hearing this right.

'So ... you're saying you *aren't* bringing us to the farm?'

'No.'

'And you *are* letting us go to Finn's beach shack.'

'Yes. Not because of the party, mind. So you can talk to Daisy. Give that girl a piece of your mind.' Nana peers at me over the rim of her glasses. Her expression is fierce.

I tilt my head to the side, trying my best to copy that puppy-dog look Obi's so good at, seeing if it works on my nana. 'So ... what you're saying is you *aren't* going to tell Mum and Dad about me and Obi?'

'No. I won't tell.'

The look *does* work on my nana!

I launch forward and wrap my arms around her neck, nearly choking myself with my seatbelt. 'Thank you, Nana.'

'Get off! I'm driving. Sit down, young lady.'

I twist in my seat to grin at Obi before I've thought it through. His dimples appear, a little tentative, but there. That makes me feel a bit better.

It isn't Obi's fault that I've confused everything between us. And I shouldn't have been mean to him back at the fairground. If I feel weird, that's for me to deal with. I just have to survive the rest of this trip with him first.

I sit back in my seat, chuffed. I'm not going to argue with Nana. If she wants to deal with Dad's wrath when we come back, then whatever. I'll just say she kidnapped me. Except then Obi taps me on the shoulder and mouths silently, *your nana is going to crash Finn's party?*

Oh.

That part is less good. Already my heart is seizing up. 'Um, Nana?'

'Speak, Pearl.'

'Er. You're dropping us there, right? At Finn's coast shack? Right? Dropping us and driving away?'

She barks out a honking laugh. 'Did you think I wanted to go to some boring party? Don't be ridiculous. I'm going whale watching down the coast.'

I'm filled with acute relief, giving Obi a discreet thumbs-up behind my seat. Then I frown. 'Whale watching?'

I'm pretty certain whale watching is strictly a winter pastime around here. It's way too late in the year for that sort of thing.

'Yes,' says Nana, oblivious. 'There's a stretch of coast just down from your beach shack. You can see them from the cliffs.' Her thin lips pull into a pleased smile as I assess her suspiciously, memories stirring. I've seen that expression on her face before.

At the picnic table in front of the fairground.

When I first told her where Finn's beach shack was located.

A stab of indignation blooms in my chest.

'Nana! You're not driving us there because of Daisy at all, are you? This is only because you want to go whale watching.'

She peers at me disapprovingly over her big black sunglasses, pink hair flying in the wind. 'So?'

Obi taps my shoulder from behind and whispers, 'Don't look a gift horse in the mouth, Nash.'

Nana frowns into the rear-view mirror. 'Who are you calling a horse, young man?'

Obi gulps audibly from the back seat, but I'm still fuming. I'm not exactly sure why though. I mean, technically I'm getting everything I want.

But whale watching?

That sounds kind of cool. Even if it is the wrong time of year. Still, even without whales, the isolated coast and cliffs there must be pretty nice.

A small pang swells at the idea I'm going to miss out.

If things had been different with Daisy, I might have skipped out on the coast shack and just tagged along with Nana. After all, she's been alone so much lately, I'm sure she'd be grateful for the company. I glance back at Obi again. It's not something I'd ask *him* to do, though. My nana scares the hell out of Obi, I'm pretty sure he's dying to get away. From her *and* me.

He's lounging in the back seat now, milkshake in hand and dark shades on, the world rushing by outside his window. I'd never be brave enough to ask him to go whale watching. Especially when there won't even be whales.

But I allow myself to face the truth.

I'd *like* to ask him.

I'd like it if he wanted to come with me instead of going to this stupid party. I'd like it a lot. I face forward again and gape at the windshield in horror. My heart beats rapid patterns against my ribs, jumps into my throat until I can't breathe. Nana sees I'm acting weird and raises her brows. I ignore her, sinking low in my chair, feet on the dash. So it appears I have a shiny new problem.

Obiara Okocha.

And how I potentially feel about him.

Which creates a question that churns up my insides as we drive.

What will happen between me and Obi when we get to Finn's house? Will things revert to how they were before? Me awkward and hovering at the edges of things, and Obi flitting from friend to friend – and then whenever our paths accidentally cross, we'll say nasty things to each other again?

Is that all we are, after everything?

I touch my fingers softly to my chest, feeling the throb in my blood, the electricity running across my skin.

It's not what I want.

Nana drops us in the centre of town near the highway. She says she doesn't have time to drive us to the actual house, which is a little mean. I'm about to say so when Obi grasps my arm and pulls me from the station wagon, hissing, 'Gift horse, Nash. Gift horse.'

I suspect Nana is just in a hurry to find those non-existent whales. I wonder if I should tell her the truth, but decide against it immediately. I don't think Nana is really going there for the whales anyway. More likely, she's searching for peace of mind. Extending her grief break. Maybe she's feeling sad again and doesn't want anyone else to see.

My mood darkens at that idea. I remember her and Grandpa talking about whales. That they'd been to see them together? Or that they wanted to? I can't quite grasp the memory; it curls and wisps into nothing. I'd thought after our chat on the beach at the end of the world that Nana would be okay again.

But I guess that was the whole point of our chat, wasn't it?

That everyone wants her to be okay already, but she isn't. She acted so normal in the car that I forgot again.

Nana roars off in a cloud of grit and dust, leaving us coughing outside a double-storey colonial-style pub with piles of bags at our feet. The sun is hot and heavy. My skin is slick with sweat already, my white T-shirt sticking to my back.

Obi motions with his head toward the big looming pub, the air conditioning wafting from the glazed glass doors. 'Want a drink?'

He's teasing me.

I heave up the bags. 'I'm not eighteen yet.'

Obi takes two off me and bends for the rest, loaded up as he mutters, 'Isn't it weird that I can quit school and enter the workforce right now but I still can't buy a beer at a pub? Not that they pay me enough to buy a beer.'

I don't know and I also think I don't care. I'm kind of worried about my nana. The station wagon is long gone now, speeding off along the highway under the big blue sky, disappearing into the desert.

Obi glances at me over the rim of his black sunglasses, dust clinging to his throat and cheeks. He nudges me softly. 'She'll be okay, Nash. Just give her some time.'

I shrug and follow as he trudges down the main street. He's the one who's been here before. I've only got one bag: Obi's, I think. Definitely not mine anyway. It's nice and light, just filled with clothes. He's carrying two of mine, one of which is completely filled with books. I'm a little guilty, but not guilty enough to actually do something about it. The sun is really hot.

Soon I'm sweating like mad and wishing I had sunglasses like Obi's. My hair is sticking to my forehead and neck as we pass under a massive jacaranda tree. It spreads wide above a cottage that's built from sandy slabs of stone, covered in creepers. We pass all the things you'd expect to find in a town like this, to the point that I wonder if this really is a different town or if we've somehow doubled around and ended up back where Nana lives. It definitely isn't in the end, because even though this place has the pub, and a corner store and a servo (and another pub) it doesn't have any silos or a deep-water port. It definitely doesn't have a quarry. Which is a good thing. Especially now Nana is on the loose again.

I watch Obi's back as we walk, the way his shoulder blades slide beneath his thin, damp T-shirt, the way he has a really long stride that leaves me almost scurrying to keep up.

'Obi,' I call. 'Obi!'

'What?' He turns so abruptly I actually collide with his sweaty chest. 'Oh.'

I step back quickly, away from his raised hands, squinting against the sun as I blurt, 'I didn't mean what I said yesterday. I'm sorry. I didn't even mean any of it. I was just ... upset.'

His brows shoot above the sunglasses, hands clenching and unclenching. 'Oh,' is all he says.

I nod. 'Yeah, so are we good?'

'Why?'

I frown. 'Why are we good?'

'No, why were you upset?'

I gape up at him. The truth burns in my chest.

Because I thought for a wild moment you were about to kiss me and it hurt my feelings.

I don't say that aloud though.

'Just ... you know ... Nana stuff.' I choke on my words.

Obi nods. 'Right.' I can't read what's going on behind his sunglasses. 'It's fine, Nash. Whatever. I didn't care anyway.'

He didn't care?

Good. Well, that's good.

That's freaking great.

I scowl and keep trudging. Soon I'm puffing from the exertion of trying to keep up with Obi's long strides. Mainly because of the heat. The heavy, sticky air makes me dream about the ocean, salt and cool water sliding across my skin. Better than thinking about Obi. I glance at the back of his head. He's sweating too, his T-shirt drenched and his neck beading. Maybe he'd like to go swimming too.

I'm getting up the courage to ask when he stops walking. It's abrupt enough that I almost collide with him again, but this time I manage to hold myself back.

I make a face as he announces, 'We're here. This is it.'

'Really?' I squint at the shack. It appears deserted. And dilapidated. Overgrown garden practically obscures the weatherboard house, the windows covered in cobwebs and grime.

Beach grass gone wild lines the edges of a cracked concrete path passing beneath a twisted banksia tree. 'When was the party meant to be again?'

Obi is frowning too. 'I think the big party is on the second last night of everyone's stay, right? So there's time to recover before they have to drive home.'

So that's tonight. We don't move. The house doesn't stir.

'Maybe everyone left already,' I suggest hopefully. Now we're here, I'm actually not sure I'm up for this at all. Already my chest is tightening. Daisy I can deal with. Maybe Lachlan. But Finn and Sophia and the rest?

I'm scared.

Obi glances down at me. 'It'll be fine,' he says. He doesn't sound very confident though. Something moves across his face. I can't quite read him beneath the dark glasses. Maybe he's worried. Lachlan did chuck Obi out of his car, after all.

That kind of makes me feel better.

I mean, not the car chucking part, but the bit where Obi is back on my side, sharing my fears. That part is nice, a bit of added strength that makes me think that maybe I can do this. And maybe things are normal between Obi and me again.

Or at least, as normal as they've ever been.

Which, I suppose, isn't really that normal.

I take a deep breath.

I can do this.

Without waiting for Obi, I march up that overgrown pathway and pound my fist on the fibreglass front door. Loudly. Something stirs within the house. Footsteps pad in dull thuds toward the door. I wait, twitching and wringing my hands, heaving Obi's bag higher onto my shoulder.

The door swings open, darkness spilling out. A girl stands blinking in the sunshine through the flyscreen. Her hair is salt-dried, like she's been hanging out on a beach for days. I force myself to smile.

'Hi Daisy.'

18

GRASS TREE

Daisy is clearly a little bit drunk. Even though it's only mid-afternoon. But I guess that's what you do in a house filled with teenagers, most of whom have just graduated high school. I guess for them it's a sort of desert-coast schoolies.

I'm sitting on the couch in a darkened room and at least two of my schoolmates are passed out on the carpet. I glance at them, wondering if they're dead or just sleeping. Beyond them, in the kitchen, Daisy and Lachlan chat about tonight's big costume party.

'I guess every night here is a party,' I say nervously, still observing the bodies on the floor, and then immediately wish I hadn't said it. Daisy looks at me like she wishes I hadn't either and in the kitchen, Lachlan snorts. At me. Like he thinks I'm funny. I'm pretty sure it's not the good kind of funny either.

I try again. 'I thought Stacey and Lucas and them were coming ...'

'They did come,' says one of the bodies on the floor. 'They all went down the beach.'

'Right.'

So I definitely hate this. This is not an improvement on my

past experiences at events like this at all. I'm pretty desperate by the time Obi comes back from the bathroom. It's nice to have a bathroom again after all that hiding in the bushes stuff while on the road. I'm over that. I nod at Obi nervously and clamp my mouth shut before I can ask him if he had a nice bathroom break. It's like my brain is on overdrive. I either can't speak at all or I say stupid things.

Obi collapses on the couch beside me. He's at ease here. These are all his friends, after all. Everyone except me and Daisy. Though I guess Daisy must be his friend by now. I glance over to where she's making out with Lachlan in the kitchen. I'm getting the distinct impression that she's ignoring me. Or like, using Lachlan's face as a shield.

Finn and Sophia are sitting at a small rickety kitchen table, her on his lap. There's clearly some tension between the two which everyone else is trying to ignore, so I decide to ignore it too. We all sit around and pretend we can't hear them fighting in hushed tones about some other party. It's a weird vibe because Sophia's clearly pissed at him, yet she stays sitting on his lap. I try very hard not to look at them. Or at Daisy and Lachlan, who are still making out. Instead I focus on my hands clenched in my lap.

This sucks.

Obi's glancing around the room, kind of frowning. I wonder if he's suddenly seeing it through my eyes, because he says loudly, 'Anyone want to go for a swim?'

I nod. A bit too enthusiastically. So does everyone else unfortunately. And on my way out after changing into togs in a grimy, cobwebby bathroom, I notice that Lachlan appears to be ignoring Obi too.

Whatever happened back at that servo was clearly not pretty.

I bound from the house into the sunshine, breathing deep. The hot wind ruffles my hair. Eucalyptus leaves litter the yard, along with heavy strips of bark. We climb the wire back fence to reach the dunes. Tiny white flowers pinprick the stringy creepers growing over the sand.

Daisy walks beside me on the way to the beach. She's less drunk than I thought. 'I didn't think you were coming,' she says quietly. I can't tell from her voice if she's pleased that I'm here or wishes I hadn't bothered.

I blow out a breath. 'I was just ... delayed. You know I had to go see my nana.'

I notice she doesn't ask how Nana is, even though she knows my dad was worried. Even though Daisy used to come over and hang with us in the granny flat all the time, watching stupid television shows and eating crisps. She smiles. 'Well, I'm glad you made it.'

I assess her carefully. 'Are you?'

Even after everything, a small part of me still thrills to hear those words, hope rising hot and sharp inside my chest.

'Of course I am, Pearl.' She smiles at me. It feels genuine. 'Why wouldn't I be?'

Daisy's acting so normal now. I can't figure it out. Did our sort of fight not faze her at all? Has she seriously not noticed how *wrong* everything is between us, even after I attempted to confront her about it?

Maybe she still has no idea, even now.

That throws me off balance.

I wonder if there are different kinds of grief. Grief over someone dying. Grief over losing a friendship. Grief over losing who you thought someone was.

Daisy flings an arm across my shoulders and for a moment, it's like everything is back how it used to be. It's now or never.

'Daisy, I really have to talk to you. Do you wanna ... like, go for a walk or something?'

'What, right now?'

I nod and Daisy laughs. 'Later, Pearl. There'll be all the time in the world to talk tonight at the party.' Then she's off and running down the beach, feet digging deep into the sand, shedding her clothes to plunge into the ocean alongside Lachlan.

She's most definitely avoiding me.

I follow more slowly, the ball of bitterness inside my chest growing, and Obi appears at my side. 'You getting in?'

'No.'

'Come on, Nash,' he drawls. 'I'll be with you the whole time.'

I frown at him, still reeling from Daisy's indifference. Trying to focus.

'You came all this way, and you're just gonna sit on the sand? Come on, you can do better than that. I promise I won't leave you alone out there.'

I think of Daisy, of how she'd drag me to parties and always make promises to not leave my side. Yet I'd be abandoned within five minutes of entering the house. I glare up at Obi, annoyed. 'I'm not afraid of the water!'

'I know that.' His tone implies he knows exactly what I'm scared of. And it embarrasses me. Lachlan is still within earshot and I already know he thinks I'm a joke. Someone who clings to his girlfriend.

'Go away,' I hiss at Obi, and it's like we've immediately reverted to our old ways. Maybe hating someone really is a habit.

I don't get in the ocean, though I want to. Instead I sit on the boiling sand, pretending to read my romance novel. I don't even bother to hide the cover. I can't concentrate on it, though it's a great one. Instead I watch Obi in the water from the corner of my eye, as he chats animatedly with Lucas and Jamie. He uses his dimples on Stacey, who waves at me happily, and none of it makes me feel good.

I wish I'd gone with my nana to watch the whales. Or whatever it is she's doing out there in the desert by herself.

I'm lying in the sand, sweating, the back of my T-shirt soaked and my bare legs crisping, an arm thrown over my face. My novel is discarded and I'm pretending to nap, listening to everyone's chatter and thinking about Daisy. About why I even came to this place. I'm trying not to get worked up about it, but I guess I'm pretty upset. My eyes are squeezed tight and they feel sandy. Gritty.

There's no way I'm crying over Daisy here on the boiling hot sand. Lachlan would laugh his head off at me.

It's just that it's real now. And the expanding bitterness inside my chest has made me realise something I can no longer deny, though I've been trying to hide from it for days.

The truth is I don't want things to go back to how they were.

Even if Daisy listens to everything I have to say. Even if she apologises to me. I've realised she already used up her last chance, back at my house in the city when I tried to tell her how I felt. This new truth hits me square in the chest, winding me.

I don't want to be Daisy's friend anymore.

I'm going to do this. It's why I came. I'm going to tell Daisy why I've made my decision and then I'm going to leave her behind. My heart beats faster just thinking about it. And my stomach hurts. I wish it wasn't real. I wish I could go back in time to before all this started, and just fix it so it never happened.

That makes me picture my nana, and I shift on the hot ground, other arm covering my face now. She also wants to turn back time, yet the world just steams ahead. Grandpa always said it. You can't go back, only forward.

It makes things feel so final. And it makes my eyes sting.

Water drops cold onto my skin.

Drip, drip.

Obi stands above me, ocean sliding in shimmering droplets off his face and shoulders, speckling me with water.

'Hey,' he says.

I grimace back, wary. I'm starting to worry that maybe once I've finished with this awful Daisy thing, I'll just be walking out of here. And then I probably won't see Obi again for the whole summer holidays. Until next year when school starts again. Except he won't be coming back to school next year, which means ... what?

This is it?

It makes me feel sick.

I don't get up off the sand, still lying on my back. 'Hey.'

He looks nice. Like, really nice. Even though he's not smiling. Even though his bad skin is extra bad today. He just looks nice.

Obi bites his lip.

Just stands there.

'Sorry,' he murmurs eventually.

I blink. 'Huh?'

'About before.'

I say nothing, still lying on my back in the hot sand. He keeps dripping water on my face and I wipe it off, my fingers cool and wet.

'I didn't mean to sound so patronising. About coming in the water? I know you can handle yourself.'

I blink up at him.

He thinks that? I can handle myself?

I don't know if *I* even think that.

I sit up fast, a spray of sand in my wake. I push sweaty hair from my cheeks. 'Oh,' I say. 'That's okay.'

'Cool.'

'Cool,' I echo.

The ghost of a smile tugs Obi's mouth and he collapses beside me, sitting close but not too close, shoulder to shoulder. He's not wearing a shirt and I'm trying hard not to look at his chest. I focus straight ahead on the ocean instead, blue waves breaking white on the sand, a flat expanse of water that rushes to meet the horizon in a pale haze. I can't tell where the sea ends and the sky begins. I concentrate on that and not on the fact that just a few days ago, I was pressed against Obi's skin. I had my hands on him. On his face. I'm pretty sure I helped him pull his T-shirt off.

Weird.

All of it is pretty weird.

I'm blushing, my cheeks burning hot. I hope he'll think it's because of the beating summer sun, the dry heat in the wind, the boiling sand.

Obi clears his throat. 'So ... what are you wearing tonight?'

I turn to him blankly. 'What?'

'For the costume party.' He smiles with his eyes, tentatively. It makes me stare at him harder. Is Obi nervous right now? He seems nervous.

'Nash?'

Oh.

The costume party. I blink. And then glance down at my body, at the clothes I'm already wearing. A sweaty white T-shirt and jean shorts.

Obi groans. 'Nash. You've got to make *some* effort.'

'What are *you* wearing, then?'

He wiggles his eyebrows. 'Guess.'

'A character from *Dune*,' I say right away.

Obi's face falls. 'Oh shit. I didn't even think of that.'

He's so disappointed it makes me laugh beneath my breath. Things feel more normal now, our new normal, and I'm doing quite well at ignoring the bare chest. Mostly. 'Okay then, not *Dune*.' I try to think. 'Han Solo?'

Obi scoffs. 'I can't go as Han Solo, Nash. No one would know who I was. I'd have to explain it all night.' He rolls his eyes. 'They'd all think I was Lando Calrissian.' He makes a psshhing sound, like he finds the whole thing very annoying.

'I give up. Who are you going as, then?'

He grins, flashing teeth. 'Me.'

I gape at him.

'Yeah, I totally forgot,' he snickers, running fingers over his buzzcut. Salt stains his skin in crystallised patterns, clinging to the lines in his throat.

My cheeks are burning again. I mutter, 'I can't believe you made me guess.'

Obi doesn't seem to hear me. He coughs softly. Suddenly awkward again. 'Look, Pearl, I was thinking ...'

A spray of sand whips into Obi's face, making him flinch. Lachlan shouts an apology that doesn't sound entirely genuine and Obi launches himself off the ground to follow, calling after his friend (sort of friend? ex-friend?). And that's it. Conversation over. It gives me whiplash. A sense of stirring disappointment sneaks into my chest, and lingers.

I stay where I am, sitting by myself. Everyone else is gathered in groups. Daisy is talking to Sophia just down the sand, her hair stiff with salt. So I reach for my romance novel again. It feels like progress that I'm reading it openly. I decide I don't care what anyone thinks. I'm not sure if it's completely true, but it feels good to say it inside my head. My mouth curls into a smile, which is wiped away at the sound of footsteps tearing toward me from the water.

I drop my novel as Stacey Green comes flying up the sand. She's wearing a tiny string bikini and looks lovely, her wet hair hanging like streamers down her back. And she's also really happy to see me. Which feels surprising. I mean, we know each other because of all the parties I tagged along to this past year and she's part of the group we sit with at school. But still. I've always thought of her as Daisy's friend more than mine. Like the rest of those girls. We hang out at lunch and sit together in class, but I'm not in their group chats, and we don't really hang out on weekends. Not without Daisy, anyway. Which means not at all, these last few months. I'm enveloped in a wet hug, and I must admit it feels good that at least one person seems pleased I'm here.

Maybe I'm not quite as alone as I thought.

Maybe some of Daisy's friends are my friends too. An unexpected thought, which fills my chest with warmth. Until I notice that Daisy's watching us with a stony expression. I ignore her. She's the one who said we'd talk later. I turn my back on her purposely, because I need some time to think.

When Stacey asks why I arrived so late, I tell her. Everything. About finding Obi at the service station, my car breaking down. I even tell her about losing my nana.

I leave out the bit about the rainstorm and the Bedford obviously.

By the time I'm done, Stacey is laughing so hard she's crying, which makes me feel rather pleased. Perhaps being friends with other people isn't that hard, after all. I strip down to my togs and we swim together, me steadfastly refusing to check if Obi is watching. We talk about exams, a more sobering topic but one we both need to get off our chests. When we've run through every possible mistake we could have made on our tests, we talk about the others we sit with at lunch, who couldn't come on the trip. Stacey mentions jokes they made at school, and things they're all worrying about (exams, mostly), and I realise I was part of most of these conversations, that I was there with them when they spoke about it. So when Stacey invites me over to her house during the holidays to hang with the others, I don't even hesitate before agreeing, even though the idea makes me nervous.

Stacey doesn't invite Daisy though, and I realise this is the point where I'd normally bow out. I always presumed I was *Daisy's* friend, not theirs, but this time I don't withdraw.

By the time dusk is falling, I've lent Stacey two of my

historical romance novels and I feel much better about everything. It makes me wonder why I spent so much time this year concentrating on my failing friendship with Daisy, instead of looking around me. It occurs to me that maybe there are a lot of people at school I've been ignoring.

Like Stacey. Like Mish, who loves books as much as me, though she prefers different genres. And Georgie, who likes football above all other things. Blake and Tory and all the rest, too. I guess we're all pretty different. But maybe that doesn't matter. Maybe we fit together anyway.

It hits me hard. Like a sledgehammer. Was it a mistake assuming that everyone still thinks of me as the weird country kid? It's been four years already. Maybe I've been so preoccupied with what I *believe* everyone thinks about me, I haven't noticed that things were gradually changing. Or actually, even if they still do think I'm a weird country kid, whatever. Maybe it doesn't mean much at all.

Right now, Stacey is offering me her company. I don't have to strive and earn her time. I don't have to fight for it. Maybe some people like me just as I am.

I grin at Stacey, sudden and wide. She grins back.

It feels like something new.

A possibility.

19

FREE FALL
Two Weeks Ago

School was over and we tumbled toward the gate, Daisy at my side with Stacey and Tory close behind, trying to keep up. I was attempting to hurry Daisy because we were meant to be catching the train in a minute and the station was still all the way down the street. She was dragging her sneakers, checking her phone every two seconds.

'Daisy, hurry up,' I said. 'We won't get home in time for the show if we miss the train. The next one's not for ages.'

Behind us, Tory was glaring at Daisy's back, whispering something to Stacey behind her hand. Stacey bit her lip. It made me feel protective of Daisy, because I knew what was going on. It was true that Daisy hadn't been the best kind of friend since she'd started going out with Lachlan, but she was still Daisy. She was still the girl who'd saved me when I turned up at this school with no friends and no clue, and I refused to give up on her like the others were starting to do. She was still Daisy. She'd come around.

She just needed time.

'Daisy, hurry up,' I said again. 'Please! We'll miss the train.'

She sighed and stopped dead on the cracked pavement outside the school. Stacey and Tory stumbled to a stop behind her. I could tell from Tory's expression that she already knew exactly what Daisy was about to say.

And she was right.

'Sorry, Pearl, Lachlan just messaged me. He said Obi has stuff with his parents now and can't go with him anymore. He wants me to come and keep him company. He said it's the last night that it's showing at the cinema.'

I blinked. 'But ...'

No. No way.

Not again. She'd already said she *wanted* to come over to mine tonight to hang out in the granny flat. I frowned, annoyed, as I remembered how Daisy had changed her mind immediately after I'd said yes to her coming, because she had thought Lachlan was going to ask her to the movies.

He didn't. He offered his free ticket to Obi instead.

So then Daisy had come crawling back to me, saying she wanted to come over to my place. Again.

I gritted my teeth. This was a whole *two days ago*, and by then I'd already agreed to take Sam to the library so he could play video games (because he's banned from them at home right now for being such a ratbag). He *begged* me, and I eventually agreed, because that's what older sisters are meant to do (even if their little brother really is a total ratbag).

My chest constricted and my fists clenched tight.

I told her I'd already promised Ash, but Daisy had still convinced me, like she always did, to ditch my little brother and spend Thursday night with her instead. And I'd agreed like an idiot, like I always did. Just like I'd agreed to drive her out into the desert for this stupid end-of-year party at someone's beach shack. Only this time, I'd agreed just to ... what?

Get ditched by Daisy again, at the very last minute?

The *ding ding* of the railway crossing rung out from down the street, the barriers flashing over the road. The train swooped by, rattling like crazy.

'We missed the train,' I said stupidly, pointing. I suddenly felt close to tears.

We'd missed *Billionaire's Secret Penthouse* now, too. Not like I couldn't watch it online later. But it had been our ritual: mine and Nana's, then mine and Daisy's. Watching it the old-fashioned way, on Nana's old TV, on a mountain of crochet, at the time it was broadcast.

I caught Tory's eye over Daisy's shoulder and she made an *I told you so* face at me. That sucked my tears right back up.

No. No way.

This wasn't the kind of person Daisy was. I didn't care what the others said. Daisy was just so caught up in Lachlan and what *he* wanted, that she'd forgotten about the rest of us. It made my heart hurt, because she'd always been so good to me in the past, going out of her way to be my friend. It was like she'd forgotten everything.

I stared back at Tory. Shook my head.

No. No way.

Daisy's other friends could all ditch her if they wanted to, but not me. I knew the real Daisy was still in there, underneath all this new obliviousness.

Tory just shrugged, like she didn't care. But I knew she really did. I knew she was hurting too. Just like Stacey, who was staying silent beside her.

'Daisy,' I tried again, turning back to my best friend. My voice turned shrill, even to my own ears. 'You said I shouldn't take Sam to the library! You said you needed me tonight. Come on, you're not really going to go with Lachlan are you? After all that?'

Daisy peered up from her phone, a confused look on her face. 'Pearl, he said Obi *can't go*! What else am I supposed to do?' She made a soft sound beneath her breath, like I was irritating her, and her fingers flew over her phone, typing messages. Presumably to tell Lachlan she'd be right there.

Tory's glare turned harder. She placed her back to Daisy, who didn't even notice, and instead looked at me, her gaze softening. 'Me and Stacey are meeting Georgie at the kiosk for some fish and chips.'

I nodded, mind still swirling with Daisy, everything inside me focused solely on my best friend as she walked away with only the barest of slack goodbye waves. I watched her move off in the opposite direction to the station.

'You've missed your train, anyway,' said Stacey.

'Yeah,' I nodded. It was weird. Since Nana had left home to go back out into the country, it felt like everything had been falling apart. It was no fun sitting in her granny flat alone, watching *Billionaire's Secret Penthouse* by myself. Sometimes, I even caught myself missing the smell of her burning cooking.

I pressed my fingers to my eyes. Shook my head again. Is this who I was? A girl who was going to mope around in her nana's empty granny flat alone and missed the smell (not the taste) of her burnt pancakes?

No. No way.

I stood taller suddenly, straightening my shoulders and lifting my chin. 'I gotta go home,' I announced, already stumbling toward the station.

Tory called from behind me, 'But what about fish and chips?'

I frowned back at her. Fish and chips? What was she talking about? I had to do something about Daisy. This was it. I'd had enough. I waved to Tory and Stacey, calling back, 'I have to talk to Daisy about what's been going on. It'll get better soon, I promise.'

I turned back around before they could answer, and stomped off down the street to wait for the next train. It took ages to come. But by the time it did, rumbling and rattling along the hot metal tracks, I was more determined than ever.

I was going to talk to Daisy. I was going to make her listen.

I was going to fix this.

20

SPIDER FLOWER

Music blares, the floor thumping beneath my feet. I'm sitting awkwardly on the threadbare couch, while people in terrible costumes crowd the tiny, low-lit room. I'm still wearing my sweaty T-shirt and the house is still stifling, which is just making it worse. I don't feel hugely out of place though. Everyone else is sweaty too. My sunburnt legs are tender to the touch. Nana will give me hell when she sees them.

I'm sitting next to a ninja turtle, or at least a boy in a lycra bodysuit painted like a turtle (Jamie Gorecki) and across from an actual cupcake (Stacey Green). It's pretty fascinating really.

Stacey is a bit tipsy and I've noticed the way Sebastian Lewis (who is dressed like Batman) is giving her the eye. I'm trying to decide if I should go save her or if she's giving him the eye back. It's very hard because half her face is obscured by a smaller cupcake. Also, Sebastian is dressed like the old-school version of Batman in a pale-blue bodysuit, little dark underpants on the outside and pointy white eyebrows painted onto his mask. He keeps grinning at Stacey like an enamoured loon.

I decide she's pretty happy about it, so just stay where I am on the couch, feeling rather awkward. I'm not drinking, mainly because I haven't managed to have *the conversation* with Daisy yet and feel strongly that alcohol would not be helpful in that situation.

I catch Obi's eye across the dark room. He's leaning against the kitchen counter talking to some boys from school. He still has salt stains on his neck and is holding a beer bottle. It's definitely the same one from the beginning of the night, so either he's a slow drinker (I wouldn't know) or he's using it as a bit of a prop. He lifts it to his lips every now and then, but I'm not convinced he's actually drinking.

He catches my eye and mouths silently, *the start of a horror movie*. I frown, not getting it, until he does a scan of the room around us, raising his eyebrows and grinning.

Huh.

I peer around at all the teenagers partying it up, wearing cute, cheap costumes and getting progressively drunker in this isolated beach house. I turn back to Obi with wide eyes.

This really *is* how teen slasher movies start. I notice the front door is unlocked and ajar, night spilling in along with the gentle hum of the ocean and the buzzing of insects.

When I turn back to Obi, he's lost in conversation again. I sigh, lifting my glass of cordial to my lips. It's tart and sweet, and I'm pretty sure it's staining my tongue red, but I don't care. I need the sugar rush to get through what I have to do.

I peer around the room searching for Daisy. Every time I go near her, or ask her to talk, she disappears. She's avoided me for hours, but she can't do it forever. I notice she isn't drinking either. I guess it's been a big week here at the coast shack. Maybe she's had her fill.

Suddenly Jamie Gorecki (ninja turtle), who's been blathering on in a very slurred way to Lucas (Dora the Explorer, with tiny shorts and a little bobbed wig) slams into my side. He was trying to make room for Lucas to sit on the couch beside us, but got a little too enthusiastic about it.

'Sorry! Sorry, Pearl,' he mutters. His beery breath is warm on my face. 'Pearl! Pearl, what do you reckon? How would you rather die – a crocodile in a river or a shark in the ocean?'

Both boys wait expectantly.

I blink back at them.

'Um ... I guess, a shark in the ocean.'

Lucas whoops loudly and Jamie Gorecki appears devastated. 'Why, Pearl?' he whimpers. 'Why would you say that?'

Again, they both fall silent and wait, so I guess they actually expect me to answer.

'Uh ... well, I guess if I really had to choose, I'd rather die in the nice clean ocean than in a muddy river. I think it'd be less terrifying.'

Lucas smiles in agreement. 'Yep. That is the correct answer.' He squints at me blurrily, sticking his face close. 'I like your braces. They are ... cute.' I'm taken aback and jump when he suddenly claps his hands. 'Okay. Your turn, Pearl.'

'My turn what?'

'Give us a *would you rather*.'

'Uh ... right.'

And just like that, I'm drawn into their conversation. Like I was always part of it and hadn't previously been sitting right next to them like a silent lump of wood. It might just be because Jamie and Lucas are quite drunk, but I'm definitely not complaining. Though I'm having a lot of trouble coming up with my own *would you rather*.

I also notice that Daisy is observing me with a weird expression on her face. She'd been talking to Stacey Green for most of the night, until Stacey drifted off to Sebastian. Now she's sitting with Lachlan and Finn at the rickety kitchen table (a Rubik's cube, Wonder Woman and another ninja turtle), all playing some drinking game, though Daisy's cup could possibly contain the same as mine. Red cordial.

I ignore her. She's avoided me all night, and *now* she wants to talk to me? *Now*, when I'm finally (sort of) having fun? I blurt, 'Would you rather be a serial killer or be serial killed?'

Both boys frown. Very serious, thinking hard.

Right then, Stacey and Sebastian collapse beside us, shoving Jamie into my side. He slings an arm over the back of the threadbare couch behind my head, and Stacey sits on Sebastian's lap, the two of them talking animatedly about whether our principal, Mr Virk, has real hair or not (it's not real).

Lucas disappears into the kitchen and I catch Obi watching me with a frown as Jamie leans in close to say, 'I guess I'd rather be serial killed. As a ninja turtle and defender of the innocent, it feels a bit wrong to become a serial killer.'

He's clearly upset at this unexpected fate though, and I giggle behind my hand. His fingers have crept closer to my shoulder over the back of the couch. 'Alright, Pearl. Let me ask you this. Ready?'

Jamie bends his head closer and I lean in to hear him above the general hum in the lounge. Stacey is laughing so hard I suspect she's going to fall off Sebastian's lap at any minute.

Jamie says, 'Would you rather—'

But I never get to decide what I would rather, because a shadow appears right above us, a looming body blocking out the dim light from the camping lantern in the kitchen.

Obi.

He looks weird.

'Nash, can I talk to you for a second?'

I nod slowly. And he just walks off. I blink after him. And then shrug at Jamie. 'So I guess I'm ... going to follow Obi.'

Jamie waves me away and once I've stood up, he immediately scoots into my place, closer to Sebastian and Stacey, to ask, 'Would you rather be a serial killer or be serial killed?'

It makes me giggle again as I pick through the crowded dark room toward the back hall, where Obi disappeared. It's very shadowy back here, and I weave past a boy I don't recognise dressed as a big baby. A bark of laughter escapes my throat. He grins at me and I grin back. Too silly.

Am I actually having fun now?

Amazing.

The noise from the lounge travels heavy and thick down the hallway, leading past a few open doorways that spill shadows and emptiness. My sneakers scuff across the threadbare carpet. An old, ripped flyscreen looms at the back, and because I can't see Obi anywhere else, I push it open. It leads down concrete steps into a small undercover laundry. Stacked dusty boxes lean against the green fibreglass walls and there's a big, cracked concrete sink next to a water boiler. It's dark and I step lightly so I don't trip, calling Obi's name.

He's right there. Always was, but I just thought he was part of the piled boxes and the sand-covered towels slung over the string washing lines. The lines sway and shake in time with the thump of the distant music, voices from the party billowing into the laundry from upstairs.

'Is everything okay?' I whisper. I don't know why I'm

whispering, except that it's dark and the air is hot and thick. Stifling, with all the windows closed and the door to the yard shut up tight. My back hits one of the damp towels and a shower of sand dislodges into my hair. My knee presses against a big cardboard box, gone brittle with age. Laughter rings from the house, a ripple that passes through my body, making my skin warm and my ears buzz.

Obi steps closer in the dark. Pushes the towel off my shoulder in another rush of sand. My hip presses into the box as I lean away. He's so close it's making my pulse race, my fingers clench tight. And he's not saying a word.

I lift my chin, peering up. His eyes glimmer in the dark. The towel swings behind my head, cool against the back of my neck as Obi's fingers reach for my T-shirt, softly touching the hemline resting against my collarbone.

I grow still, unable to move, to breathe, head slung back and attention only on that glimmer of his face. Slowly he tugs, gently, pulling my T-shirt so softly I could just stay where I am, ignore it.

I don't. I lean after his hand, let him draw me forward. The sound of him breathing in the darkness. The wash of distant noise and thudding music from the house spills over from the back door, down the stairs, the whole laundry heavy and still. Just Obi and the sound of his breathing.

In the dark, his fingers dance to my throat, my jaw, up into my hair, until his nose is pressed against mine, mouth so close, warm breath and beer on my lips, almost touching. He kisses me long and deep, in a way that arches my body back, the sandy towel enveloping us both, scratchy against my throat and shoulder. I don't care.

Obi's arms push around my body, pressing me against him, pulling me tight and I lift my hands to his face, thumbs across his cheeks, scars rough beneath my fingertips. He's almost lifting me up, my sneakers on tiptoes, his body curled around mine. My hip slams into the brittle cardboard box again and we're thrown off balance, yet Obi doesn't stop. He kisses me harder, longer, pressing me back until his hand reaches for the far wall, palm spread against the fibreglass to hold us up. The towel creates a quiet bubble, a secret place, his breath sharp and loud, a soft sound escaping from within his throat.

He stops kissing me, his voice a breathless murmur. 'Pearl, do you wanna ...' Mouth against mine again. I'm almost sitting on the cardboard box and it's collapsing beneath me. I don't care, pulling Obi closer, fingers curling around the back of his neck.

He pulls away again, only a little, noses still pressed together, breathless as he murmurs against my mouth. 'Next week ...' He kisses me again, and it's hard to concentrate on words. 'Next week ...' he says again. 'Do you want to ...'

I'm not really listening because my skin has electricity running through it, like I'm drowning in him. Obi tastes of salt like the ocean, the gritty film of it beneath my fingertips running over his skin. 'Pearl,' he tries again. 'Please, Pearl ... I'm trying to ...'

I clasp him closer and kiss him hard, and he pushes me so far back with his mouth against mine that my skull connects with the wall.

It really hurts. 'Oww!'

He lets go. Properly.

Turns out Obi was actually holding me up, because now the cardboard box beneath me collapses inwards until, with a yelp,

I'm sitting on a pile of dusty sheets and stacked books. My neck is squeezed against the wall. Obi leans overhead with his hand splayed against the wall, breathing heavy and fast. We're not touching at all anymore.

'For fuck's sake, Nash, I'm trying to ask you out!' He sounds annoyed.

I stare up at him, blinking dust from my lashes. 'You are?'

'Yeah.'

My body turns heavy, my heart beating fast. 'Okay,' I say.

'Okay, what?' he snaps, like I was the one kissing him and he had nothing to do with it. 'Okay, you agree that I'm asking you out, or okay, yes you want to go out with me?'

'I want to go out with you,' I answer straight away. No hesitation.

That shuts him up. His lashes flicker in the dark, the beginnings of a smile curl his mouth. He breathes, 'Yeah?'

'Yeah.'

'So ... you like me, then.'

I suck in my breath, feeling dazed. 'Yeah, I like you.'

'Love me even, potentially, I'd say.' He sounds pleased with himself.

That snaps me out of my dreamy, fugue-like state. 'Excuse me? I think you're getting ahead of yourself.'

'I don't think so. It's pretty obvious. You've been following me around for days.'

I frown. 'Obi, you were in my car. I've been *driving* you around for days.'

'In your *car*,' he repeats, wiggling his eyebrows and leaning closer. I know he's thinking of the Bedford. And what happened in the back of it. He's clearly about to kiss me again, still grinning wide enough to bring the dimples out, but I shove him off with a hand to his chest.

'I'm about to fall on the floor.' I can't help the low laugh that escapes my throat. I feel ... happy. Flush with it, like it's tingling beneath my skin and growing inside my chest.

Obi really is on my side.

I like it so much.

He grasps my arm and drags me from the dusty collapsed box. We stand and assess the damage. It's completely destroyed. Obi slings an arm around my neck, pulling me into his side gently as he presses his mouth against my temple. 'Maybe Finn won't notice,' he says hopefully.

It's completely destroyed, sheets and dusty books spilling onto the concrete floor. 'I think he's going to notice.'

Obi nods in agreement. 'Okay, let's go.' He tugs me to the top of the stairs, pushing the flyscreen open into the dark hall. The music gets louder now we're back in the main house, thumping beneath my sneakers through the carpet. Obi's still holding my hand, walking backward and grinning at me. 'He'll never know. We'll never speak of it again, right?'

I raise my brows. 'None of it?'

A glint surfaces in his brown eyes. 'Some of it's okay to speak of.' He hovers close in the shadowed hall, fingers to my stomach to push me back, grinning down at me. Dimples. Pushing until my back thuds gently against the wall. Other than his fingers through my T-shirt, he doesn't touch me at all, until his mouth presses against mine, soft and then deeper. He still doesn't touch me and I'm attempting to follow his lead, but my body is on fire and my breath is caught in my throat and I'm just about to give in and reach for his shoulders when a loud voice barks out behind us.

Lachlan.

Laughing at us.

21

SPINY EVERLASTING

Obi jerks away from me.

Lachlan is standing, beer in hand, at the corner of the hallway, pissing himself with laughter. 'So ... I guess *that's* why you got so defensive in the car. I should have known, mate.' He's clearly drunk.

Obi grows stiff and tense beside me, and I notice the way he draws himself up, stands in a way that makes him seem bigger.

'It had nothing to do with it,' he snaps. 'I just thought you were being a dick.'

'Yeah, mate, being a dick about a girl you clearly had the hots for.' Lachlan runs his gaze over me in a way that makes it clear he thinks I'm not worth it. Not worth Daisy. Or Obi. I dunno. Either way I don't enjoy it.

Obi's voice is low and dangerous. 'Be quiet, Lachlan.'

'You should've just said you were into her, mate, instead of storming off like a little girl.' Lachlan's words are very slurred. 'We wouldn't have left you behind if you weren't such a tool about it.'

Obi's hands clench into fists and he's literally vibrating with anger. It hums off him in waves. I see all this, and my brain explodes with multiple things.

One. Obi likes me back and I guess we're together now.

Two. Lachlan appears to be implying the reason Obi got left behind at the servo was because of me. Interesting. Even a bit fascinating, I admit.

Three. I don't want Lachlan and Obi to fight because fighting is stupid.

Four. Lachlan sucks. I always knew this about him, but here in this moment, it really hits home.

I push off the wall and step around the shelter of Obi's body. Then I march up to Lachlan. My heart beats a drum roll against the inside of my ribcage. The noise of the party in the lounge rolls down the hall, a wash of happy laughter and shrieks. I scowl at him. (Lachlan is very drunk so can't properly look back at me, but I can see that he's trying to, which feels like almost the same thing.) Taking a deep breath, I inform him, 'I don't like you, Lachlan. At all.'

He barely reacts. Just scoffs in a slurred way, turning back to Obi.

It doesn't seem like much. My words. Yet I still feel a surge of power at having said them. At hearing my thoughts out loud. I don't need Lachlan to like me. I don't need him at all.

I glance over my shoulder at Obi. 'You coming?'

He smiles at me, tight and tense. 'In a minute.'

I get it. I'm done with Lachlan, but it's different for Obi. They were friends and I guess maybe now they're not. Seems to me that maybe Obi has outgrown him. So he needs to deal with that, however he feels is right.

Like me and Daisy.

I leave Obi alone with Lachlan, giving them space to sort out their shit, and walk through the lounge room like I'm inside a dream. I realise with a surge of pride that I'm not even upset about the Lachlan thing. It hasn't fazed me. Instead, I'm still thinking about Obi and the dark laundry, and those thoughts are good and warm in my chest.

Everything is noisy and hectic; Stacey, Sebastian and Jamie still playing *would you rather* on the couch. It actually looks like fun, but my brain is on overdrive. Too much noise, too many people, too much, too much. I need some space and quiet and stillness just to find myself again.

I figure Obi will know where to search for me whenever he's ready, so I decide to head down the beach. I slip out the front door into the overgrown garden, and it's only when I'm sliding through the long grass beneath a huge sprawling banksia tree, that I realise I didn't even check if Daisy was still in the lounge room before I left.

Our friendship must truly be over, because I always used to care about where she was. Always wanted to know, so I could stand beside her and laugh at her jokes and bask in her sunshine.

It's quiet outside. And cooler. A relief.

I walk through the long, wavering grass toward the dunes, and then I kick off my shoes and hold them as my bare feet sink into the sand. The beach is shadowed and empty, a salty wind rising from the churning water to ruffle my hair. It feels amazing on my sweaty skin.

I paddle in the waves for a bit, sloshing around contentedly, chin lifted to the sky. A blanket of glittering stars streams overhead, like a banner through the inky night. The moon is glowing pale blue, a little thicker tonight, but still like a fingernail.

Rustling erupts from the dunes, followed by sandy footsteps.

I turn, expecting Obi but instead finding Daisy standing there, frozen on the beach, staring at me.

She's dressed like Wonder Woman except not in a sexy way. A wrinkled, skin-coloured bodysuit of cheap lycra, the Wonder Woman one-piece printed on it. It's kind of hilarious.

It looks good on her.

It makes me sad at what's happened to us.

Angry too.

I blink. Then slosh out of the waves, walking up the wet sand with my feet sinking deep. I stop in front of her and open my mouth, ready to finally do it. Say my piece. Except Daisy gets in first.

'How come you told Stacey your nana went missing but never bothered to tell me?'

I gape as Daisy crosses her arms over her chest. She's sharp and sober, unlike Lachlan, and I remember she hasn't been drinking. Yet she still has the gall to ask me such a dumb question. She actually appears to be annoyed at me.

Something inside my chest explodes. It could be my heart.

'Excuse me?'

'You heard me.'

I'm so angry it hums in my ears, caught on the tip of my tongue. 'Are you seriously asking me that? I kept trying to talk to you *all day* and you just ignored me.'

She turns away. 'I never ignored you.'

'Yes! You did!'

She lifts her chin, her voice wobbly. 'I thought we were best friends, Pearl. I'm trying to talk to you and you're just yelling at me.'

For a moment my breath is gone. She's going to cry. I hurt her. Daisy. I'm about to say the words ...

Of course we're best friends.

... except they just die on my lips.

She always does this. Every single time.

It's like she has me wrapped around her finger. I don't know if it's on purpose, this push and pull, but she's always been the one holding the power in our friendship. I always come running when she calls. I wonder if that's even her fault. If she's even aware of it.

Maybe I enabled it. By always bending and changing to fit in with whatever she wants. Always shaping myself around her.

I don't want to do it anymore.

I stare at her. For a long time. Daisy shifts from foot to foot and I can tell it's making her uncomfortable. This silence. Making her annoyed. It flashes across her face, and that in turn makes my own anger erupt, tight and bitter. I'm recognising the patterns now.

My voice turns dangerously low. 'We *were* best friends. Until you consistently treated me like shit for a whole year and ditched me for your boyfriend.'

She's surprised, mouth falling open. 'I never ditched you. I invited you everywhere.'

'Yeah, to all the places you were going with *him*! To all the places you know I hate going. You never bothered to do anything I wanted to do.'

'You don't get it because you don't have a boyfriend, Pearl.' Daisy sounds frustrated, like she can't believe she has to explain it to me. 'It's *normal* for me to want to spend time with him. That's what you do when you fall in love. When you get a boyfriend, you'll be like that, too. You'll see.'

That statement pricks me, and I flinch.

Is that true? Now that Obi and I are ... whatever we are. Is that what love does?

I don't want that to be true.

But I guess I've seen it happen with more people at school than just Daisy. Maybe not to such an extreme level, but still. I've seen it.

I stand there in the wet sand with the wind rustling my hair and think this is the exact kind of problem that I would have liked to discuss in depth with Daisy. About the way things have changed between Obi and me, and what it's going to mean.

We really used to tell each other everything.

Except ... well, I guess now there are things between me and Obi that feel secret and private, things I'm not sure I'd even want to share with Daisy.

Does that mean I'm just the same as her?

Already wanting to ditch a friend over a boy.

I shake my head. 'I don't think the only thing wrong with our friendship is you spending time with your boyfriend, Daisy.'

And my words, now said aloud, slowly seep through, sink deep, carve into me. This idea that it's got to be more than that with Daisy. This problem between us is deeper than just her ditching me. It's deeper than her not wanting to spend time with me.

'I know Lachlan says mean things about me,' I blurt. Then I lift my chin, challenging her to say anything different.

She doesn't.

I surge onwards. 'He doesn't like having me around when you

guys hang out.' My voice wavers and I keep waiting for her to challenge me, but she doesn't. Her face is hard to read, but her lip could be quivering. Maybe this is getting to her. Maybe she's finally listening.

I take a deep breath. 'I know Lachlan says stuff about me and ... I know you don't stop him, Daisy.'

She's still silent, her face caught in shadow, and I'm wounded, teeth sinking into my lip. I'd hoped she would at least deny it. For some reason, that would have been better. If she'd at least cared enough to pretend it wasn't true.

Tears are welling, sliding down my cheeks. Because it's happening. And she isn't giving me a reason to backtrack. She isn't even fighting for us.

A big part of me wishes I could be flippant and indifferent when I do this next part. I wish I could be cool. I wish I wasn't crying.

I don't want her to know how much she hurts me.

'Daisy,' I say in a shaky voice, trying to ignore the way my throat is closing up. I wipe tears from beneath my chin. 'I didn't come here to talk about this stuff with you. I came to give you a final chance to be my friend.'

I pause and take a deep, shaky breath, taking some control. Clawing it back through sheer willpower. 'Except, to be honest, on the way here I decided you already used your final chance. I tried to tell you how I feel already, before you left with Lachlan. You didn't want to listen. That was your choice.'

She says nothing, her expression blank.

I shrug, tears wet on my skin. I'm embarrassed but also it feels fitting. Like an ending. It's okay to be sad when something is ending. It's okay to grieve its passing.

Or if Nana was here I guess she might say our friendship wasn't *passing*, it was *dying*, and if I'm completely honest with myself, I'd have to admit that it's already long dead.

So I say it.

I swipe the tears away as I whisper, 'So in the end, I guess I came to tell you that I don't think I want to be your friend anymore.'

Daisy's eyes are so wide I think they're gonna pop out of her head. And something finally occurs to me.

She never thought I'd actually do it.

She didn't think I'd have the guts.

Because we were so close for so long. We *did* have fun together, we *did* enjoy being around each other, we *did* love each other, except ...

I can't remember the last time I had fun with her.

It must have been months and months ago.

The wind picks up, Daisy's hair flying and the dangling streamers of her wrinkled costume wavering madly at her hips. I feel stupid, for holding onto something that was already gone. I wanted so badly for things to be how they used to be that I was lying to myself.

All year.

I picture my nana. She doesn't have the luxury of lying to herself about Grandpa. She *knows* he's gone. She *knows* he's not coming back. And she's doing her best in her own way to meet that head on. Which is courageous.

You can't go back, only forward.

I want to be courageous too.

'So ... I guess ... that's it,' I whisper. 'What I came to say.'

It's like a weight lifted from my chest. My stomach is still bitter and sick, but at the same time I feel better too. Lighter.

Daisy says nothing. Just stares.

I don't know what I'd do if she broke down crying, if she tried to hug me. If she told me she was sorry. That she'd been wrong. Already I feel myself wavering.

But she doesn't even move.

Daisy's features are tight and sharp, like a mask. I can't tell what's underneath. And I don't know what to do about it.

So I take a step away.

Another one.

My feet sink deep into the sand, and just as I'm turning toward the beach shack in the darkness, really truly leaving, Daisy's hand grips my elbow hard. Holding me back.

I grow still, the inky ocean swelling softly beyond the sand, wind brushing against my hair, pushing it into my eyes. My throat feels heavy.

'Pearl, you can't just leave.' Her voice turns shrill and when I turn back, her mask has finally cracked. She looks shocked. Like she didn't see it coming.

I don't know how she didn't see this coming.

'We've got to talk about this,' she pleads, eyes wide and glittering in the darkness, salt-heavy hair wavering in the breeze. 'We need to talk about it.'

I stare at her as she plonks down heavily onto the sand, her fingers still gripping my elbow like a vice. She tugs me down with her until I'm kneeling.

'I've been *trying* to,' I hiss. 'I tried to tell you everything back at home and all you did was ditch me and drive here with Lachlan. And I still followed you all the way out here, Daisy. To talk with you. You avoided me all day. *You've* been ignoring *me*.'

She shakes her head. Suddenly she looks desperate and it makes my body stiff with anger. Because I've seen everything crumbling down for almost a year, but she's only just noticed now.

It makes me feel even more alone.

'Admit it,' I whisper. 'You've been avoiding me.'

She doesn't say anything for the longest time. Until finally, 'Yes.'

It still hits me like a shovel, even though I already knew. 'Why?'

'Because I was scared of what you'd say,' she murmurs. 'And I was right. You don't want to be my friend anymore.'

'That's because you only want me when you need me, Daisy. The rest of the time you're happy with just Lachlan. I don't want to be your second best.'

She's silent a long moment. Looking at her hands. 'That's just how it feels when you're in love though, Pearl. You can't help it. You'll see. After it happens to you. It's normal.'

I draw breath inwards through gritted teeth. 'It's *not* normal. I get that you have a boyfriend now and you want to spend time with him, but it's not okay to just ditch everybody else.'

And that's not going to be me. Not now that I've realised I actually *do* have other friends. I won't do that. Even if things go the way they seem to be with Obi, I'll make sure of that.

I have to.

'Okay, here's the truth, Daisy. Are you ready? Lachlan is not nice to any of your friends. He thinks he's better than most of us. And I'm not sure if you've noticed, but a lot of your old friends aren't really bothering to hang around with you anymore.'

She shakes her head, as if it isn't true, but our faces are close now in the darkness, and something is spilling into her eyes, like a light turning on. She doesn't sound so certain anymore. 'I still hang out with all my friends.'

I huff. 'When? When did you last hang out with anyone?'

Daisy's mouth opens and closes. She says nothing. She looks sick, swaying on the sand.

'What do you think is going to happen next year, then?' I ask. My voice softens in a way that surprises me, an unexpected swell of pity rearing inside my chest. She's starting to look desperate again, sweat beading her forehead, fingers clenched. And she's listening now. Really listening.

'Next year?' she whispers.

'Lachlan's graduating, Daisy. So are his friends. Who are you going to hang out with now you've ditched everyone for a full year?'

She breathes in slow, closes her eyes. 'They said that?'

'*I'm* saying it,' I snap. 'Me. Just … think about it, okay?'

I stand abruptly, in a shower of sand. My chest aches like there's a pressure building inside it and I can't be here anymore, kneeling on the beach in the dark beside Daisy. Who looks as if she's breaking apart. Her expression shocks me, because it's hard for me to understand how she could truly not have noticed all her friendships dissolving around her.

She's noticed now.

I can see it shining sick and desperate in her eyes.

Turning, I slowly trudge away up the sand, leaving the slow sounds of the dark ocean behind me, leaving Daisy too. She calls after me, her wavering voice wafting on the warm breeze.

'I can fix this, Pearl.'

'I don't think you can,' I call back, my voice thick. I swipe tears from wet cheeks. Looking back, she's just a small, huddled figure beside the water in the dark. Just a shadow.

Yet her voice is shrill and determined. 'I will. Wait and see.'

I watch her a long moment in the rising wind, holding my shoes tight in my hands. Finally, I call out, 'Okay.'

I don't know why I say it. But I do.

She doesn't answer. For the longest time.

Eventually I just walk away. My last look at Daisy is of her huddled form sitting on the sand under a vast night sky. So tiny compared to the world.

I thought I'd feel some sense of closure or triumph to have finally stood my ground.

I don't.

I just feel sick. And confused. It's messy and complicated and Daisy isn't letting go. Except I can't be sure whether she wants to fix things between us because she likes me and doesn't want to lose our friendship, or because she listened to me and has finally realised she'll need me next year, after Lachlan leaves. She'll need all her friends.

I don't want to be needed. I want to be *wanted*. Valued.

I don't think there's any answer here. Everything feels just as bad as it did before I confronted her. Worse even.

But maybe that's just how life goes. No neat endings. Everything tangled and complex and lingering.

Just like Nana and Grandpa.

Just like Dad and my uncle.

Nana and Mum.

Daisy and me. Me and Daisy. Things left half-resolved and half-ended and mostly just painful.

I don't know what's going to happen next.

I walk up the beach, shoes in hand. Over the wire fence and out through the overgrown garden to the wide, empty street, where I hesitate under the sick orange glow of a single street lamp. The dilapidated houses on the other side of the street are dark. Only Finn's is lit up like a beacon, windows alight and thumping music spilling onto the street. Three cars are parked in the driveway and the one closest to the road has the keys in the ignition.

I burst out laughing. A hysterical, slightly crazed sound. I mean, I know we're in the country, but come on, that's just stupid. Also, I can't believe I said what I said to Daisy. Suddenly it's like madness, the giggles bubbling up in my chest. I feel wrecked. Exhausted.

Brave.

Nothing is resolved. It's tangled worse than before. But at least I told the truth. I didn't hold back.

Maybe that's something.

The laughter dies as I slide into the driver's seat, tossing the keys up and down in my hand.

I don't want to stay at this party anymore. I need some space to breathe.

Also, I think I kind of need my nana.

I slide the key into the ignition and turn it, the engine coughing to life. I can't believe I'm actually doing this. It is terrible. Inconceivable. Ludicrous.

Also a bit exciting.

'What are you doing?'

The voice makes me jump in fright, holding a hand to my chest. Obi is standing by the car, lounging by my unwound window with his arms resting on the frame.

'Um …' I don't know what to say so I opt for the truth. 'Stealing a car?'

'Oh.' Obi bites his lip. Shrugs. 'I guess I'll come, then.' He jogs around the front, slamming a hand against the bonnet as he goes. The door swings open and he slides into the passenger seat, reaching to buckle his seatbelt. He peers around the inside. 'Isn't this Lachlan's car?'

'Yeah. I kind of figured he deserved it.'

Obi nods. Hesitates. 'You been crying?'

I peer back at him. Bite my lip and then finally just say, 'Yeah.' The engine is still running and my hands are curled tight around the steering wheel. Obi wipes my streaked cheeks with the palm of his hand and I murmur, 'I think we should probably leave a note. If we're taking the car. Right?'

'Right,' he agrees.

We spend the next few minutes searching the car for pen and paper, upending the contents of the glove box before finally finding what we need beneath the driver's seat. I scribble a note out with Lachlan's name at the top. Something about how we only borrowed it and will return it tomorrow.

'Do you think he'll mind?' I ask when Obi comes back from handing the note to Stacey inside the house. He's grabbed our bags, too.

Obi laughs. It sounds a bit evil. 'Oh yeah, he'll mind.'

I squint at him, assessing. 'So you're really coming with me? To hang out with my nana instead of staying at a fun party?'

'Uh huh.' He's facing straight ahead out the dark windshield. 'There was only one part of it that was fun anyway, and I can do that with you anywhere.'

I snort. 'Not in front of my nana, you can't.'

Obi looks a bit ill. 'Mmmh,' he says.

I start the engine, back out of the driveway, which is when the figures run out of the house into the dark yard behind us. Obi sees too, his hands gesturing in panic. 'Drive, Nash.'

'I *am* driving.'

'Well drive faster!' He's staring at the running figures getting closer. 'So uh ... I may have added some extra content to that note before I left it with Stacey.'

I glare at him, pulling onto the road. We're already halfway down the street before the figures reach the curb. One of them is wearing a Wonder Woman costume. A twinge erupts in my belly. 'What did you say on it?'

'Nothing that isn't true.'

Now that we're definitely going to get away, Obi is all smiles again, eyes crinkled and dimples on full display, sneakers on the dash and elbow out the window. His T-shirt billows in the wind.

We're silent for a while, just the wind whistling through the car as we drive down the main street onto the highway. I dunno where we're going exactly but we have a full tank of petrol and the highway only goes one way. I know this is where Nana went. The rest I'll figure out later.

I glance across at Obi, still sort of in shock that he's here. 'So ...'

'Yes, Nash?'

I say it in a rush, my voice teasing. 'So, you defended my honour to Lachlan when he was being a dick because you had it so bad for me, right?' I flash a grin so he knows I'm joking, braces on full display.

Obi isn't smiling. He says, 'I just didn't like the things he said. It wasn't cool to say stuff like that about anyone. That's all.'

I snap my mouth shut, smile wiped clean away.

'Oh,' I say weakly. That's ... heavy.

Obi grins suddenly, breaking the tension. Dimples in both cheeks. 'Maybe I didn't have it bad for you then, Nash, but I do now.'

Warmth blooms inside my chest: something softly unfurling. I can't meet his eyes. Changing the subject, I clear my throat and stutter, 'Did you tell everyone, then? About maybe leaving school next year?'

'I did, actually. And I *am* going to leave, I decided. It's what I want. It's what I've wanted for ages, I was just … freaking out.'

I glance across at him, surprised. 'So what did they say? Were they happy for you?'

'No.'

'What do you mean, no?' My heart sinks.

'Actually, they were all too trashed to even get what I was trying to say. Lucas just kept asking if I'd rather be a serial killer or be serial killed! Can you believe that?'

I giggle. 'What did you say?'

Obi gapes at me. 'Be serial killed, obviously. I'm not a monster, Nash.'

'I don't think you'd make a very good serial killer, anyway,' I say with a laugh. 'You're too scared of everything.'

'I take offence to that.' He hesitates, then adds, 'But also yes, that's true.'

'So … what are you going to do? About telling them, I mean.'

Obi just shrugs. 'It's no big deal. I'm hanging out with them next week when we get home. Not Lachlan, but you know, the others. I'll try again then.'

I nod, hiding the way my mouth curls at the edges. He doesn't seem that worried anymore. 'Good plan.'

Obi's got his hand out the window. The dark desert landscape flashes by. 'Things will be different, but life isn't ending. I can still hang around them next year. If I want to.'

I smile as the dark road slips away beneath us. I'm thinking of Obi in the laundry again, but the grin dies on my lips as my mind travels to Lachlan laughing at us afterwards. I glance at Obi, curious. 'What happened in the hallway? You know, with Lachlan after I left?'

'I gave him a piece of my mind.'

'Really?'

'Useless though, he was so drunk I doubt he'll remember any of it tomorrow.' Obi leans his head back on the seat and closes his eyes. 'Parties are exhausting. You have to say everything twice. What happened with Daisy?'

'I ... broke up with her, I guess.' I take a deep, shaking breath. 'She reckons she's gonna win me back. All her other friends, too.'

Obi raises his brows in the dark cab. 'Win you back? Is that ... good? It's good, right?'

'I dunno.' I bite my lip, focusing on the expanding road. Miles and miles of flat land and space, stretching out before us. 'Maybe she wants to win me back because she values me and our friendship, or ... maybe it's because she's finally realised that she'll need friends next year. I don't know. It's—'

'Complicated,' finishes Obi.

'Yeah.'

He shifts around on the passenger side, getting comfortable for the long drive ahead. 'What's going to happen, then? Will you ... you know, accept her apology?'

'She didn't actually apologise.' A thread of anger rises when I mutter the words, because it's true. Daisy never actually said she was sorry. Clearly my feelings on this matter are in no way resolved. I sigh heavily. 'But no. I mean yes. I don't know. I don't know what I'm going to do.'

'It's complicated,' echoes Obi softly. He tilts his head in the passenger side, jostled by the car. Stares at me. 'Are you okay?'

I lift my chin, breathing deep.

I don't know what's going to happen between me and Daisy. I don't know how I feel about it now, or how I'll feel about it next year. I don't know if I want to forgive her or not. But I'm here in the desert with Obi. We're going (sort of) whale watching with my nana. I've got a home and a life to return to.

The world's still turning.

'I'll be okay.'

22

MALLEE TREE

We follow road signs in the dark to find the whale-watching lookout. At one point we have to pull over while we search the map on my phone, heads bent together and fingers pointing across vast desert spaces.

After we figure it out, I notice I actually have reception, and I feel guilty enough to text my dad, telling him where Nana is and that we'll be back at Uncle John's farm soon. I figure I'll drop Obi back to Finn's beach shack along with Lachlan's car, and Mum and Dad will never actually have to know what I've been up to.

Fingers crossed Nana doesn't spill the beans. I know she won't mean to, because she's promised me now, but still ... I'm not sure if Nana is to be trusted. Especially if she's fighting with my mum, because she loves using my wrongdoings as ammunition against hippy parenting.

Poor Mum.

It occurs to me suddenly that I'm actually quite looking forward to getting back to Uncle John's so I can see my parents again. Which is surprising. I spend most of my time in the city trying to get away from them. But I guess it's been ages since I was gone from my family for this many days. Not since I went camping with Grandpa and Nana when I was little. And besides, I suppose I've been doing a bit of thinking out here in the desert and I feel like there's lots I want to tell my mum. Lots I want to talk to her about. About the past and Grandpa. About me.

And I suppose it'll be nice to see Sam too, absolute terror that he is.

I pull back onto the highway, smiling. This time, Obi does a better job with the map. I suspect he does better because it's actually easy, just a long, straight desert highway and then a left turn (heavily signposted with a cute drawing of a whale). This new road leads through more flat desert toward the ocean. It takes ages and by the time the light of a campfire flickers ahead through the black, I'm yawning heavily and rubbing my face.

Obi leans forward. 'Is this it?'

I frown. 'You're the one with the map. I should be asking you. Is this it, Obi?'

Straining against the seatbelt, he studies the flickering campfire suspiciously through our dust-covered windshield. 'I dunno,' he breathes. 'That looks more like a serial killer than a nana to me.'

I pull into the car park, rolling my eyes. I cut the engine. The quiet roars in my ears. And then the ocean does too. It sounds wild out there, like waves crashing against cliffs. 'Don't start this again,' I order. 'It's not a serial killer.'

'And how do you know that, Nash? This is literally the middle of nowhere. It could be anyone.'

He's clearly about to refuse to get out of the car again, so I point sleepily to the only other vehicle in the unsealed car park. A station wagon.

'That's Nana's car,' I yawn. 'Yeah?'

Obi's shoulders relax. 'Yeah,' he agrees happily. And with that he's gone, unbuckling his seatbelt and launching from the parked car in one swift movement, running off into the shadows with a whoop. I don't know what he's so excited about and follow at a much slower pace. I feel a bit grimy after all this travelling. I also feel like now that Obi has expressed an interest in me, I should be making more of an effort with my appearance. I frown. Or is it that I don't have to make an effort anymore because he already likes me?

I yawn again.

Oh well, whatever. I'm too tired to work it out. Besides, he's grimy too.

I trudge along the sandy track, wondering how Nana managed to get the fire going with all this blustery wind. The ocean is crashing and whooshing, but I can't see it. Can't see anything beyond the faint glow of my mobile's neon torch, just the winding sandy track and a camping ground ahead. Barking erupts from the dark and suddenly little Potato is winding his way in circles around my legs. He yips excitedly, scratching me with his sharp little nails. I lean down and give him a quick pat behind his woolly ears.

What a cutie.

He slobbers on me and I pull a face. Now my legs are covered in salt, sand, sweat, dust *and* dog saliva. Lovely.

Nana's sitting hunched in front of the fire, while Obi lays out blankets close to the crackling flames and eyes the uncooked fish waiting beside the fire with a worried expression. Nana turns as I approach, her fairy-floss hair floating about her head. She smiles at me, thin lips and papery skin. 'Pearl,' she calls, waving me over. Potato crawls straight into her lap. 'I didn't think I'd see you tonight.'

'The party sucked,' I say. Not strictly true. Actually, some of it was quite fun. Hanging on the couch with Stacey and the other boys was fun. Hanging with Obi in the laundry was funner.

I grin and collapse at her side. 'So where are these whales?'

'Well you can't see them now, can you?' Nana points off into the dark. 'And don't walk off that way at night-time because you'll fall off a cliff.'

Obi's head perks up. 'Excuse me?'

'It's a spectacular view,' continues Nana. 'Wait until dawn. If you're lucky, we'll see whales then.' She fluffs her pink hair. 'There weren't any this afternoon, but I'm sure they're on their way. It'll be very nice.'

'Sounds good, Nana.' I snuggle up to her side and she leans a pudgy arm across my shoulders.

Obi's finished with the rugs and is eyeing the raw fish. 'Er. Do you mind?'

'What?' snaps Nana.

'Um ... do you mind if I do the cooking tonight? Just to, you know, help out. To be useful.'

Nana waves her hand at him like she doesn't care, and Obi grins like a maniac. I give him a thumbs-up behind Nana's back and he winks at me.

'Did you talk to that girl?'

'Who?'

'Daisy.' Nana's voice is icy cold, like she can't even stand to say Daisy's name. It's a little much, considering Nana never had a problem with her until yesterday, but I kind of like it. It's nice to have someone just take my side, no matter what.

'Yeah, I talked to her.'

'And?'

I shrug, my throat tight again. 'I dunno. I just told her how I feel. I'm not sure what's going to happen, though.'

'Good girl. You gave her a piece of your mind.' Nana rubs my back. More like thumps it with her fist, but the thought is there. Except then she says, 'And do you think Daisy will be okay?'

I frown. 'What do you mean?'

Nana peers down her nose at me. 'Well, that boy she's stepping out with doesn't sound very nice, does he?'

'Lachlan?' I've told Nana lots about him over the past year, but I hadn't really thought she was listening. 'No,' I admit, surprised. 'He's not very nice.'

'So, he's not good to her, then. And how does that make Daisy feel?'

I open my mouth but then close it again.

How does that make Daisy *feel*?

What's Nana trying to say?

I sit still, thinking. Is he *good* to her? No way. Lachlan has Daisy wrapped around his little finger. Everything's always on his terms in their weird, unbalanced relationship. Daisy loves him and gives him all her time, as if under a spell. And Lachlan just calls her when he needs her. And she comes running.

I blink.

Kind of like a worse version of how she's been treating me this past year, now I think about it. And I know how much that hurts: to feel like you care for someone more than they care for you.

'Lachlan's definitely … not good to Daisy,' I say finally.

'Mmmh.'

Nana doesn't add anything else, just pointedly raises her brows. It makes me think of Daisy sitting on the sagging couch in Nana's granny flat, eating Nana's gross cookies with us and watching our silly television show. A thought burrows deep in my chest, like a seed unfurling.

Maybe Nana has been missing Daisy too. And also … maybe Daisy isn't okay. Maybe I've been so wrapped up in myself and how hurt I've been that it never even occurred to me that Daisy was in trouble.

I rummage in my bag and find my phone. Still with reception bars! It takes me forever to write the message.

Daisy. You rescued me when I first got to the city, and I think maybe I leaned on you too hard. Now I've figured out I'm okay on my own. I'm okay without you. But that means it's my turn to rescue you. Things aren't okay. Lachlan is a douchebag and he shouldn't treat you like he does. Call someone and ask for help. Or call me. I'll rescue you. If you want me to.

'Pearl Nash!' Nana's sharp voice breaks through my whirlwind of thoughts. 'Using electronic devices when you should be enjoying the scenery! Kids these days!'

I grin as I tuck my phone away. 'Thanks, Nana. For everything.'

Maybe she really *is* a wise old nana, just like Obi said. A surprising development.

Nana huffs. 'What did Daisy say?'

'I only *just* texted her, Nana. That's not how texts work!' Then I shrug. 'I'll just have to wait and see what she wants to do.'

Nana nods, but I think she still looks worried.

I pat her arm. 'It's okay, Nana. Daisy will be okay. I'll make sure of it.'

She nods. 'Do you feel better now?'

I think about it for a minute. 'Not really,' I admit. Things are even more complicated than before. I shrug. But maybe that's okay.

Obi's still busy cooking and the scent of crackling fish wafts across from the fire, mixed with smoke and ash. It makes my stomach hurt because I can't remember the last time I ate. As Obi works, I realise I never knew he could cook. I guess there's lots of things we don't know about each other.

I suspect we're going to have time to find them out.

He catches me watching and grins, genuine and unabashed. Like he's enjoying himself, sitting on this clifftop in the middle of nowhere, cooking dinner for my nana and me. Like there's nowhere he'd rather be.

'That's alright, hon,' says Nana, drawing me back to her. She's rubbing Potato's pink belly, her calloused fingers lost in his woolly fur. 'I don't feel much better, either.'

I bite my lip. 'Even after you came all this way?'

She breathes in, long and deep. The air smells like the desert and the sea, fish and smoke. The sky overhead is immense, inky black and pinpricked with stars. Beyond the cliffs, waves crash heavily down below. 'I think your grandpa would have liked it here.'

I'm surprised. 'I thought it was somewhere you'd been with him. I thought that's why you wanted to come?'

Nana shakes her head, leaning down to drop a kiss onto Potato's hairy head. 'No. We always meant to. But we never made it.'

I'm indignant. 'But you lived so close!'

'I know, Pearl, but there just wasn't enough time.'

My heart sinks. 'You had fifty years, Nana.'

'Fifty-two, to be exact.' She shrugs, still focused into the distance. 'Not enough.'

I peer into the wild darkness, at the wheel of stars flying overhead. 'So you never went.'

'No. We never went.' She frowns and waves at the pitch-black landscape. 'And look at all the native flora here! There's even desert flame. And you know how your grandpa felt about desert flame.'

I don't, but I peer dutifully around at the darkness anyway. I can't see anything, but I don't think that matters. Nana coughs and mumbles softly, 'Your grandpa never got to enjoy this place.'

The crack and pop of the fire rises above the wind, the scent of frying fish wafting across the flames. Sparks shower into the sky.

'That's sad,' I breathe. 'That's so sad.'

My eyes sting and tears slide onto my cheeks. My chest turns tight.

'It *is* sad,' agrees Nana. She hugs me tight, upending Potato, who falls on the ground. The woolly dog yips and then shuffles off toward the smell of Obi's cooking. 'But it'll be okay. It's just a very sad thing. You just have to deal with it, love. Do the best you can. Keep going. That's all.'

'I miss Grandpa,' I say and Nana kisses the top of my head, holding me tight.

'Me too, love.'

23

DESERT FLAME

'Nash.'

The hissed voice breaks through my heavy dreams. I ignore it.

'Nash! Seriously, wake up.'

I open my eyes sleepily. I'm tangled beneath blankets in Nana's tent. She's not here and Obi's crouched at the entrance by the canvas flap. I groan, rolling over so I can ignore him. I feel like this is the first proper sleep I've had in ages. I'm not ready for it to end yet.

'Pearl!'

This time it isn't Obi's voice at all. My eyes snap open and I sit up fast in a tangle of blankets, trying to smooth down my hair. Obi's staring at me across the gloomy tent, sunshine pouring into the opening behind him. His face is tight and scared.

I poke my head out beside him.

And come face to face with my dad.

He's standing on the other side of the smoking campfire in the dirt. Short and balding, his beer belly bulging. Wearing a Hawaiian shirt for some unfathomable reason. Dad drops his bag to the ground, glaring at me. At my bedhead. At Obi.

His face is like thunder.

Behind him I spot the Bedford in the car park, and my heart would sing at that impending reunion if my mum and Sam weren't also picking their way toward us across the sandy trail. My ratbag of a brother sees me and immediately screams my name, tugging on Mum's skirt. Even from here, I think he possibly looks quite sticky.

Mum looks up and waves at me, dressed like she's going for a cruise through the South Pacific with martini-drinking friends, huge dark sunglasses perched on her face. She looks like a celebrity and Dad looks like he bought a cheap shirt from a souvenir shop.

Obi and I don't move. Even when another vehicle pulls into the car park and spews out Uncle John and his family too. Sam spots his cousins and screams their names now, pelting back toward them across the sand. A very sticky child party.

I gulp.

My dad's glowering at Obi. 'So this is the boy I've been hearing about, is it?'

Right at that moment, Nana strolls up, pink hair flapping in the wind, which saves me from answering, but also kind of makes things worse. 'That's Pearl's boyfriend.'

My lashes flutter shut. Oh no.

Dad scowls and I expect Obi to protest this new label that we didn't actually discuss yet, except he doesn't. He just says weakly, 'Hello. I'm Obi. Nice to meet you, Mr Nash.' He holds out his arm like he's offering a handshake, except my dad is way over on the other side of the charcoal pit and we're here squashed together on the ground in the tent entrance. I elbow Obi hard in the ribs.

He lowers the hand awkwardly and tries on his best smile.

The dimples come out but he still looks physically sick. It all feels a little early to be meeting the parents. Considering we only just got our shit together last night.

Dad readjusts his gaudy surfboard-print shirt, which I suspect he believes is fancy. Though I guess for him it is, because he usually wears hi-vis yellow at all times. I wonder if he knows he's in the middle of the desert in boiling-hot rural Australia and not on a beach in the South Pacific sipping cocktails. He's puffing up his chest, sucking in his beer belly, ready for the interrogation to begin. 'So. Obi. Where are you fr—?'

'He's from school,' I snap. I'm feeling a bit worried that everything is about to fall apart. Nana is poking at the fire, motioning for my dad to sit as she re-lights it.

'I'm making fish,' she announces brightly.

Obi and I glance at each other and then scramble out of the tent in a jumble of arms and legs. 'Obi can do it!' I practically shout.

Everyone turns to stare at me. I add in a small voice, 'You know ... to help out. While we all talk.' Obi nods enthusiastically and grins wide when Nana hands him the tin plate. She winks at him.

The day is searing hot already, blue skies stretching overhead and not a scrap of wind. I can't even hear the waves beyond the cliffs, though their edges are visible where the flat, scrubby landscape just drops away into nothing.

It seems we keep turning up at the end of the world.

Dad clearly hasn't given up yet. 'So. Pearl. I hear you've been gallivanting across the countryside with some boy from your school?' He looks quite annoyed. I guess him and Uncle John are speaking again. I just wish it wasn't about me. 'Yet you said you were with *Daisy*? Was that a lie?'

'No! No, I really was with Daisy.'

Last night.

On a beach outside Finn's beach shack.

Obi agrees eagerly and then stops when he sees Dad glaring at him.

I add hopefully, 'And we've been with Nana the whole time.'

My dad squints suspiciously at Nana as Mum finally joins us, dropping her sequinned handbag into the dirt beside the campfire. Nana doesn't even seem to notice.

'Yes, they've been with me,' Nana says at the exact same moment Mum says, 'Fish!' She blinks at Obi. 'Is this the boy?'

It's my dad who answers. 'Oh this? Yes, this is indeed Pearl's secret boyfriend who she neglected to tell us about and who she's been—'

'Oh sit down and get over yourself!' explodes Nana. 'Who are you to grill your daughter? She's a responsible, intelligent young woman and you're just an idiot who didn't even notice your own mother was missing for months!'

My dad opens his mouth and blinks. And then closes it again. Slowly he sits. Mum leans over and pats his arm.

The sun beats heavy and the sand stirs in the barest whisper of wind off the ocean. It tastes of salt and the desert. Already I'm wiping sweat from my forehead. What I need is a swim. I hope there's a way down to the water from the cliffs.

My dad clears his throat in a softer and much less aggressive way, and then a moment later raises his eyebrows to smile weakly at Obi. 'Been travelling with my mother, have you?'

'Er. Yes, Mr Nash.'

Dad makes a face of deep pity and I hide a giggle behind my hand.

Nana will be using this one to control Dad for years to come.

Rose and Lily come bounding across the sand with my brother, kicking up a cloud of choking dust, and soon my aunt and uncle follow. They're laden with camping stuff.

It feels weird. Sitting by the smoking campfire and watching everyone getting in each other's way, the kids underfoot while Uncle John hugs his mother. I wonder what happened back at the farm? Because right now everybody looks almost like a family. Like we're all on each other's side.

Which is weird.

I guess Nana must think so too, because she frowns suddenly. 'What's this? Everyone's here?'

'To see the whales,' Mum says without looking up. I'm fairly certain she knows it's the wrong season too. She's tucking into Obi's fish happily. He found salad leaves and dressing in the esky this time. It smells pretty good.

'You have tents,' Nana points out.

Aunty Sue shrugs. 'It's been a long time since we had a family holiday.' She glances at Uncle John, and I remember how spaced-out he was back at the farm. The slogans lining the roadside. The dark shadows beneath his eyes. She adds, 'Or any holiday at all, for that matter.'

Dad nods and flicks dust from his Hawaiian shirt, puffing out his chest so everyone can see. 'That's why I'm wearing a holiday shirt,' he announces.

I cringe and glance at Obi. Surely this is all too much, but he doesn't even flinch. An amused grin stretches across his face.

'A perfect outfit,' chimes in Mum. I swear she's making heart eyes at Dad, patting the surfboards stretched over his belly and looking pleased with where they've found themselves. Out here in the dusty desert.

Nana scoffs, her face turning sour, but I notice she doesn't actually protest the notion of a family holiday. I think secretly she's pretty happy about it. And maybe that's a tear or two glistening in her eyes. She coughs harshly and stands up, suddenly shouting orders on where everyone should set their tents. She's quite bossy.

Mum moves to sit next to me while Uncle John and Aunty Sue scurry to do Nana's bidding. Mum's never been afraid of Nana. Which is probably why they don't get on. I place my head gratefully against Mum's shoulder and she strokes my hair. Dad leans close to Obi and stage whispers, 'Did my mother feed you her burnt fish?'

'Er.'

My dad shakes his head. 'Disgusting.' He climbs up to fetch the tents from the Bedford and for a surreal moment I suddenly feel like everything is clicking into place. It feels like coming home, all these clashing pieces of my life suddenly locking together.

Like maybe things are almost perfect.

I whisper to Mum, 'Did Dad and Uncle John sort out their shit?'

'Pearl! Don't swear.'

'Nana said it like that!'

Mum sighs. 'Sort of. Nearly. I don't know.' Then she smiles at me, exasperated. 'They're both trying, I suppose.'

Okay, so not perfect. But that's okay.

How perfect could things ever be, anyway? Grandpa's gone. My parents live in the city, far away from this landscape my dad clearly loves. The farm is in some sort of financial trouble and my friendship with Daisy is completely fractured. Also, Mum and Nana are still narrowing their eyes at each other across the campfire, even though Mum's been part of this family for over twenty years! You'd think they'd give it up already.

I sigh.

It's definitely not perfect, but it is what it is.

Besides, the future is looking very interesting.

I glance over at Obi and smile. He's still sitting beside the fire, distracted by the controlled mayhem occurring all around him. Also, I feel a bit sorry for him, because apparently my little brother has decided Obi's his new best friend, a friendship that so far seems to involve Sam placing his very sticky hands on Obi's arm to wipe them.

I grimace, but can't bring myself to move from Mum's side, even to save Obi. He looks like he's doing a pretty good job of saving himself, lifting Sam into the air and turning him upside down while my brother giggles manically.

I grin and nestle closer to Mum, breathing in her scent. I missed her.

Waving my hand vaguely toward Dad on the other side of the carpark, I ask, 'Did they tell you what their fight was about, then? Why they stopped speaking in the first place?'

Mum laughs, a low chuckle in her throat. 'You know, your dad did tell me. Or he tried to.' She leans in against my ear and whispers, 'It honestly didn't make any sense, Pearl. I swear they've been angry at each other for four years over some dumb tractor part your uncle was meant to order. But didn't.

Or something. Honestly, I don't even know. One of them was meant to order it.' She pauses for a long moment. Then adds, 'It sounded stupid.'

Huh.

But then Mum says, 'Well you know how it goes, though. The tractor issue wasn't really the problem. Of course, it was other things. That was just the excuse they both used.'

I'm interested now, sitting up. My face is reflected back at me in her big celebrity sunglasses. 'What other things?'

Mum tilts her head to the side, long hair flung over her shoulder and face caught in shadow beneath her enormous floppy hat. 'Well, think about it. Four years ago, a lot was happening. Your dad's new job, us moving to the city. Your grandpa being diagnosed. Tensions were running pretty high, back then. And honestly, me and your nana weren't getting along terribly well.'

I raise my brows. 'And you do now?'

Mum gently shoves me with a husky laugh. 'Actually, yes, Ms Smartypants. We rather do now.'

I wrinkle my nose. That means it must have been *really* bad between them back then. I lower my head to her shoulder. 'I guess I always thought something big had happened, like a huge secret.'

'Well yes, wouldn't that have been exciting?'

'Mum!'

She laughs, her shoulder rumbling beneath my ear.

I turn it all over inside my mind. It makes me think of the past differently. And it changes things. Like looking back and seeing the truth instead of the glimmering sheen of how you thought things were. Things were not great back then.

And things aren't perfect now either, but at least everyone is talking again.

Right then, Dad comes loping over, laden like a turtle under piles of bags and eskies and tents. 'Pearl, whose bloody car is that? The blue one?'

'Oh that?' I search wildly for some excuse for having Lachlan's car. Find none. 'It's just a car that Obi and I stole.'

Obi stiffens across the fire, but my dad just rolls his eyes.

'Har Har. What an amusing daughter I have.'

I grin at Obi as Dad thuds away to find out where Nana wants him to put the tent. She's directing everyone to pitch them in a strange formation that makes no sense.

Sam and the cousins beg Mum to go walking with them and eventually she relents, standing and stretching in a wave of floating skirts. 'We're going to find some whales.' She winks at me, then turns to Obi. 'Are you staying with us for a few days, Obi?'

He glances at me and raises his eyebrows. A question.

I shrug. He can do what he wants.

'Yeah, I think I am,' he says to Mum, smiling wide, which kind of makes my heart burst with happiness. Except it's also clear Obi's trying to use his bloody dimples to charm Mum and I'll definitely need to have a talk with him about that. He's not allowed to use his special powers on my family. It just doesn't seem fair.

He adds, 'But I need to borrow a phone first.'

And I guess there's the little matter of returning Lachlan's stolen car. But whatever. We'll figure it out.

Ahead, everyone is getting rounded up by Nana, ready for a walk to see the whales. Nana motions for us to follow, pink hair flapping in the wind, and slowly Obi and I walk after my huge, jumbled, complicated family toward the cliffs. Potato barks at my dad's heels and the kids shriek.

It's not very peaceful.

'You know, you don't really have to stay, Obi.'

'It's okay.'

'But if you stay, there's no way my parents are going to let you share my tent. You'll have to sleep with Sam.'

Obi smiles.

'He's gross,' I point out. 'And sticky.'

Obi just shrugs.

I shake my head. 'No, like *really* gross and sticky. I don't think you know what you're getting yourself into.'

Obi grins wide, his eyes crinkled. 'I think I do, Nash.'

Acknowledgements

Thank you, reader, for spending your time on my book. I really hope you enjoyed my story. Thank you especially to lovely Vivien, Emmey, and all of the fantastic #LoveOzYA crew (readers, writers, librarians, booksellers, bookstagrammers and bloggers). It feels incredible to be part of such an enthusiastic book-obsessed community. Thank you also to Novelist Circle and the YA Circle.

This story took a huge amount of collaboration to get it off the ground. Firstly, a huge thank you to Writers SA for awarding me the 2019 SA Writers Fellowship residency at Varuna Writers House, and to all the people who work tirelessly behind the scenes to help authors at both incredible organisations. I wrote the first draft of this book while at Varuna (surrounded by rain and mist!), and being gifted the dedicated time and space to do so felt like a miracle. Thank you.

A huge thank you to my agent, Jane Novak, for not only being an excellent agent, but also for all your help and suggestions in making this manuscript stronger. It is so lovely to have you on my side. Next up, a massive thank you to Margot Lloyd, who spent a lot of time helping me with this one, even though she was very busy and about to move interstate! I am so grateful!

Thank you SO MUCH to the wonderful team at Wakefield Press (for so many reasons!). Michael B, Maddy, Liz, Jonny, Clinton, Mark, Milly, Jesse, Michael D, Julia, Trevor and especially Jo, whose insight helped this book so much and who is an absolute joy to work with! You guys are all the very best, and I am so grateful to be part of the team!

Thank you to all my fellow authors who lift me up and help make everything better. I can't name everyone, but a special thank you must go to the incredible Kristy Fairlamb and S.J. Morgan. So glad I met you both! And thank you to Sarah Epstein for the emails!

Also, thank you to Jaclyn Moriarty for the beautiful endorsement and her help with the ending. I am so incredibly grateful. It feels particularly surreal for me to be writing Jaclyn's name into my acknowledgements, as her book *Finding Cassie Crazy* was the main inspiration behind my debut novel and a book I treasured (and read over and over) while growing up.

Thank you also to all my supportive friends: Kirsty, Nicole, Teegan, Ngaire, Lizzie (for the excellent online chats!), and everyone else!

Thank you to my wonderful and supportive family, both here in Australia and in Ireland. As always, lots of love to everyone and a special thank you to my sisters (in law) on the other side of the world, Ozi and Ima! Big thank you to my dad for being the absolute best dad. Our trips to the art gallery and the sea are my favourite. Always a special thank you to my lovely mum.

And lastly, for Gus. Because I love him.

Trouble is my Business
Lisa Walker

Olivia Grace, recently retired teen PI, has her priorities sorted. Pass first-year law, look after her little sister, and persuade her parents to come back from a Nepali monastery to resume ... well, parenting. But after Olivia's friend Abbey goes missing in Byron Bay, a short drive from Olivia's Gold Coast home, she can't sit back and study Torts. It's time to go undercover as hippie-chick Nansea, in hippie-chic Byron Bay, hub of influencers and international tourism, and home of yoga, surfing and wellness culture.

Olivia's looking for answers, with the help of her stash of disguises, the PI skills her irresistible ex-boss Rosco taught her – and a nose for trouble. Her suspects include a hardcore surfer who often argued with Abbey in the surf, a charismatic cult leader and an acrobatic botany student.

And then there's Rosco, officially assigned to the case, and proving impossible to avoid.

Lisa Walker's second Olivia Grace novel is another rip-roaring excursion into madcap sunshine noir, with nods to Nancy Drew and Sherlock Holmes, and a flavour of Veronica Mars meets Elmore Leonard.

ISBN 978 1 74305 844 2

For more information visit www.wakefieldpress.com.au

Hometown Haunts
#LoveOzYA Horror Tales
Edited by Poppy Nwosu

One bite of an apple from a family shrine unearths hungry ghosts. A poison garden unfurls a polite boy's deepest, darkest desires. Interfering with an Indigenous burial site unleashes ancestral revenge, to a metal soundtrack. An underground dance party during Covid threatens to turn lethal. And on the edge of a coastal rainforest, a grieving sister waits to witness a mysterious 'unravelling'.

This #LoveOzYA anthology – the first to focus entirely on horror – unites a stellar cast of Australia's finest YA authors with talented new and emerging voices, including two graphic artists.

Contributors are Wai Chim, Sarah Epstein, Alison Evans, Lisa Fuller, Margot McGovern, Poppy Nwosu, Michelle O'Connell, Emma Osborne, Emma Preston, Marianna Shek, Holden Sheppard, Jared Thomas, Vikki Wakefield and Felix Wilkins.

From body horror to the supernatural, hauntings to transformations, and the everyday evil of humans to menacing outside forces, *Hometown Haunts* will have you glued to your chair ... until you leap out of it!

ISBN 978 1 74305 864 0

For more information visit www.wakefieldpress.com.au

Wakefield Press is an independent publishing and
distribution company based in Adelaide, South Australia.
We love good stories and publish beautiful books.
To see our full range of books, please visit our website at
www.wakefieldpress.com.au
where all titles are available for purchase.
To keep up with our latest releases, news and events,
subscribe to our monthly newsletter.

Find us!

Facebook: www.facebook.com/wakefield.press
Twitter: www.twitter.com/wakefieldpress
Instagram: www.instagram.com/wakefieldpress